COLOSSUS

EPIC ADVENTURE SERIES

Colin Falconer

This one's for my dear mum, wherever you are now - in heaven, as you deserve, or in Fiddler's Green with the rest of the card players and sherry drinkers. Thanks for all your love and support in your good and long life.

RIP Doris Bowles, 1921-2012.

CHAPTER 1

Babylon, 323 BC

'Kill him! Kill the monster now!'

Colossus has sent everyone scattering. He has ripped out the stake chaining him to the ground and the heavy iron links now trail his hind leg, as light as a flower garland, bouncing this way and that. He has knocked down a small building by ramming it with his head and shoulder. His *mahavat* – handler - lies stricken on the ground nearby.

Someone must have scared him. He is screaming with rage.

He turns toward another of the mahavats and swats him like a fly with his trunk. The man rolls across the ground like tumbleweed and thuds into a mud brick wall. Colossus finds a straw cart and stamps on it leaving behind just splinters.

The captain of the elephants has lost his fine turban and his swagger. He is panicked and his face is covered with dust and sweat. He is deciding where to place his spear, but it is not easy to kill a fully grown elephant. It takes an army and a forest of darts. Even without armour, there are few places a man can strike with a spear and even offend an elephant, let alone kill him.

He must somehow get underneath him, avoid his tusks and feet, and strike upwards. To do that the beast's attention must be distracted and Colossus is not of a mind to take his eyes off the captain for even a moment.

The fool tries to run around him but whichever way he turns, Colossus turns too. It is clear now that he is the target for the animal's fury. Gajendra supposes he has been beating him with the bull hook, the *ankus,* again. How many times has he told him not to do that?

Colossus tramples down several tents and knocks over another cart. It is pandemonium. The other elephants are agitated now, and if someone doesn't do something about it they will all stampede.

Gajendra doesn't like the captain and will happily see him squashed like a beetle, but someone must help him for the sake of the entire regiment.

So Gajendra steps out in front of Colossus.

The world stops. He can hear only two things now: his own blood pounding in his ears and his Uncle Ravi shouting at him to come away. He sees horses galloping down the road, a hawk soaring high overhead.

He cannot let them slaughter Colossus. The beast needs someone who knows how to handle him, that's all. If someone had put that bull hook up the captain's ample fundament instead, everything would be all right.

He stands in front of the big bull and Colossus bellows, trunk raised, ears flared. The tusks are terrifying. He once saw a man gutted and near torn in half by one of those. He still remembers the inhuman cry as the bull tried to shake him off.

Never mind the tusks, watch what he does. The tusks are the least of your worries. He can just stamp on you if he wants, leave behind a red stain and stringy fibres like betel nut.

Colossus swings his front foot, a sure sign he is going to charge. He starts at a gait, trunk curled. The ground shakes under his feet. The captain screams and tries to run but he trips in his haste and falls on his face in the dirt.

Hold your ground now, Gajendra thinks. Go down on one knee like Uncle Ravi showed you. Don't let him see you're afraid even though you're near pissing yourself. Remember, on one knee and point to the ground.

'*Hida, Hida!*' Lie down!

The effect is dramatic. The elephant's ears crack out and he unrolls his trunk. He shakes his huge head, showering Gajendra in a cloud of sand, and backs off.

Impressive. He has only once before seen an elephant break off an attack at full speed. On that occasion it was Ravi himself standing in front of it.

'*Hida!*'

Colossus is slow about it, but he does it, settling into the dust. The captain runs forward with his spear. Gajendra sees what is intended and throws himself at the captain, taking him in the midriff, knocking the wind out of him and sending him sprawling on the ground. The spear bounces across the dirt. Colossus gets back to his feet, picks it up with his trunk and tosses it casually over his massive shoulder. He does not see where it lands.

Greece, perhaps.

After all the trumpeting and screaming, the silence that follows is eerie. A shadow falls across Gajendra's face. He hears the jangle of trappings, realizes that a horse and its rider have stepped up to him. The rider has his back to the sun and Gajendra must shield his eyes to look at him.

'Well, that was smartly done,' the newcomer says. He sits on a huge white Arab stallion. The captain scrambles back to his feet and almost immediately puts his head back into the dirt, this time without the assistance of one of his own elephants.

The rider steps his horse forward and turns to the officer beside him. 'I can make an oriental kneel, but this one makes an enraged elephant grovel. Which of us is greater, do you think?'

Unsure of the correct response, the officer is not keen to venture a guess.

The rider slides from the saddle and stands, legs apart, surveying the scene. Gajendra realizes who it is and gasps, falling to his knees behind his captain.

'Don't bother with all that now,' Alexander says. He grabs him by the tunic and pulls him back to his feet.

Gajendra is surprised to find that the great Alexander is shorter than him. Squat, golden and broad, his legs are bowed from spending his life in the saddle of a horse. And yet he feels as if he is standing next to a giant. He had heard legends of his general long before he was conscripted into Alexander's army. It is like standing next to the sun. The energy burns off him.

Alexander nudges the captain of the elephants with his foot. 'What's your name?' He has a high-pitched voice, this lord of war, it grates on the nerves.

'Oxathres, my lord,' the captain says, without raising his face from the dirt.

'You might as well lick his boots while you're down there,' one of Alexander's officers says and guffaws when Oxathres actually does it. Apparently it was a joke.

'You're a fool, Oxathres. What are you?'

'A fool, my lord.'

Alexander winds up and kicks him hard in the ribs. He turns to Gajendra and asks him his name.

'It sounds a little like my own name. Gajendra the Great!' he says and his officers chuckle, which is why he keeps them with him, Gajendra supposes.

Alexander nudges the captain of the elephants with his boot a second time as if he is something in his path that he is unsure about. 'You're in charge here. How did all this come about?'

The captain says, 'Beg pardon, my general, but the beast is mad. It should be killed immediately.' He wipes the sweat off his face and smiles up at his general in an ugly way, something like a grimace. 'The animal is a menace and will not be properly trained.'

Alexander starts to laugh. He throws back his head and roars. Oxathres starts to laugh too, though he doesn't know what the point of the joke is. Now the officers laugh; even one of the horses snickers. Then Alexander draws back his boot and kicks Oxathres in the ribs again. It is a terrifying sight because Alexander is still laughing as he does it.

'Who made you captain of these beasts?' *Kick.* 'Was it me?' *Kick.* 'I shall have to put myself on a charge for incompetence. What was I thinking, I must have been drunk!' *Kick, kick, kick.*

Oxathres starts to cry. The fault is not his, he whimpers. The beast is unnatural. It will not submit to direction. Forgive me. I am Alexander's most faithful soldier. I would follow you to the ends of the earth.

'Only to the ends of the earth?' Alexander says. 'I've been there. I don't remember seeing you.'

He suddenly loses interest in his captain of the elephants. He is as easily distracted as a child.

'Well, look at this,' he says. He walks up to Colossus and stands in front of him, hands on hips. Gajendra watches Colossus carefully; the imperceptible flick of the pink tip of his trunk, the slow blink of his eye. No sudden movements please my lord, he thinks, or you will follow the captain's spear over that wall.

'What is his name?'

'*Fateh Gaj* – it means Victory Elephant. But your soldiers have called him by a different name. They call him Colossus, my lord.'

Alexander laughs. 'Colossus. It suits him.'

Gajendra moves closer so that he can intervene should Colossus take exception to his general's behaviour. The elephant reaches out with his trunk and touches Gajendra's head and face with his trunk. He makes a deep rumbling in his stomach as he does this.

'He is the biggest beast I have ever seen; even at Gaugamela I never saw the like,' Alexander says. 'How did you tame him?'

'I spoke to him.'

Alexander walks around the grey mountain of leathery flesh. Colossus has tufts of greyish hair all over him and ears as big as a man. Alexander folds his arms and frowns.

'You're telling me this beast can talk.'

'No, but he can understand.'

'And what's that language you use?'

'It's the language of elephants, my lord.' He doesn't know how to explain that it is the language Uncle Ravi spoke as a child and even he doesn't know what that tongue is, or even if it has a name.

Alexander gives Gajendra a pained look. 'Elephants have a language?'

'He is trained to obey certain commands and that is the only language he understands.'

Alexander indicates Oxathres with a dismissive nod of the head, 'Does he know that?'

'I have tried to tell him, but he pays no attention to me.'

'Are you Indian? You look Greek.'

'My mother was Persian.'

'What was your father doing with a Persian. Besides making you?'

'The Rajah gave her to him. As a gift, for his exploits in battle. He said he was the best mahavat in his whole army. But then he was wounded and could not be a soldier anymore. He went back to farming.'

'It seems to me that you are the only one here who knows how to control this animal.'

'Yes, lord.'

'Then why has it done all this?' He looks around the enclosure. Two men lie motionless in the dirt, two small buildings are partially destroyed, and three carts are now only of use for firewood.

'The captain of the elephants took to him with a bull hook.'

'Where were you?'

'I was mucking out the straw.'

'But isn't this your elephant?'

'The captain won't give me an elephant, lord. He says I'm too young.'

Alexander sighs, theatrically puffing out his cheeks. He walks over to Oxathres, who is still curled up on the ground clutching his ribs. This has not been a good day for him, and it is about to get worse. Alexander grabs him by the hair and cuffs him smartly about the ears. 'From now on, this boy here is this animal's mahavat.' He nods to one of his officers. 'Give him five of those new *siglos* I had minted yesterday.'

The officer drops some coins into Gajendra's hand. He gapes. It is as much money as he might make in a year.

Alexander takes a last look at Colossus, who is still kneeling, playfully blowing at the dust with his trunk, mild as a kitten. Alexander shakes his head.

Then he looks at Gajendra and grimaces with distaste.

Gajendra looks down at his tunic. He is covered in slime, half a pint of it from where Colossus has expressed his affection. 'We have known each other a long time. He is fond of me.'

'I should not like anything to be that fond of me,' Alexander says. He gets back on his horse and rides away, his staff officers in tow.

Oxathres gets to his feet. His ear is bleeding. He tries to straighten up, but his ribs will not let him. He looks at Colossus and then at his new mahavat. He points a finger at Gajendra.

'You're dead, boy,' he says and staggers away.

Gajendra looks over his shoulder at his elephant. All the madness has gone out of him. He flaps his ears and tastes the air with his trunk. Now that Oxathres has gone, he is perfectly at ease.

'Now look what you've done,' Gajendra says to him. He taps the *ankus* behind his tail and Colossus does as he asks and trails him across the enclosure, leaving the water boys to clear up.

CHAPTER 2

The moon is tentative, slipping in and out between dark clouds. The night wind collects the fallen leaves and whispers them up the trail that winds along Elephant Row.

Gajendra cannot sleep tonight. He wonders if Oxathres will slide a knife across his throat in the dark.

He gets up to check everything is all right. A few of the elephants are asleep, others sway in the darkness, still awake; he can feel the rumbling from their stomachs through his bare feet. A lone water boy is about his work.

Gajendra has been around elephants since he was nine years old. Uncle Ravi taught him how to talk to them, to rub their bristly hides and the smooth hind side of their ears, then feed them melons and whisper to them that one day when they were grown they would be spoken of in the same breath as Ganesha himself.

The torches are sparking. In his mind he goes back to when he was nine years old, walking into the Rajah's camp for the first time, Ravi's hand on his shoulder, the hard faces of the other mahavats scowling at him.

Ravi had said, in a loud voice, 'He is my new water boy.' Just like that. In just a few weeks he had changed from being a boy who cried for his mother when he fell in the river to a soldier in the Rajah's army.

Tonight, Gajendra has an *ankus* in his right hand. It is made of steel and has a small, blunt hook. Some mahavat*s* sharpened the hook to a point but Ravi always said that a good handler would never hurt his elephant.

'It is for guiding them only,' Ravi had told him. 'A good mahavat uses his voice to command. The elephant should obey because he loves you, not because he is afraid of you.'

A massive shape looms out of the dark and the rumblings grow deeper. Gajendra hears the tinkling of the bell Colossus has around his neck. They all have one; when you are working around animals the size of a house you need to know where they are.

Especially Colossus. Gajendra has to stand on another man's shoulders to reach the top of his head. Uncle Ravi could walk under him without even touching his belly.

Colossus finds Gajendra with his trunk and explores his head and his chest. The tip of it is wet and soon he is covered in slime. Now he'll have to bathe in the river before bed or sleep on his own in the straw.

He finds a melon with his foot, picks it up and tosses it into the great pink maw. Look at him, playful as a kitten now. But two men still lie groaning in the hospital tent because of him.

'You've got to keep a rein on that temper of yours,' Gajendra says to him. 'Be clever about these things. I know the captain's a dog. I know he beat you with the hook. But you must learn to bide your time. Wait for your moment and give it back when they're not expecting it.'

He finds the puncture marks the bastard captain has made with the *ankus*, in the elephant's knees and the base of his trunk. It's not supposed to do that. He always tested his own hook on his finger and if it drew blood then he knew it was too sharp. The captain must have been sharpening his, wanted it to hurt.

Colossus is done with the melon, and he searches Gajendra out with his trunk, hoping for another. He sneezes in his hair.

Gajendra knows that Ravi and the others won't let him near them now. He finds a pile of straw next to Colossus and settles down on it. It's safer anyway, no one's going to stick him with a knife with the big fellow standing guard.

Besides, sometimes he prefers the company of elephants to that of other men. With the tuskers at least you know where you stand.

Colossus keeps at him with his trunk, nagging him for another melon, but finally gives up and lets him sleep.

Gajendra sleeps soundly. He knows Colossus won't step on him in the dark. Even the biggest elephants are strange like that. They never hurt anyone by accident.

But when they set out to do harm, well, you had better watch out.

The next day Gajendra takes Colossus down to the river, watches as he splashes water over himself with his trunk. There is a basket of apples on the bank. Colossus decides on one and places it in his mouth with great delicacy, like a courtier selecting a grape. He swings his trunk from side to side. He appears happy.

Nothing like a good scrubbing bath. Gajendra uses his *ankus* to scrape the mud off his back. He talks to him the whole while. He is so engrossed he does not see Uncle Ravi until he is at his shoulder. Gajendra likes to call calls him Uncle, but there is no blood tie.

He has no idea how old Ravi is. Even Ravi himself can only guess. Ever since has known him, he has always looked the same; hard, wiry and nut brown. He says he is from the south, but the south of where? He left his home so long ago he can't even remember the name of the place.

He only has one arm, lost his left arm at the elbow in a nameless battle.

'Uncle! I didn't hear you.'

'I've been watching for a while.' He scratches his head and says in a whisper, 'Do you trust him?' All the mahavats, even Ravi, talk in whispers around Colossus.

'I trust him more than I trust Oxathres.'

Ravi has something behind his back and now he brings it out. 'Here, I brought you something to celebrate your promotion. You're one of us now.'

It is an *ankus* made of teak root, as long as a man's arm. The end piece forms two dull points, one straight, one curved back towards the handle. It is trimmed with silver and copper, the shaft inlaid with sculpted silver elephants. There are a series of engraved initials of the mahavat*s* who have owned it before.

'But this is your *ankus*,' Gajendra says, bewildered.

'And now it's yours. One day you'll pass it along, as I'm doing now.'

'I can't take it.'

'No one else can manage this elephant, you're the only one. You've earned the right to have this.'

Gajendra laughs in surprise. He shows it to Colossus.

'See, I'm your new mahavat,' he says to him. 'I'm the boss now.'

Oxathres appears on the bank. He keeps his distance. Colossus sees the bull hook at the captain's side and his eyes turn cold. Why would he come near Colossus again holding a bull hook? His stupidity is alarming.

'Get him out onto the *maidan*,' he croaks. 'We are having a drill.'

It takes a long time to get the elephants ready, even without adding their warrior paint and the sword tips on their tusks, which they would need in a real battle. First there is the armour: a metal sheath for the trunk and the head. A camelhair blanket must be thrown over the beast's back before the heavy timber *howdah* is mounted in place with the aid of broad straps of woven hemp. Colossus bears it but he doesn't like it; he bellows and thrashes around. It is a long and exhausting process.

'Hurry!' Gajendra shouts at the handlers. The water boys are not accustomed to being bossed around by someone so young, and grumble about it.

They are still securing the wooden *howdah* onto his back when the others are already filing out to the *maidan*. Oxathres marches over, tapping the bull hook on the ground. His face is red. This is what he wanted, has been spoiling for it since he woke up this morning with his sore ribs.

'Why are you not ready?'

'We are almost finished.'

'What good is almost in a battle! You are not ready to be a mahavat!'

'Alexander thinks I am.'

At the mention of Alexander's name, Oxathres goes berserk. He screams at the man tying the ropes of the *howdah*; he screams at Gajendra; and then he screams at Colossus and strikes him a glancing blow on the hindquarters with the bull hook.

Colossus bellows, red-eyed with rage, and lumbers to his feet. The boys scatter.

A chain is attached to an iron stake in the ground and that's supposed to hold Colossus. It will when he is calm. But when he is angry he forgets he is tethered. He forgets everything. He whirls around and the stake skitters across the dust. It hits one of the boys on the legs and he goes down howling.

Gajendra jumps on Oxathres. The bull hook bounces away from him into the dirt. Gajendra picks it up and throws it as far away as he can. He turns around to face Colossus.

'*Hida! Hida!*'

Colossus shakes his head, ears standing straight out.

'*HIDA!*'

Oxathres staggers to his feet. 'You assaulted your senior officer!'

'I saved your life.'

'I'll have you bullwhipped!'

Colossus looms over them both, stock still, not even his trunk moving. While Gajendra is there he holds back. A truly mad elephant would have run over the top of both of them. Right now, this one is doing something he thought a wild animal could never do.

He is considering his options.

'That elephant is a menace!' Oxathres shouts. He looks at the bull hook lying in the dust.

Gajendra follows his eyes. 'Pick that up and he will tramp us both into the *maidan*.'

The captain hesitates. The boy with the broken leg is howling. 'Get your elephant to the drill,' Oxathres says. He gets up and walks away.

Colossus stands at Gajendra's shoulder. His rubbery trunk nudges him in the back, knocking him off balance. Gajendra looks over his shoulder at the mountain of grey flesh. The elephant picks up some dust in his trunk and blows it over him.

He is as calm as a lapdog again.

The boys finish roping the *howdah*. They carry away the one with the broken leg.

Gajendra climbs on Colossus's neck. 'We're in big trouble,' he says to him. 'That dog Oxathres will kill us both, sooner or later.'

Colossus hoists his trunk and bellows. Everyone scatters, thinking he is crazy again, but then he settles into a slow walk, the *howdah* swaying wildly on his back. It's as if he understands.

The purpose of the battle training is simple: to get the elephants accustomed to the horses and the horses accustomed to the elephants. Horses despise elephants and it takes months of patient training before they will approach one.

The elephants are from India, a gift from the Rajah of Taxila, and few of them have been in a combat. They are like men in that they all have different temperaments. Some will run at the bugle or at the first clash of steel; others will wade into the fight before their mahavats are ready.

Now is the time to discover their mettle.

The infantry is formed up into ranks, the cavalry on each flank. Their horses are beautiful, steel grey Arabs. They are all high-prancing and nervous with elephants around.

Gajendra recognizes their commander. His name is Niarchos. He is the officer who was with Alexander the day Colossus went berserk, the one who gave him the five silver coins. How fine he looks in his red cloak, cocksure, joking with the front row of infantry.

Niarchos sidesteps his stallion towards them, along the line of elephants. He controls him with his knees, hands resting on the withers. He shouts his orders, but Gajendra cannot hear a word above the bellowing of the other bulls and the rush of the wind. There's grit in his eyes. He wants to get this over with.

The cavalry ride in pairs to the heroes' wing, on Gajendra's left. The infantry put on their helmets, pick up their shields and weapons and get ready for the drill. The tuskers around him scent the air with their trunks, flaring their ears and trumpeting, frightened by the noise and the confusion.

Colossus is quite still.

Gajendra wonders if this is what it feels like, the real thing. He has been told that in battle he will be the first to die. Kill the mahavat and you kill the elephant, as the saying went.

But I'm not going to die, Gajendra tells himself. I am going to charge to glory. I will show Alexander what elephants can do, that's my destiny.

Niarchos' equerry waves a short-staffed flag in the breeze and the cavalry charges over the plain. He can feel the vibration of their hooves even up on Colossus's neck. The foot soldiers advance, beating their swords against their shields, making as much noise as possible. They give their battle cry in unison, and it is like there is no more air left to breathe.

The cavalry close in first, dust rising from their horses' hooves in a brown fog. They reverse their spears and swarm along the line, poking and jabbing the tuskers on the legs and flanks.

Gajendra feels Colossus twitch.

He kicks him behind the ear to set him going. They will meet the charge head on. He screams at the archer in the *howdah* to hang on; not that he has a choice.

Some of the elephants have broken away already and the cavalry chase them, whooping, into the river. One goes down, crushing its mahavat and sending the *howdah* spilling into the dirt. The bowman is trampled by the horses' hooves. Just because it's a drill does not mean you can't die.

Colossus coils his trunk and flares his ears. He's game for the fight and charges the infantry phalanx. But the soldiers don't want to tangle with him, not even for a drill. They saw the destruction he caused in the *maidan*. They part and let him through.

The archers on the ground aim without arrows. One of them waves cheerfully to Gajendra, letting him know that if it were a real battle he'd have an arrow in his neck. Gajendra looks back at his own archer in his *howdah* behind him, but he would be useless in a fight with Colossus running full tilt like this. All he can do is hold onto the sides to keep from being pitched out.

The dust kicked up by the horses and elephants has obscured everything except what is directly in front of him. Gajendra sees a rider go down almost under Colossus's forelegs. The horse struggles back to its feet and the cavalry officer scrambles back into the saddle, with a panicked look over his shoulder. He is right to be afraid. Colossus would have gored both him and the horse if Gajendra had not kicked him hard behind the ears to stop him.

He hears the boom of a drum; the signal for the manoeuvre to end.

His heart is hammering, and he is covered in sweat. He has no idea where the rest of his squadron has gone. All their battle plans have been forgotten in the chaos.

Is this what a real battle is like?

He yells for the boys with the wineskins. As the dust clears, he sees that only five of the twenty elephants are left, the rest have run off into the river.

Niarchos rides through the lines, a spear overhead held level to signal that the two sides are to pull back. The soldiers throw down their weapons and flop down to rest.

Gajendra turns Colossus towards the river, finds the water boys with the melons and wineskins. Colossus lets him down and follows him into the water.

Oxathres appears, ranting again. Niarchos is most unhappy, he shouts at them. If that had been Numidian cavalry, they would all be dead. You will all stay out here in the sun until you find a semblance of order.

Gajendra and Oxathres exchange a glance. For all his cant, the captain of the elephants would have enjoyed it if Colossus had been one of the tuskers to run. Colossus ignores him, happily spraying water over his back. The sounds of trumpets and horses and drums hasn't troubled him at all.

Gajendra watches the other mahavats fighting over the wineskins, but he stays in the river with Colossus, patting his trunk and telling him how his mother would have been proud. Colossus may not know the words, but he knows the meaning behind them, he's sure of that. He tips in another watermelon. They wait for the next drill.

Soon Colossus's trunk and face plate are smeared with watermelon pulp. His eyes sparkle behind the iron mask. It's as if the beast can read his mind.

We have to do something about Oxathres before he does something about us.

CHAPTER 3

Carthage

'You must throw the baby into the pit.'

She stands, swaying, before the well. Her eyes are turned inward. She is concentrated on the past, a time when the child was alive and warm in her arms. She is unsteady; one gentle push and she would topple forward into oblivion also.

The child is mottled and grey. A girl. She is wrapped in a shroud. Mara arranges the linen neatly around the child's face, so it will not trouble her in death. She wants her to look at her best in the afterworld, neat and well attended.

'Let her go.'

Mara shakes her head. The priestess glances at her father. What shall I do? the look says. We cannot stand here like this forever. She puts a hand on Mara's shoulder to encourage her, but Mara does not move.

The wind roars inside the well. 'See, child,' the priestess whispers. 'The goddess grows impatient. She wishes to take her now. Your baby will be safe with her. She is a good mother and a kind one. There is no pain down there.'

Mara shuffles forward a half step, then another.

'You must let go now.'

Mara lowers her face to the shroud. She doesn't smell like her baby anymore. She was all curds and warmth once.

She starts to shake. The priestess guides her forward another step.

'Just do it,' her father says.

At his command, she drops her baby into the well. She falls to her knees. Her father puts his arms around her.

Grief swallows her up.

CHAPTER 4

Babylon

Alexander has ordered that his pavilion be guarded, night and day, by elephants in full battle armour. There are two hundred elephants, and they all take their turn at it. It is not necessary; a handful of bodyguards who know what they're about are deterrent enough for any would-be assassin. Gajendra supposes that he wants the elephants to intimidate his friends more than his enemies.

It is during one of these guard duties that Gajendra first sees Zahara.

Alexander leaves his headquarters to make a sacrifice at the temple of Marduk. His whole court is with him. He has more ass lickers than anyone in history. Perhaps they sweep up his dung too, like the water boys with the elephants.

Gajendra feels like he knows the great man now and almost expects a cheery wave every time he sees him. Today Alexander is in full regalia, the sun shining off his burnished ceremonial armour so that Gajendra must shield his eyes.

He is mantled in gold, edged in silver. He sits squat in the saddle, jaunty and smiling. Niarchos rides at his shoulder with Ptolemy, Perdiccas and the others he calls his Companions.

His bodyguard rides behind, all ostrich plumes and iron, trappings jangling. Alexander's harem is with him also, mostly Persian princesses and concubines. He hands women out like markers: here take one, it's a favour, now you owe me. Gajendra has heard that Alexander would rather drink or fight than screw, and even then he prefers boys to girls, like most of these Macedonians – or Macks, as people call them.

The women are veiled, as much to protect them from the sun and the dust as the hungry eyes of men. But the wind takes the scarf from one of them and Gajendra catches a glimpse of the most beautiful woman he has ever seen. In that instant he understands the meaning of longing.

The procession passes and he watches her until she is out of sight, a splash of violet lost in the dust thrown up by the rear guard. He closes his eyes, commits to memory the black eyes, the haughty look. She is the embodiment of perfection.

'Did you see her?' he asks Ravi later that day when they are relieved from duty and are washing down Colossus and Ran Bagha in the river. Ran Bagha is Ravi's elephant, smaller than Colossus and with only one tusk. The Macks think it is hilarious: a one-armed mahavat with a one-tusked elephant.

'What are you talking about?'

'Didn't you see that woman riding behind Alexander?'

'There were dozens of women.'

'The one with the dark eyes.'

'They're Persian. They all have dark eyes.'

'That one was extraordinary. I'm going to have her one day.'

Ravi shakes his head, feeling sorry for him. 'Why would you even think about something like that? Alexander's harem is not for the likes of you, boy.'

'He gives his women away to his best soldiers. Perhaps one day he will reward me for services on the battlefield.'

'They're not rewards, they're bribes to keep the Macks from mutiny.'

'Why would the army want to mutiny against Alexander? He's the greatest general in the world.'

'Not the army – just the Macedonians, the ones he relies on most in a fight. They're sick of it, Gaji. Some of them are old men now. They've been campaigning for years. They miss their home.'

This makes no sense to him. The Macedonians seem to him like they are built for war and nothing else. They are formidable on the battlefield, clannish and tough as spit. But they are a miserable lot when they have no one to fight. They sit with their scars and their silence, hating everyone with their eyes.

He has been told they are a mountain people, raised in high valleys they call *creases*, which they talk about as if they are a Rajah's pleasure gardens. He thinks what they really miss is rolling about in mud and conjugating with pigs.

They grumble constantly that there are too many foreigners in the army now. Foreigners like me, he thinks.

But if that's their mettle, then Alexander is better off with exotics; strong brown lads like me who are hungry and up for it, not these three-fingered old hacks.

'Alexander wants to march on Carthage.'

Gajendra wonders how Ravi hears these things so fast. He has a fly on every wall. 'How do you know this?'

A shrug. 'I thought everyone knew.'

'I thought we were aimed at Arabia.'

'He has to keep the Macks happy. Carthage is his compromise. He has told them they can all go back home if they help him take Carthage on the way. He'll sail them back to Macedonia from Sicily. He tells them it will be easy and there's profit in it.'

'Is that true?'

'I don't suppose it is, but you know what he's like. A few lies here and there won't bother him. He won't stop until he has slaughtered and plundered every corner of the world and back, then he'll start thinking about conquering the sky.'

'Then I want to go with him.'

'Be careful what you wish for, Gaji! Rise too high and the gods will knock you down.'

They start back toward Elephant Row with Colossus and Ran Bagha trailing behind. 'You're wrong,' Gajendra says. 'The gods like a man who believes in himself. That is why they have favoured Alexander. If you believe it can be done, you can get whatever you want.'

'You frighten me, Gaji. I don't know what will become of you if you keep talking like this.'

'Do you remember that archer in Taxila?'

'Mohander. He wasn't an archer. He was an officer in the cavalry.'

'He saved the Rajah's life at the river crossing. As his reward he gave him the most beautiful girl in his harem.'

'And what good did it do him? Three months later he got a poison-dipped arrow in his thigh, and he died screaming at phantoms. Karma is karma. You can't change it.'

'I'll make my own karma, Ravi. That's what a real man does.'

That night they sleep in the straw. Gajendra listens to the elephants and wonders what it is like to sleep next to a princess.

He imagines sliding a filmy gown off a bare shoulder, the feel of satin skin, a woman smelling of jasmine and oils. Then he imagines riding a white horse like Niarchos does, moving with speed and intent, not lurching from side to side on top of an elephant. He thinks about holding a sword, wearing armour and a red cloak, looking brilliant, purposeful.

An officer, a lion.

He stares wide-eyed at the stars and thinks about the little boy he left behind a decade ago. He wonders again why the dacoits left him alive. Perhaps no reason. Because they felt like it.

He feels no especial pity for his younger self, just a bitter impatience. It is only when he revisits the memory of his father dying, shivering and shouting at ghosts, that he experiences any sense of real grief.

Ravi is right, a man has his karma and there is nothing he can do about it. It is the way of the world. You catch a fever, you are left unprotected when the bandits come, you marry a princess, or you sleep in the straw. All luck, the fall of the dice.

But how can a man feel safe in a world where the gods control everything? Look at Alexander. He rules the world and makes his own luck. He has become a god himself. That is how you stop it, the one way you can rid yourself of this unholy dread.

You make yourself divine.

He remembers how his mother held out her hand to him as she died. The bandit who had raped her was still lying between her legs when he stuck the knife in.

Help me, she mouthed at him. *Help me.*

He rolls on his side and tries to sleep. In his dreams he crucifies the men who did it, watches them turn black in the sun and die by inches. In reality he supposes they are still out there somewhere on the banks of the Indus river, laughing around the slow coals of a campfire.

CHAPTER 5

Carthage

Mara is propped on cushions in her bed. Hanno, her father, stands in the doorway. He has two of his sergeants with him.

He bawls for the servants. 'Why did you not send for me before?'

Mara knows how she must look from the way he stares at her. He has this same face when he comes home from a campaign or an execution.

Her chamberlain arrives. 'Look at her,' Hanno says. 'Have you been bathing her, feeding her? She looks like a body on the street. Why did you not send for me?'

'She forbade it!' the old man protests, but Hanno will have none of it and boots him out of the door.

'It's time to get yourself back on your feet,' he says to her and throws open the shutters. She winces at the light.

He gets her maidservant to fetch water and turns his back while she washes her. He folds his arms and gives directions.

'How long has she been like this?' he demands of the servant girl.

The girl mumbles a reply. Mara feels sorry for her. It's not her fault.

She suspects that he blames himself for the state she is in. It is weeks since she has seen him. He cannot ignore his employer's demands. He may be a general, and responsible for the safety of the entire city, but they can just as easily turn on him. He lives as much on a sword's edge as any of the city's enemies.

The servant girl lifts Mara from the bed and carries her to the hip bath, now warmed with scented water. She is surprised that the girl can lift her so easily. She rests her hand on the girl's shoulder.

When she is done the maid wraps her in a long towel and her father takes her. He cannot look at her, the sight of seeing her so wasted distresses him so. 'You will come and live with me. I will make sure you are looked after.' This is what he is good at: giving orders, taking charge.

There is a litter and bearers waiting in the court.

'You will love again. You are young. You turned men's heads once. You shall again.'

Was this how he got over the death of her mother; dusted off his hands and straightened his tunic once she was cold. She has never seen him grieve.

The chamberlain rushes after them across the courtyard, calling her name. He holds in his hands a ring and a small blanket. He hands them to her, and she accepts them gratefully.

'What are they?' her father asks.

She does not answer, so he asks the chamberlain.

'The blanket is the one she used to wrap her baby when she was born. The ring was given her by her husband before he sailed to Panormus.'

'Is it necessary to be continually reminded of the past?' he says to her. 'There is no sense to this continual grieving. They are gone and they are not coming back. You must live and carry on.'

The lush suburbs of Megara are out past the great triple city wall and overlook miles of vineyards and farms, where goats stand in the black shade of olive trees and red water gurgles between date palms.

Her father brings her a broth and feeds it to her himself. As he spoons in the soup, he tries to lure her in with his imaginings of a new future, another husband, pink babies. He is going to take a broom to her grief. Tidy it away and assign it to the whimsy of the gods. She hears him form up his philosophy and would like for a moment to reach inside and transfer a little of her own grief into him, watch him shrink and wither also, from the bitterness of it.

But the effort of contending with him is too taxing. She nods as if she agrees with his visions and revisions, his summation of life, fate, and loss.

'You are looking better,' he says when he has fed her the broth. He stands up, satisfied. She feels like one of his soldiers: there, you have lost an arm and a leg and your manhood, but never mind, some of my excellent soup and you'll be as good as new.

'You cannot give up,' he says.

I wish I had my father's stout courage, she thinks. I have watched the way he forms up his troops, reorganizes the ranks after every bloody defeat, straightens lines, makes new strategy. Life surrounds him in a better tactical position, and he shouts bloody defiance and charges its flanks.

He stands in front of her, massive and helpless. He has the salt and pepper hair of a survivor and there are few enough of those among the generals of Carthage. Here is a man who cannot countenance defeat, ever.

'Tomorrow I will take you for a walk in the garden,' he says and his voice cracks. It startles her. The moment passes. He straightens, gives her a smile like a rallying cry. 'Yes, a walk in the garden will make you feel better,' he says and walks out before he breaks ranks and weeps.

Peacocks call from the darkness beyond the silvered lawns; the sound of the cicadas is deafening. She lies on a fresh linen sheet in a strange bed.

Her father's servants feed her and wash her while he hovers, worrying that she is still too thin; he sends musicians to play music, always tiresomely cheerful.

Her arms feel empty. She thinks about soldiers she has seen begging in the street without limbs. Do they feel like this?

The servants whisper about her.

'She's gone mad,' she hears the chambermaid say to a serving girl.

'She lost her husband and her baby within a few months, and it has turned her mind.'

'Have you seen how thin she is?' another whispers.

'She looks like a skeleton. And so pale! The cook says she cannot keep her food down. And they say she was a real beauty once!'

'I wish she would get better or die, for she is driving the poor master mad like this. And we are the ones who pay for it!'

The lawns of her father's villa stretch down to the sea wall, where the fat boles of the palm trees plump themselves in the sand like old women out for the sea air. From her bed she watches a slave pruning an ilex tree. His limbs are black and shine in the sun.

She decides to go downstairs and surprise her father at his breakfast. Her appearance has the desired effect. His face registers astonishment, then delight. He thinks she is better and his long campaign against doom is won.

'Well, look at you. I do believe you've put on a little weight.'

She sits down. 'Thank you for all you have done.'

He stops chewing and throws the hunk of bread on the table. He senses from her tone that a pronouncement is coming, and he doesn't like those.

'I am going to devote my life to the service of Tanith.'

At first he is incredulous. Once he sees that she is serious, his shoulders sag. His force of will has carried battles and councils but he cannot overrule shattered hopes.

'It's too soon to decide these things,' he says. Look at this big house and all these servants. Why doesn't she rest, he thinks, take her ease in the garden and listen to his lute player? Use her time to pray for his success when he goes to Sicily to fight the damned Greeks in Syracuse.

'For weeks now I have done nothing. My mind is made up.'

'But the priestesses are all women without hope.'

'As am I.'

'But you are not without hope. I have told you. I will find you another husband.'

'I do not want another husband. If the gods wanted me to have a husband, why did they take the one I had? I'll never find one better, so I really do not see any point in it.'

'Right, so shall we understand this then? The gods play fast and loose with my daughter, tear out her heart and take away everything she lives for. After she has dragged herself back to the land of the living, she says she will go and light their incense every day, clean their statues and say prayers for them.'

'We cannot fight the gods.'

'Watch me,' he growls, with a tilt of his chin.

She thinks he should be pleased, at least her thoughts have turned away from self-destruction.

He hides his face from her. He is calling for reinforcements he does not have. She understands how much he loves her, but it is not enough. She wants only what she had before.

In truth, he has lost as much as she has. She imagines the life he could have had; grandchildren around his knees, piles of bread and steaming meat, shouting and laughter. Instead here he is at the head of an empty table, with fresh baked bread he has no appetite for, arguing with a childless and bereft daughter.

Woodenly, he gets to his feet. He leans on the table with his knuckles. 'Why would you do this? There have been widows before and there will be widows again.'

Mara considers his question. Why does she miss her husband so much? There are so many reasons why love is a difficult thing to quantify. He would have known how to comfort her if he was here now. She recalls how he would take her head in his hands when she was sad, hold her, not saying anything, his silence as reassuring as any consolation.

Unlike her father, he never tried to take away her sadness, only reshape it. Feeling sad with someone you love is the greatest consolation she knows. He had reminded her of the palms along the road to the port, all of them bending with every breeze so that they would never break.

She wonders if he had even fought for his life when his ship had capsized. Knowing him, he would have simply shrugged his shoulders when he saw the sea rise up and slid in without even a splash. The waves would have been disappointed with him. The sea prefers its victims to put up a fight.

'You will come around, you'll see. You just need time. Sometimes life takes us along strange and painful byways. But it will come out alright in the end.'

She bows her head and does not answer. There is no point in debating with him, her mind is made up. After she has been ordained at the temple, he will miss her at first. When he realises she is not coming back he will be angry. But finally he will accept her decision. He will rejoin his army. He will go on.

'Why Tanith?'

'She has my baby. If I am at the temple every day, I will be near her.'

'Your baby is gone.'

Mara shakes her head. 'Sometimes at night, when it is quiet, I can still hear her crying.'

Now her future is decided she feels better. It is the struggling that's hard; once you accept that you cannot have what you long for, then life becomes so much easier to bear.

CHAPTER 6

Babylon

By autumn, Alexander is ready. They are going to march north-west to Tyre, then down to Egypt. Ravi says it was once ruled by a race of kings called pharaohs. Alexander has installed his own satrap in their place and has named a new capital after himself.

It is a dark place, Ravi says. The people eat the brains of the dead and keep their vitals in jars. Then they wrap the bodies in sheets and put them in coffins that look like women.

From Egypt, he will launch their campaign against Carthage. It will mean a hellishly long march across the desert. They will not be able to take all of their elephants because there will not be enough water along the way. Even if they survive the trek, it is said that the city is protected by three stout walls, as high as ten men.

Alexander's veterans don't like it. They shout their discontent at him as he rides past.

He appears untroubled by it, does not take their displeasure seriously. Why should he? He is the great Alexander. Men will always follow him, whether they like how he does things or not. There is not a city or state he has not conquered, a battle he has not won. The word is that he will not be content until he has the entire Mediterranean in his jaws.

Gajendra is excited. He knows his time is coming.

'They have never seen elephants where we are going,' he says to Ravi. 'We will carry the day in every battle from now on, and one day I will be captain of the elephants!'

In public Alexander's generals are all smiles, riding behind him like peacocks. But rumour has it there have been drunken arguments in Alexander's pavilion, food thrown, daggers produced. Surely, it is only a matter of time before someone is carried out dead. Everyone knows how Alexander once put a handy spear through one of his best friends when he dared to challenge him. He is dangerous sober. When he is in his cups, it is suicide to even debate the time of day with him.

What really has the Macks seething is that their great king has gone native. Did they go to all the trouble of defeating these foreign pansies just to have them take over their army? There are Persians among his elite Companion Cavalry now. And what do they need with barbers and bath masters, wine stewards and pastry makers? Alexander even has a night porter. They despise the fops with greased ringlets and perfumed beards that hang around the court. Their great general has taken too much of a liking to all their bowing and scraping.

To head off trouble, Alexander has sent the more disaffected of the Macedonians home with one of the few generals in his army he really trusts: Kraterus. He has orders to assume the regency from Antipater, who currently rules in Macedon in Alexander's place. Antipater is then to return to Alexander's side with fresh troops to assist in his current campaign.

Everyone knows what that means: Antipater is out of favour. No one knows what he has done to offend Alexander; become too efficient perhaps. No king can afford able princes in times of discontent, even one old enough to be his father.

Two of Antipater's sons are already in Babylon. Iolaus is Alexander's cupbearer and Kassander arrived just a few weeks before to plead his father's case and keep hold of the regency.

Apparently, the audience did not go well. Kassander left the pavilion with blood on his face.

So perhaps we will not get as far as Carthage after all, Ravi says. The Macks may turn on each other like dogs fighting over a carcass, long before that. He thinks that this is the best of the possible outcomes. 'You cannot take elephants across the desert. They will all die and us with them. He is mad!'

'All gods are mad,' Gajendra replies. 'If anyone can do it, Alexander can. Besides, I did not join this army to march elephants up and down the *maidan*. No soldier ever found his destiny in peacetime.'

Ravi shakes his head. 'You may have to rein in your ambition, lad. This time, the Macks say they have had enough.'

'Enough of what, enough of winning battles?'

'You can say that because you have never been in a battle yourself. Some of these old goats have been with him for years, since he first came to Persia. What's the point of winning all this loot, like they have, if you don't live to spend it?' He leans closer. 'He'll never get near Carthage. There's talk that Alexander will not even leave Babylon alive.'

More likely they would pull Zeus out of the sky and kick him to death, Gajendra thinks. It is a bizarre notion. 'Impossible! He is immortal.'

'So is every king. Until he dies.'

That night in his sleep Gajendra goes home. His mother is outside their hut with his sisters pounding the rice. He listens to the rhythmic *tonk-tonk* as they work in unison. They are talking and giggling as girls do. His mother chides them for being slow.

He hears men approaching on horseback and he runs out. The strangers are silhouetted against a copper sun. He feels the earth shudder under his feet.

Then he wakes. The sweat has risen on his skin like cold grease. These memories are a constant torment. He wishes he could rid himself of his own past.

Unable to sleep, he checks the patrols on Elephant Row. He finds Colossus in the straw. He will not rise no matter how he chides him. He lies there like a grey, heaving mountain. His trunk flicks feebly at the dust. It occurs to him that the horses he heard in his dream was actually Colossus, struggling to breathe.

'So, we must fetch an elephant doctor now?' Oxathres says, when he hears that Colossus is sick, and he positively glows with satisfaction.

Ravi and the boys stand around, helpless. They bring Colossus water, and apples which are his favourite, but nothing will tempt him to rise or show interest. A scour runs out of him. He stinks.

Gajendra sinks to his knees. 'What about the rest of the elephants?' he asks Ravi.

'All the others are fine. It's just Colossus.'

Gajendra feels the elephant watching him with his small, flat eye. He expects him to help. But what can he do?

Gajendra talks to him, tells him he's going to be all right, tells him how they will build a statue for him one day, right in the main square in Carthage, then one in Alexandria, in Athens, in Macedon; that he will be the most famous elephant in the whole world.

The elephant's eye follows him as he moves around, though he cannot move that massive head. Death pours out of him in a dark brown stain. The flies torment him. Gajendra fans him with a palm leaf, keeps them off him as best he can. He supposes they sense a great feast here in a day or two.

He tries to remember the things his uncle taught him about elephants and their ailments, but he has heard of nothing like this.

Ravi comes to sit by him. They watch the great creature suffer. Ravi breaks a twig off a nearby tree and places it inside his trunk to keep his airway open.

Gajendra has tried Soldier's Friend, dried yarrow petals, used to stop bleeding and for fever, but how much do you give a tusker the size of a house? He put a handful in a bucket of hot water but getting Colossus to drink the mixture was a labour that took him half the day. It did no good anyway.

They seek out one of Alexander's physicians. He claims to know something of animals and fries the leaves and flowers of the Beni Kai plant to make a potion. He tries to coax Colossus to swallow it but, because he's lying on his side, it just dribbles out. And he's too weak to stand up and drink, even if he has a mind to.

Gajendra imagines the massive workings inside; lungs like bellows as big as a man, labouring to push that massive chest up and down; a heart as big as a chariot hammering the beat like a slaver's drum but slowing with every strike.

He goes back to Alexander's physician, looking for another remedy.

'There is this,' he says. 'I brought it back with me from Taxila. One of the Rajah's doctors gave it to me, but the dose is uncertain. Give him too much and will kill him anyway.'

He hands him the powder, tells him to mix it with warm water.

Gajendra sniffs at it and winces. 'But how can I make him drink this? It's foul.'

'It's not for drinking,' the old quack says, grinning. 'You have to find another way to get it inside him. Strip down and get to work!'

So now here he stands, up to his elbows in elephant shit, pale and drained from lack of sleep. Oxathres walks in.

He takes one look at Colossus and frowns. 'We move soon, with or without him. Alexander's orders. If he is too sick, I will replace him with Asaman Shukoh.'

'We cannot leave him behind.'

'It looks like we have no choice. The other beasts are better managed than this one.'

'He's the best warrior elephant we have.'

'Not anymore,' Oxathres wrinkles his nose. 'You like sticking your hand up an elephant's ass, son?' He walks out, laughing.

'Don't listen to him. I won't let you die,' Gajendra promises Colossus. 'And I won't let them leave you behind.'

Occasionally the elephant bellows, a pitiful sound that leaves them all covering their ears.

'He is dying,' Ravi says. 'He is scouring from the inside. There's something in his vitals. Something he has eaten. What can we do?'

'While we have breath in us, we keep going. And so will he.'

He imagines his father sitting with him through the vigil that night. 'The resin the quack gave you will settle him,' his ghost whispers. 'If he can see his way to the morning, your old tusker will be all right.'

CHAPTER 7

Gajendra wakes to a shadow across the moon.

Colossus is standing upright. He waves his trunk weakly side to side.

He wants to laugh aloud. He kicks the boys awake, gets them to fetch buckets of apples and river water, plenty of it. Another few days before they are set to march and Colossus must have his strength back by then.

What had seemed impossible is now merely difficult.

A young Macedonian officer arrives on his horse, self-important and sweating. Alexander himself is to pay Gajendra a visit. He is concerned at the news he has been hearing. Is he to lose his best elephant?

Gajendra sets the boys to scouring him. They use rags to remove the stains from his hindquarters, then paint him with henna to make him look fierce. Soon he is polished like a newborn and caparisoned in red and ochre.

He stands before the animal himself and issues new instructions. I want him looking ready for the charge. Gajendra tells his boys. Set to on the ivory, paint the tips scarlet. Braid his tail!

Colossus looks baleful.

'Don't look at me like that. If he sees you stagger, he will leave you behind or carve you up for the pot. Bellow at him. Stamp your foot. Don't let him see you weak. He despises weakness. He once fought a whole battle with an arrow through his chest!'

Alexander strides in, wearing his golden armour. 'I heard the beast was dead,' he says.

'As you can see, my lord, he is not easy to kill.'

He glances at Oxathres who stands to the side, looking sour.

'I don't want to lose him,' Alexander says. 'They don't have these where we're going.'

'He will kill ten thousand of your enemies on his own,' Gajendra says. He looks at Colossus, who sways dangerously, like a tree about to come down. Their eyes meet. He swears the animal winks at him.

Alexander turns on his captain of the elephants. 'I suspect that you have risen above your ability,' he says and walks out.

That's it. The audience is over. They are all going to Carthage.

Gajendra finds a melon. Colossus opens that huge pink mouth. Gajendra tosses it in and laughs. He would have hugged him if his arms were long enough.

CHAPTER 8

Every girl in Babylon, once in her life, is required to offer herself to the goddess. It is a sign of great piety to give Astarte her virginity. The courtyard temple is always packed with women, sitting in sombre rows, separated from each other by scarlet cords. The first man who tosses a piece of silver into her lap can have her, and it is her sacred duty to the goddess to comply without demur.

No woman is too fine to overlook her obligation; no man so low that he might be rejected.

Princesses sit on silk cushions, perspiring with exquisite delicacy while their slaves stand to the side with fans; peasant girls with calloused hands and sun-hardened faces sit glum and alone on the baking marble.

Men stroll between them as if they are at a horse fair. They might as easily find a lady today as a farmer's daughter. It is all there for the taking. Some of the less favoured girls are there for days on end. A beauty might not sit long enough to warm the stone.

Gajendra has Alexander's silver, and he plans to use it well for his first time. They are heading to Carthage soon. Who could know if a first time might also be the last?

He arrives at the temple just after dawn, hoping to avoid the crowds. He wants to do this with dignity, not get into a shoving match with a drunken ferryman over who saw who first. He strolls along the lines, avoiding outstretched hands. He is flattered that he is so sought after; he supposes that as he is young and better favoured than most, the girls would rather him to a ditch digger with bad teeth.

And then he stops, catches his breath. It is her, the girl he saw riding behind Niarchos in Alexander's procession. She appears surreal in a white diaphanous gown. It has a scarlet belt with a gold chain dangling from the buckle. Her blue-black hair is braided down her back.

She has only recently arrived. She has two slaves with her, one to choose the perfect place for such a delicate bottom to rest, another to fan away the flies. The other girls eye her bitterly, jealous of her looks and her wealth. There is a commotion around her; it will be a while before she is settled. As if she thought she might be there long enough to catch her breath.

He experiences a thrill of panic; he must get there before any other man sees her. She has her back to him, is waiting for her slave to finish brushing dust from the marble and set out her pillows.

Gajendra takes Alexander's silver *siglos* from his leather pouch, hurries over and holds them out to her. 'May Mylitta prosper you,' he says, using the correct words.'

She raises her eyes. Her casual glance leaves him gawping like a bumpkin. She cups her hands for the coins then passes them to one of her slaves. Later she will offer them to the goddess, and her duty to the temple will be done.

Then she gives a little tremulous sigh and holds out her hand.

He leads her through the temple, past the glares of the less favoured. 'She didn't even get to sit down!' he hears one of the girls hiss as they pass.

She walks with her eyes down, but there is no humility in her; she looks as if she is going to her own coronation.

'My name's Gajendra,' he tells her.

Not even a nod. It is as if she had not heard him.

'What is your name?'

'Zahara.'

'I have seen you, riding with Alexander.'

'You have paid for my virginity, not my conversation,' she answers, and this haughty reply is what changes his mind and makes him decide on a different course.

She keeps her eyes to the ground even after they reach the privacy of a grove of orange trees. A pair of hairy buttocks writhes in front of them; a carter skewering a poor girl against a fig tree. They almost fall over another coupling on the ground. She does not comment.

Over there a man is at it like a dog, taking his choice from behind and making a sound very much like howling. Gajendra is disgusted. He looks for a quiet spot, secluded by bushes.

He lets go of her hand. She gives another forbearing sigh and waits.

He takes her chin and tilts her face to look at him. 'Listen to me, there's something I have to tell you.'

She still looks faintly bored.

'My name is Gajendra. Remember my name, and my face. Gajendra. Right now I am a mahavat in Alexander's army, but one day I will be counted among his finest officers. Nothing will stop me from achieving that aim, nothing.'

Still no response.

'I know I could never possess a woman like you as I am. I do not want a moment's pleasure up against a tree, that is not why I chose you. What I want from you is not something I can buy for a few pieces of silver. I want you for my own, forever.'

Her eyes widen a little. She doesn't look bored now; just scared.

'So you can leave the grove with your duty to the goddess done and your maidenhood yet intact.'

She frowns, not understanding.

'Remember me. One day you will be mine by right and for always.'

And then he turns and walks away from her. For a moment there is a feeling of pure exhilaration. It lasts until he is outside the temple and then he almost doubles over with the horror of what he has done.

'You idiot!' he mutters, as he fully realizes his loss.

But as quickly as his sense of exhilaration dissipates, so does his self-loathing. What remains is a sense of pride and resolution. He has set the stakes, made his dream real, declared it in front of the gods. The only thing to do now is to perform the impossible, as Alexander has done.

To conquer the world or to marry a princess, a man must first believe it can be done. He has come close enough to touch his dream, to feel her sweet breath on his cheek. He will move heaven and earth to have her as his own.

One day she will say his name, and she will say it with a sigh.

The camp is like a small town and gossip travels fast.

Alexander has decided to delay the march to allow Colossus time to recover. He has never done anything like this before. Well, that is not quite true; he once threatened to lay waste an entire country after someone stole his horse, even though the beast was old and lame in one leg. He wept like a boy when the tribesmen who took it brought it back.

But this is not the same thing.

The morning clatters on to the sound of men playing dice, the clash of swords from the practice yard and the boys mucking out the yard where they keep the beasts. Colossus sways his trunk as he dips into the apple barrel, trumpeting loudly.

Two days ago, he could not even find his feet.

Gajendra has put a guard on him. No one is to feed him unless I am present, he has told them. No one!

There is a hazy sun. The trees are a lurid green. The wind picks up a gritty sand that stings the eyes and sticks in the throat. Everything smells of the shit the locals use as fertilizer.

He will be glad to get away from here.

'I know who did it,' he tells Ravi. 'I know who poisoned Colossus.'

'You don't know it was poison. He got sick just like a man does. It is a foul humour that brought him down.'

Gajendra shakes his head. He points to Oxathres. 'It was him. I am sure of it. I could put a knife between his ribs right here in the yard. What do you think Alexander would do to me?'

'You know what he would do. Let it go. Do your Uncle Ravi a favour instead. I need a loan.'

'What do you need money for?'

'I'll pay you back. Just two *siglos*.'

'Two *siglos*? Don't tell me you lost that much playing dice.'

'Come on, help me out. It's not that much. I saw one of Alexander's cronies give you a lot more than that, that day Colossus went berserk in the yard.'

'I don't have it. I spent it.'

'On what?' He sees the look on Gajendra's face. 'On a whore? What tart charges that much?'

Gajendra doesn't answer.

'Must have been a pretty one. What was it like?'

'It was fine.'

'Fine? You get yourself a girl at last and spend half a year's ages on her and that's it, *fine*.' He narrows his eyes. 'You didn't do it, did you?'

Gajendra looks the other way.

'Tell me it isn't true.'

'Leave me alone.'

'You couldn't get it up, but you still let her keep the money?'

'I can get it up.'

'I don't believe you.'

'I don't care what you believe. It's none of your business. I have to go into the city.'

'You can't go. There's a drill.'

'Colossus is not well enough for the drill. I'll be back later.'

'What's so important you have to go now?'

Gajendra doesn't answer. He walks off, leaving Ravi staring after him, bewildered.

Babylon means *Gate of God*. The black walls were built by a king called Nebuchadnezzar when Alexander's ancestors were still living in caves and eating their young. The walls look like cliffs and there are over a hundred gates of solid bronze. It would take a man two days to walk around them.

There is a hot dry wind, ideal for flying kites. They love kites here, or anything that snaps in the wind. Out on the *maidan*, kite masters fly extravagant creations of pressed flax, dyed to dazzling colours, in every imaginable shape; there are swallows, butterflies and carp.

Their camp is on the other side of the river from the city. Gajendra pays his coin to the ferryman and crams into a water taxi with the lovers, the merchants and the hawkers, for the short trip across the Euphrates. As they draw closer, he looks up at the towers of the great city, burned brick and bitumen, so high they seem to merge with the sky. Ravi says that from the top you can see all the way to Macedon.

He goes in by the Ishtar Gate. Inside it reeks of incense from a hundred temples. The city is a riot of greenery; it seems everyone has a roof garden. The people jabber to each other in Sumerian but will take your money in any language you care to choose.

The shops cater for every kind of depravity. These Persians would rather fuck than fight, or so Ravi says. He gapes like a farm boy; do they need these whips and phalluses between dusk and dawn? There is an olive wood penis so big it would not have shamed an elephant. He's just a country boy. He never knew there were such things.

He asks a hook-nosed hustler for an apothecary. There are two worthy of the name, he is told. It takes him all morning to find the first, but when he tells him what he needs the man laughs at him and says that it's impossible.

The second shop is no more than a hole in the wall. Inside there are shelves lined with jars and flasks. A crocodile gapes its jaws at him, terrifying even though long dead. There are dead men's skulls, a still, a set of scales. It smells like a tomb.

The shopkeeper is cautious. He has a certain look about him. If he is not guilty of the crime against his elephant, then he is surely guilty of many other things just as bad.

Gajendra tells him he wants white hellebore.

'That will be difficult.'

'Come on, not that difficult, surely. You got it for my captain!'

The apothecary's eyes drop. He looks around the room, searching either for a weapon or a route of escape. 'I don't know what you're talking about.'

Gajendra grabs him by the throat and pushes him against the wall. The apothecary would like to scream but he can't get his air. 'Now listen,' Gajendra says and lodges his knee into the man's groin to sharpen his concentration, 'all I want from you is the truth. Otherwise I'll slice you up and put you in a jar up there with the snake's droppings.'

The man's eyes acquiesce. Gajendra releases his grip on his throat a little. 'Tell me what happened.'

'I only supply. It is not my fault what a man does with such things.'

'It was hellebore! What did you think he was going to do with it?'

'He said he wanted it as a purge. I told him to take care with it, that he should not use more than a pinch each morning.'

He releases the man, but the fellow's legs won't hold him, and he flops onto the floor. He tells him to describe the man. It is Oxathres, right down to the squint. He was right.

He reaches into the apothecary's belt and takes out his purse. He extracts two silver coins to pay off Ravi's gambling debts. Then he steps over him and goes to the doorway.

'You are robbing me! Is that what this is all about?'

'I'm accepting a loan on very favourable terms. If I ever see you in the street, I will slit your throat.' He leaves.

Now for the captain of the elephants.

49

CHAPTER 9

Gajendra stands at the waterfront among the bustle of hawkers, pickpockets, merchants and procurers. He smells spitted meat and baking bread. His stomach growls, but he cannot eat. There is too much murder in his heart.

When he gets back to Elephant Row, he cannot find the captain. The water boys say he disappeared after the drill that morning and they haven't seen him since. It is towards evening when he sees him heading out of the camp. He follows him.

Oxathres looks furtive and Gajendra takes pains not to be seen. A Macedonian officer is waiting for Oxathres near an olive grove. They are up to something; it is clear from the way they are talking. They make their way along one of the irrigation channels to a hut sometimes used by the government officials, whose job it is to inspect the complex system of waterways that patchwork the plains around the city.

They go inside and Gajendra hears them bar the door.

He creeps closer, takes off his sandals and climbs up the wooden ladder at the back of the hut onto the flat roof. A hole has been cut for a cooking fire and if he lies beside it, he can hear them talking below.

'You look like you have the flux,' a man's voice says. 'The state of you! Get a hold of yourself man, or we'll never get this done.'

Then another voice. It is Oxathres. He would know that grating whine anywhere. 'My lord, you don't understand the risk I am taking.'

'You think the danger is any less for me? I'll die with you if we're discovered.'

'I won't betray you.'

'Of course you would if his torturer is at you with his knives and irons.'

This is bad business they're about. The gods have shaken the tree and dark and dangerous fruit have fallen into his lap. This is not about elephants. Oxathres has more on his mind than murdering Colossus.

His heart starts pounding so hard, he is afraid Oxathres and the Greek can hear it down there. Any moment they will look up and wonder who it is pounding on the roof with a stave.

With the twilight the mosquitoes come out and start swarming. He dares not swat at them. They buzz impudently in his ear as if they know his predicament.

'You have the poison?'

'I had an apothecary in the town make it up for me,' Oxathres says.

'And you have tested it?'

'Well enough.'

'It must be slow. If he dies quick, it will raise suspicion and give his friends reason to accuse me.'

'They say it resembles a fever, like the one he had in India. Once it takes hold a man dies measure by measure, from the inside out.'

'You had better be right. We cannot fail at this.'

'You have the means to deliver it?'

'My brother is Alexander's cupbearer.'

The itching on Gajendra's bare legs is maddening, but there is nothing he can do. Start slapping away at these midges now, and they will be up here with their swords out to fillet him. They have said enough yet he wishes they would say something more. He has enough for accusation but not for proof.

The first stars blink above the desert.

'It is harsh to kill him this way.'

'I would rather he died frothing, than be dragged across that fucking desert for yet another campaign. The men will laud us as their saviours. When it's done, my father will assume command and bring an end to this madness.'

They light a candle in the room below. Gajendra resists the urge to peek down. He got enough of a look at the captain's fellow conspirator back at the olive grove: reddish hair, broad shoulders in a red cloak, the bearing of a general. He believes he has seen him before, in a procession; it is Kassander, the son and envoy of Antipater, who rules Greece in Alexander's absence.

'You will remember me when all is done?' Oxathres says.

'You will get your reward, never doubt that.'

They leave separately and Gajendra waits till their footsteps have receded before he dares a glimpse above the parapet.

They are silhouetted against the evening, headed in different directions and on foot.

At last he can take his revenge on the midges, one of them so fat with his blood that when he squashes it he looks as if he has been knifed in the leg.

Above him the stars are swinging across a deepening sky. Only the gods that ride them know their future promise. But if he gets back to the camp alive, he knows what they foretell for Oxathres.

Alexander no longer sleeps alongside his men. Gajendra comes from a place where you would expect nothing less of a Rajah. But the

Macks are in a froth about it. They say it is another sign that he has forsaken them. The general can do nothing these days without the phalanx muttering into their beards and spitting into the fire.

But they may be right. Alexander has even abandoned the grand pavilion he captured from the Persian king, Darius. It is the size of a parade ground; you could stable horses in it. But it is not fine enough. Instead, he has gone to live in the palace and leaves his soldiers to sleep rough on the other side of the river.

He fears assassins, some say; others think that as he now considers himself a god, he believes he should live like one.

Guard dogs yelp and growl behind the palace gates. A sentry looks Gajendra up and down and laughs at him when he requests entry.

'What the fuck have you done to yourself?' the guard asks him. 'What's wrong with your face?'

'I was bitten by mosquitoes.'

'You look like you've been in a fight.'

'I have to see Alexander.'

'Who the hell are you?'

'My name's Gajendra, I'm a mahavat with the elephant squadron.'

'Well, see here, Gajendra. Fuck off.'

'But I must see Alexander.'

'Leave a petition with his scribe in the morning.'

The gatehouse door slams.

He hammers again with his fist. The guard reappears, asks another guard to hold his spear and then kicks Gajendra across the street. 'Look here, lad, I won't have this. If you do that again, I'll grab your ankle and bash you up against the wall like a cat. Now get out of here.'

But the commotion has woken the captain of the guard.

He storms into the torchlight, still buttoning his tunic. He has been screwing a servant girl in the guardroom and all this noise has put him off his stroke. 'What's going on out here?'

The guard snaps off a salute. 'We have here a skinny little gyppo. He wants to see Alexander and won't fuck off when he's told.'

'I'm not a gyppo. I'm a mahavat with the elephants. His finest.'

The captain's face is a study. All his men have to do is guard the door and open it only when given the password, not get into brawls with elephant boys. It is surely a simple enough task.

'What are you doing here?' he says to Gajendra, buckling his sword belt.

'I have to see Alexander. There is a plot against him.'

'Keep talking.'

'I overheard two men speaking. I know one of them. I saw him riding with Alexander in procession. He plans to poison him.'

The captain stands there, considering. Gajendra feels blood trickle down his forehead where the guard has struck him.

'The plot is real. He fully intends to carry it out.'

The captain grabs the guard by the tunic and pushes him out of the way. His dilemma plays on his face: there's a promotion or a horsewhipping for him in this.

'You'd better come with me,' he says to Gajendra, finally.

They go deep into the palace, the captain's studded sandals echoing on the stone. Torches flare in brackets on the walls. Gajendra counts six gates. Once all there was between Alexander and his army was a strip of canvas and a guard's good morning.

He is shocked by the change in the King of Asia, as he now styles himself. Alexander is sprawled on a chair surrounded by his generals. He is dressed in a white robe and sash with the royal purple at its border. He even has a blue and white diadem. He looks like a Persian nobleman, in other words, like a pansy.

Alexander does not have his usual bounce tonight. He is yawning and bleary. Gajendra glances at the silver goblet on the table. He hopes they have not poisoned him already. It would be easy to do when he is in this state. He looks at the men hovering around him. I wonder which one of you is the assassin.

'Who is this?' Alexander says to the captain of the guard.

'This man came to the gate saying he needed to see you urgently. He claims he has information of a plot against your life.'

'Another one?' an officer sneers. It is Niarchos.

'What's your name?' Alexander asks him.

'Gajendra. I am a mahavat in the elephant brigade.'

'A jumbo fucker,' another one growls.

Alexander rouses himself from his stupor. He swings his legs around and gives the captain signal to leave. The man looks disappointed. He had hoped for commendation. He gets none.

'I've seen this one in action before,' Alexander says. 'He talks to elephants.'

'Does he trumpet at them with his pizzle?' Niarchos says. 'I should like to see that.'

The other Companions enjoy his ribald choice of imagery. Alexander does not laugh. 'Don't make fun of him,' he says. 'That is the problem with the common soldiery. They don't think we respect them anymore. Isn't that right, elephant boy?'

This is unexpected. Gajendra did not expect to be interrogated about general morale. He is being tested before he has even had the chance to tell his news.

'I don't pay attention to the talk.'

'Well, you should. A man who does not pay attention to the talk around him cannot use it to his advantage.'

He is right, it is a test. He wants to see your mettle away from the elephants. That glittering eye is on you now and you had best speak up. There is no point in being mealy mouthed in this company.

'Some still adore you and would follow you to the end of the earth. You know this already. But others say that you have gone too far, that conquest has gone to your head. You have forgotten your crease. Forgive me, I am from Taxila. I have no idea what that means.' This last is a lie, but it does no harm to appear disingenuous in such company.

Alexander's lip curls in the torchlight. 'A crease is what we call the valley where we are raised. They mean to say that I have forgotten my own people. What else do they say?'

'That you are mad.'

There is an audible hiss as everyone in the room catches their breath.

Alexander smiles. 'Madness is divine,' he says. 'All gods are mad.'

He stands up. He is steady on his feet, despite the wine that is spilled across the table, soaking like a bloodstain into the wood. 'And what do you think. You think me mad?'

'I think you are all that I should like to be.' He has spoken without thinking. There is a moment of stillness, then Alexander throws back his head and roars with laughter.

He stabs Gajendra in the chest with his forefinger. 'Who is this pup? Tell me again why he is here.'

Gajendra addresses Alexander directly. 'I overheard two men plotting against you. They plan to put poison in your wine.'

'Which men?'

'One is Oxathres, the captain of the elephants.'

'Well, of course it is,' Niarchos shouts. 'This raggedy-arsed little fucker is out for his own advancement. If you listen to every calumny that comes wheedling up to your ear, we shall have the whole army settling scores by way of promotion.' He turns on Gajendra. 'Look at him. The gall of the boy. He comes in here, stinking of elephant, hawking yet another poisoner's story and expects us to believe him.' He reaches out and grabs Gajendra by the jaw. 'He doesn't even shave yet.'

'Yet he's a wondrous turn with an angry elephant.'

Niarchos stands so close Gajendra can smell the wine on his breath. 'Sold your ass to a corporal yet? Pretty boy like you, there must a copper or two in it.' He turns to his fellows. 'They all do that, these Indians.'

The calumny rings in his ears. The hypocrisy – being accused of buggery by one of these big-nosed Greeks – is more than he can bear. But he manages a suitable reply. 'I would not sell my ass to a corporal,' he says, setting his shoulders. 'Nothing less than a captain of cavalry, thanks. But most of them are spoken for.'

Alexander laughs. He is enjoying this.

Niarchos is irritated that he has lost the initiative. 'Who is this little wretch?' he says to Alexander.

'I got him and his fellows as part of the truce with Porus. I asked for a core of his war elephants and the handlers to manage them.'

'Well, this one's no use to you. No hair on his balls yet.'

Gajendra flinches again at these insults but doesn't take his eyes from Alexander.

'You heard what he said,' Alexander says to him. 'Speak up for yourself. What do you think about what Niarchos has said?'

'I think that I am older than you were when you fought against the Thracians, and that you'll be happy to smell my elephants when there's a squadron of enemy cavalry at your right and centre and your own line's ready to break.' He rounds on Niarchos. 'Let's see if my elephants don't smell as sweet as *patchouli* to you then.'

Niarchos looks suddenly too hot in his clothes. His face is red from drink and bad temper. Alexander decides to intervene. Another time he might have let his general skewer Gajendra for his impudence but tonight he is impressed with the lad's spunk. 'Don't mind him,' he says to Gajendra. 'He lost his nephew to an elephant at Gaugamela.'

He puts a hand on his shoulder. 'Tell me about these men who conspire against me. One was the captain of the elephants. Did you recognize the other?'

'Yes. He is sitting right there.'

He points to one of the couches, but it is now empty. One of the guests has slipped away during the arguments.

'Kassander!' Niarchos hisses.

Iolaus, Alexander's cupbearer, springs forward and grabs Gajendra by the throat, calls him a toady and a serpent. Alexander pulls him off and tells the others to find Kassander. They believe him now, even Niarchos.

Everyone is in uproar except for Alexander, who looks delighted. 'Rouse my torturer. Tell him the captain of the elephants needs stretching and twisting a little. If there's any truth to this tale, we'll hear it from him.'

The company is dispersed. At last only Alexander remains behind with Niarchos and Gajendra. Their general sits down and pours wine into his goblet from a flask. He grins. There is red wine on his teeth, making him look bloody.

'Shall we ask again how you came by this information?'

'I was following Oxathres.'

'To what purpose?'

Gajendra considers a lie, but an instinct tells him the truth will serve him better, incriminating as it is. 'I was set to brain him and leave him in a ditch.'

'You see?' Niarchos says. 'This is revenge, not information.'

'I might agree with you,' Alexander says, 'except for the empty chair at the end of the table. No matter. We'll soon get to the bottom of this.' He resumes his slump and regards Gajendra with a lazy grin. 'What a useful lad you're turning out to be!'

By the time Gajendra gets back to his straw, it seems the whole army knows what has happened. News travels faster here than fire through summer grass. Ravi rushes over to him.

'What has happened? Everyone is saying that Oxathres has been arrested.'

'You look worried.'

'Some of the Macks are saying that you were part of the plot and are to be crucified in the morning.'

'As you can see, I'm still here. What other rumours did you hear?'

'That it was you who denounced him, and that Alexander has promoted you to general and given you a palace and your own harem.'

'Sadly, the truth lies somewhere in between.'

'I was afraid for you,' Ravi says.

He puts a hand on his arm. 'I was afraid for me, too.'

Something hits him hard on the side of the head. He looks up. Colossus has taken an apple from his barrel and blown it at him using his trunk.

Gajendra pats his tusker's head. Colossus is mollified, but only after Gajendra feeds him a watermelon.

Ravi shakes his head. 'I swear he's almost human sometimes,' he says.

Over the next few days the stories flow thick and fast. It is like an army of old women, all gathered by the well. It amuses him to hear the stories repeated back to him in different ways; that Kassander paid Oxathres to make Colossus run amok in the *maidan* and trample Alexander; that Oxathres had been planning to lead a charge against the palace at the head of the tuskers; that Alexander had been poisoned with a potion made from elephant bile.

When you know the truth, the lies that spin off it become truly astonishing.

'I almost feel sorry for your friend Oxathres,' Ravi says. 'You should have seen him when they dragged him off. He was crying and slobbering like a child.'

Gajendra might feel sorry for him too, but then reminds himself that Oxathres did not blanche at torturing Colossus with the hook and then the poison.

'Kassander planned it all,' Ravi goes on. 'They found him halfway to Sidon and have dragged him back here to face Alexander.'

Three days later there are executions. The captain of the elephants is first. It is a chill morning. The men stand around huddled and shivering, warmed by the prospect of hearing somebody scream. Alexander strides from his tent in his golden armour, mounts his horse and parades in front of them. He does not speak. He rides down the lines, his horse skittish, flicking its tail and twisting its head.

Then Oxathres is dragged out, or what Gajendra believes is him. He has been badly used. He cannot stand, either from fear or from their tortures; his guards must drag him towards the cross that has been prepared. A rope of saliva spills from his mouth. He is screaming, but there are no words, just a high-pitched wail.

He has on only his tunic and there is blood matted in his beard.

Two of the men behind Gajendra make a wager. One says he will be dead by the morning, the other bets a *siglo* that he will still be groaning when the crows take his eyes out.

A man standing behind Gajendra leans forward and squeezes his shoulder. 'This must be a good day for you,' he says.

A good day? Four days ago, he wanted to pulverize this man with his fists and feet, but that was different. He wanted to do murder but not this. 'What did they do to him?' he asks Ravi.

'Hot irons and a turn on the wheel. They say he gave it all up before they started but Alexander insisted they make him scream anyway. He sat and watched while he had his breakfast.

They strip him. There are lesions all over him. Gajendra swallows down the acid in the back of his throat. 'I hated him,' he says to Ravi. 'But I never hated him this much.'

'He did this to himself.'

The executioners are expert. They have performed the task many times before. They hold him down on the cross as they apply the nails, first through the wrist bones and then the ankles separately, the legs pinned either side of the stanchion.

They have dug a hole in the ground ready to plant the base of the cross, and they haul him up. It isn't very high from the ground; Alexander's horse could look him in the eye. Gajendra flinches and cannot watch. Could they not just kill him and be done with it?

To hear a man scream like this in the silence of a shuffling parade ground is a sobering proposition. He tries to remember Oxathres lashing at Colossus with the bull hook to make himself feel better about it.

The next wretch brought out is Iolaus, Alexander's cupbearer. He looks as well as a lad might who has been flayed with horse whips. The boy is similarly prepared and hoisted up. It takes longer because he faints when they bang in the nails and Alexander insists they wake him with buckets of water so he can better enjoy the experience.

He supposes no one here this morning will be in a great hurry to be next to try to kill the King of Asia.

Alexander wishes to make his point. He spurs his horse to the front rank of soldiers, until he is close enough that they can feel his horse's breath in their faces. Then he slowly rides around the entire parade ground, as if he is looking at each man in turn, until he has completed an entire circuit of his army.

The sun rises over the eastern hills. It is going to be a hot day. The man behind Gajendra taps him on the shoulder again. 'A fine day to be out in the sun. His skin will be black by sunset. Two *siglos*.'

Gajendra shakes his head, declining the wager.

It is Kassander's turn last of all. Gajendra wonders how it might have turned out if he had kept his nerve that night and bluffed this out. Would Alexander still have believed his story if the son of Antipater had looked him in the eye and denied everything?

When he is brought out it sets up a murmur among the Macedonians. Alexander flicks at the reins and his horse spins around to face them all. He sidesteps him right to the first rank. The murmur dies to silence.

Unlike the others, Kassander walks with his head held up. Behind him comes a squadron of a dozen archers, marching single file. No cross for him. As a nobleman, he is entitled to a nobleman's death. They chain him to a post facing the Macedonian ranks.

Alexander wants the ranks to have a good view.

Kassander spares a glance for his two fellow conspirators gasping on their trees. He appears contemptuous. You have let me down, the look says.

'Look at their faces,' Ravi said. 'The Macks do not adore Alexander as they once did.'

'He'll bring them around,' another man says. 'He always does. When he takes Carthage, they'll be fighting over each other to kiss his ass.'

The archers arrange themselves in a line, facing the post and about twenty paces from it. Alexander walks his horse towards them and with a grand gesture withdraws his sword from its scabbard. The archers each select an arrow and raise their bows in unison.

Gajendra holds his breath. Kassander starts to make a speech. Alexander hits him around the head with the flat of the sword and he slumps in his bonds. 'I have decided to be merciful,' Alexander says. 'Cut him down.' He looks at Oxathres and Iolaus. 'Not those two.'

Oxathres starts weeping again. The passage of a single day is nothing when you are in a pavilion by the river, eating sesame seeds with honey. When you are hanging on a splintered cross in the desert sun, it stretches ahead like a hundred times a hundred years.

The army is dismissed and shuffles back to the camp, unusually silent. Gajendra turns to Ravi. 'Have you ever done something and you're not sure afterwards if it's a good thing or a bad thing?'

'No.'

Gajendra stares at the two men on their crosses. The cupbearer is trembling, but Oxathres is quite still, and he thinks that by some miracle he has died. But then he raises his weight on his skewered wrists and takes a long trembling breath before sagging to hang limp on the nails again. He wonders how many times he will do that before his strength and his will give out. He hopes the man who wagered him still alive by the morning will lose his money.

'Do you think Alexander will give them an hour or two and then order them killed? He won't let them hang there all day, will he?'

Ravi shrugs. 'What do you think?'

'I think he is likely to leave them to their suffering.'

'So do I. They plotted to kill a god, and gods are nothing if not cruel. Do one thing for me, Gajendra.'

'What is that?'

'If you ever rise so high that you are like him, and I try to kill you for it, don't hang me on a cross.'

Gajendra laughs. But Ravi is deadly serious.

'That could never happen,' Gajendra says.

'Oh, you never know,' Ravi says.

'You must get them all back to their drills,' Niarchos tells him the next day. 'We can't have another debacle like last time. If it weren't for your big tusker, Alexander might have given up on the idea of using war elephants.

Gajendra has been promoted from being a humble mahavat to Niarchos' second in command, though no announcement has been made.

'Hurry up and get to it.'

'It should be Ravi. He's the most experienced. I'm just his apprentice.'

'Which one's Ravi? I don't know the names of all these fucking Indians. Anyway, you don't look like an apprentice to me. They all listen to you and that elephant of yours is the best we have. Do as I say.'

A week later, Gajendra is rewarded with Oxathres' position as captain of the elephants; he is even offered a place in Alexander's outer circle. He feasts at the long table with the other junior officers of Alexander's army. Niarchos himself is given the rank of *Elephantarch;* a new position invented just for him. It is the first time a Macedonian general will be in command of an elephant squadron.

It demonstrates to everyone the importance their general places on his new weapons of war.

CHAPTER 10

Carthage, 322 BC
Temple of Tanith

Hanno is shocked at the change in his daughter. It is not so much a physical change that he notices; it is that there is finally a light in her again. Not a raging fire, to be sure, but after so long even candlelight will do.

When she greets him, she treats him with formal respect, like the head of the household giving the weekly report. Her serenity is intimidating. As they walk in the gardens of the temple, her talk is not of her lost husband and child but of prophecy. One of her fellow priestesses has earned a reputation as an oracle. She has foretold the downfall of the city, claims that it is inevitable and will happen imminently, with or without his army's intervention.

Hanno doesn't believe in prophecy, except for political purposes. But the oracle has only given voice to what everyone privately fears, which is that nothing can stop Alexander's inexorable advance. So far no city or country has been able to defy him. News of his progress along the coast came months ago. He is marching west from his new city of Alexandria in Egypt, building a road as he goes.

He could have come by sea and landed at Cape Bon if he had wanted to play the invader. He has a vast fleet of one thousand warships in Cilicia and Phoenicia. Instead he is laying a trans-African road. He is coming not to destroy but to colonize, and he is taking his time about it.

All is not well in Alexander's empire, Hanno's envoys tell him. Antipater has fomented rebellion in Macedon and has found a willing ally in Antigonus the One-Eyed, the satrap of Turkey. Kraterus has gone to deal with it, along with ten thousand of Alexander's veterans from Babylon. There are reports of the two armies massing in Tarsus.

Antipater had no choice but to rebel. Alexander crucified one of his sons and imprisoned the other, over the latest poison plot. Hanno is glad he is not Macedonian. You dare not eat anything over there unless you pick it fresh off the tree or throttle and cook it yourself.

But this internal strife has not slowed Alexander's advance. Hanno has done all he can. It is one thing to be forewarned of Alexander's intention, it is another to prevent it. He is a vast storm building on the horizon. You cannot stop the weather either.

But some good news; his spies tell him that it is not the same army that he took against Persia. There are weaknesses, or perceived ones at least. The number of Macedonian veterans has dwindled. Alexander now has Scythians and Bactrians in his cavalry, wild tribesmen with tattooed faces and bedecked ponies. His archers are Indians. His lancers are Parthians and Syrians. Only his light infantry are Greeks and Macedonians, but they are just arrived. Most of them have never seen a battle.

Alexander has another twelve thousand Persians in training, and no one with any sense trusts a Persian.

Yet the core of his strength is still there. He has his Agrianian javelineers, wild men who fight with dogs and can take the eye out of a lizard at a hundred paces. He has his Companion Cavalry, though that too is reinforced with Syrians.

Most telling of all, he still has some veterans with him, fifty-year-old warriors who were fighting battles when most of Carthage's population were suckling at their mothers' teats. These are the men who will make the difference. They are hardened by years of campaigning; they have iron discipline and are expert in weaponry and battle tactics. They are the best soldiers in the world.

Alexander will have to leave fifteen thousand troops stationed in Babylon with Meleager, to guard his rear and enforce his rule there. So Hanno estimates he will have five thousand horse and a little over twenty-five thousand infantry by the time he arrives in Carthage.

Though does it really matter how many? His reputation is such now, that people say he can take a moderately sized city on his own with a buckled helmet and a bent sword.

'You have been charged with the defence of the city,' the Council have told him. 'You have superior numbers. He will be exhausted after a long march. This Alexander is not invincible.'

Being invincible has nothing to do with numbers and battle formations. It has to do with attitude, cunning and good fortune. And what was fortune but the invisible hand of the gods?

The Council members have argued among themselves for hours: should they meet him on the plain or prepare for siege? A siege would be better. Alexander will always outwit you on a flat plain.

They choose the plain. He suspects they will all have boats waiting should the fight go against them. The weather is better in Spain at this time of the year.

Day by day Alexander gets closer. What frightens Hanno is not the battle but the seeming inevitability of their fate. Alexander has never lost a battle. He knows it, and his army knows it too.

'We must get you away from Carthage,' Hanno tells Mara.

'My place is here in the service of the goddess. I cannot leave.'

'What will you do if the city falls, and you are made a slave?'

'Accept it.'

'A daughter of mine cannot accept such a fate. I order you to leave the city!'

She smiles. Once she would have defied him, now she slides either side of him, like waves around a rock. 'Why should I leave if you are defending us? Do you not believe you can win?'

'I want to know you are safe in all eventualities.'

'I will not break my vow to the goddess. I will remain.'

He wonders what he can do. He has never told this wisp, this fragile wonder, how much he loves her. A sinew jumps in his cheek. He thinks of arranging an abduction, sending her to Lilybaeum. 'Do it for me, then.'

It is the first time he has ever asked her for anything.

Her serenity fractures. 'Father, I cannot. You have your duty. Allow me mine.'

Once, as a child, he found a pup that had been abandoned by its mother. Its eyes had not yet opened, and it squirmed warm in his hand. He placed it on a cushion in his room and tried to feed it ass's milk with a spoon. He had even slept beside it that night, murmuring encouragement. He blew on its face and whispered about the rats they would catch together when he was grown.

In the morning it was dead.

That was the way of it. You did your best to love something and keep it safe, but Mara was right, in the end it was the gods who decided who lived and died. And the gods could be relied upon by no man.

CHAPTER 11

Outside Carthage

Already Babylon seems a lifetime ago. They have been travelling for months. Apart from a brief sojourn in the Egyptian city their general now calls Alexandria, they have been constantly on the move.

They have been camped here within sight of the city for many weeks. Alexander wants the army properly rested for this next battle.

It is not yet dawn and Alexander's tent is full of generals, marshals and brigade commanders as well as the tribal chiefs of their auxiliaries, wild-looking men in fox-skin caps. They stink to heaven.

The sky is the colour of pewter, the air so thick Gajendra can hardly breathe. Sweat crawls over his body. Yet Alexander looks fresh and spirited. It could be a dewy morning in the mountains.

He wears the armour they say once belonged to Hercules, the metal greening with age, a leopard-skin cloak over it. Under his arm is a gold helmet with the wings of a bird set in white gold on either side. There are greaves on his legs. His thighs are the size of tree limbs and look about as hard.

The first rays of sun catch the purple silk of their tent and colours them all in blood.

Niarchos stands in the corner like a predator, debating with himself which of the company he might like to consume. His eyes fix on Gajendra. He forever sings one note: 'These fucking Indians, these pretty boy foreigners.' Always the same old cant. He is Macedonian and thinks that mud wrestling pigs in his youth is a sign of aristocracy. It appears to Gajendra that every true-born prince in that country fucks a goat by the time he is twelve years old and considers it a sexual conquest.

The war council is divided into two groups, each suspicious of the other's motives. Alexander's generals glower and mutter among themselves; Lysimachus, Ptolemy and the rest. They resent these Persian princes, who now make up half their king's Companions. They have grown to value the elephants but hate the fact that they have to employ men from the Rajah's old brigades to ride them.

Alexander claps his hands and laughs, as if they are all about to open a new flask of wine or go into a brothel. He looks at his officers; his officers look at him.

His height is no impediment to the force of his personality. 'So,' he says, 'are we ready to take Carthage?'

There is a parchment on the table, held down at the four corners with stones. Alexander points out the enemy's defences; Hanno has the sea on his left and the lake on his right. They have sixty thousand infantry and six thousand cavalry. Their infantry, however, is made up of recruits who do not know which end of a lance to hold. It is just a handful of mercenaries from Gaul, Greece and Iberia. Hanno also has Numidian cavalry, bare-arsed gyppos in leopard skins. One Macedonian is worth ten barbarians, he tells them. 'So I calculate we outnumber them five to one!'

The generals laugh. The Persians frown at each other. The day is not an hour old and already he has insulted half his general staff.

'Hanno has decided on open battle. He has taken up a defensive position on the plain with his infantry in the centre, his cavalry at the wings. He is showing us what he thinks are his strengths: his massed infantry, a flanking left wing. So, we already have the advantage. We can change our plans as we see fit. He has already indicated his intention.'

With a few sweeping gestures, he briefs them on the position of Hanno's battle lines. He has placed staked timber palisades in front of his infantry; he wishes to fight the battle on the wings. The troops of Carthage have never faced elephants before, and it is clear from this deployment how greatly they fear them. He has placed the Sacred Band, irregulars from the city itself, behind the main army, in reserve.

Next, Alexander tells them how they will win. His philosophy has always been simple; to win a battle you do not have to prevail at every strategic position, or even at most of them. An army needs only to win at the most telling point. In every case, it means ignoring the limbs and going to the heart.

'We must ask ourselves with our every stroke how our foe will counter,' he tells them. 'All our tactics shall seek to provoke a breakthrough in their line.'

He turns to Niarchos. As Elephantarch, he has responsibility for the most unpredictable element in his army – the elephants.

'We will distract them with our tuskers, wave them in front of their faces like a snake charmer with a cobra, while we strike elsewhere. The elephants are well-drilled and rested after the trek from Egypt. The effect will be terrifying.'

The Persians look at each other; they are terrified of the elephants themselves. They call them *ahrima* – demons – and refuse to go near them.

This plan is one that Alexander has used before, at the Granicus River. Hanno has superior cavalry numbers and Alexander is sure he will try to exploit it. They will use specially trained javelineers he calls 'stingers' to counter the threat. Meanwhile, Perdiccas is charged with several squadrons of cavalry to hold the left flank.

The elephants will attack the centre of the line. That alone may be enough. The first time any soldier faces an elephant in battle he is tempted to run. Even Alexander's own veterans, the Silver Shields, still shudder when they talk about facing up to the tuskers at Jhellum.

Alexander should be looking to me to lead the charge, Gajendra thinks. I will be the one on Colossus's neck. If Colossus stands firm, so will the rest. Niarchos has no idea what he is doing. The elephants are nothing like commanding a squadron of cavalry.

But Gajendra is not a Mack, so he will have to stay out of sight

'It is not about numbers,' Alexander says. 'It is about bringing the utmost violence to their most vulnerable point with the greatest speed. Speed is the key to all martial success.'

Gajendra goes back to Elephant Row, hears the beasts trumpet to each other as the water boys paint red circles around their eyes to make them look fierce.

That night, not one of the elephants sleeps.

Gajendra watches the water ripple in the troughs from their rumblings. They are talking to each other. It's as if they know.

Tomorrow. Tomorrow they fight.

CHAPTER 12

The Battle of Carthage, 322 BC

Gajendra has never been in a battle before.

He battles with his nerves as he leads Colossus to his position in the line. He is not alone. He sees one of the young recruits vomit on his own boots. The veterans make a joke of it until their sergeant pushes the boy back into line and orders the rest to silence.

The plain rings to the slap of leather and armour as the regiments jog into place. It is another close morning, the air again like treacle. The colours of the army are muted. Yesterday's overcast has been replaced with a fierce yellow sun and white-hot sky. Armour is scalding to the touch. Men are eager to be at it, anything but stand around boiling up in this heat.

Gajendra sits astride Colossus's neck, sweat running down his face from under his headband. His arm muscles ache from holding the quiver of javelins and his shield.

The elephants will not take much of this. They do not like to stand out in the sun. They are dressed in thick, quilted armour and will soon overheat. Colossus fans himself with his ears and trumpets his disapproval.

'Not long,' Gajendra says to him, though in truth he does not know how long it will be before Alexander starts the attack. Boys with skins of river water pour them into pots between each pair of elephants so the beasts can drink. But they are soon empty again, and they rush back behind the lines to get more.

Ensigns snap in the wind. A squall dances on the salt pan. A sand-coloured murk obscures the horizon. It will disguise our feints, Gajendra thinks. The gods are on the side of Alexander once more.

Gajendra hopes he will prove himself valiant. This is the moment he has waited for, his brief chance of glory.

He is at the centre of the line. Each of the elephants has a squadron of Persian slingers and archers between them as protection. There are more light infantry to guard Colossus's legs.

The Agrianians are out there in front, Alexander's famed javelineers. Madmen. They have no armour, no helmet. All they have is a cloak and a shield and steely nerve. They fight in pairs, father with son, brother with brother, a wolfhound to shield them if they go down.

It is both a beautiful and terrifying thing to see them hurl a spear, twisting, trembling, playing the wind. It takes years of practice, so they say; they must use a finger sling, learn to apply the right spin to the shaft. The older man is always the hurler; the younger will spot the targets and pass the javelins.

Alexander rides out. He holds his sword in his right hand, the sun blazing on his armour. His helmet is in the crook of his other arm.

Behind him his generals wait in a tight group, their horses high with excitement. They look impatient to be done with this. Only Alexander is unhurried.

He walks his massive Arab along the line.

'Men of Macedon! They do not wish us to enter Carthage. Do you know why? Because the city is a treasure house. They have all the wealth of Iberia and Africanus in there. Riches that will soon be yours! We are finally on our way home, brothers, and we will not go back empty-handed. Everything we have won so far will seem like trinkets compared to what we will find when we ride into Carthage. You left your crease as men, and you will return as gods!'

The army cheers him, though only the Macks can understand what he has said. His rallying cry was meant just for the veterans, for he will rely on them when the battle reaches its pinnacle. These are the men who will not break, who will always hold their lines.

He stands in the saddle, his sword raised, and a roar ripples over the plain. They will surely hear it in Carthage.

Someone has brought a ram. Alexander jumps from his horse, expertly slits its throat. He butchers it and holds its still beating heart to the gods. The blood runs down his arm.

The army roars again. They are following Zeus's son into battle.

How can they lose?

Hanno watches the army come. It looks too small. The battle is unfolding just as he imagined it. This seems far too easy, and the thought alarms him.

The Macedonians have advanced on the oblique, trying to draw Hanno's forces away from the centre. Already, Hanno's generals are panicking about the elephants. What if their civilian militia, the *hoplites*, cannot hold them?

Hanno has the advantage on the other flank. One bold sweep from his heavy cavalry and they will have Alexander's army surrounded. Alexander even seems to be inviting him to do it. But he would surely not leave such an opening unless he wanted Hanno to attack it.

And this is why Hanno hesitates. One after another his generals urge him to attack.

Alexander's war elephants start to move forward. Dust drifts over the plain and soon it obscures everything. Hanno can hear them coming but he can see nothing. The imagination will have you slaughtered or victorious depending on which way the wind blows. He fidgets in the saddle and waits for his outriders to return and tell him what is happening.

His generals are clamouring for him to act. How does a man direct such confusion? Where is Alexander and how far are the elephants from the lines?

'This is our chance,' someone is shouting at him. 'We should commit our cavalry to the right flank.'

'No,' he says. 'Wait. If we hold our line, we can contain him.'

'If we attack now, we will crush him!'

He looks around for one dissenting voice among his officers. The wind blows grit in his face. If only he could see what was going on.

An outrider rushes in. The enemy are weakened on their left. The captain wants permission to attack.

Hanno's instinct tells him to hold his cavalry in reserve. What if it is a feint and Alexander is bluffing? Yet Hanno has the greater numbers, and a good general is never timid.

But still he holds back. If Alexander invites you to attack him at a certain point, isn't it better advised not to?

His generals are all shouting at him at once. We must seize the opportunity now, now! He relents and gives the order. His courier gallops away.

At once, he experiences a tide of misgiving. He tries not to think about defeat. There will be thousands dead on the battlefield if he has made the wrong decision.

Gajendra spits the dust out of his mouth. Ravi is pointing to the left, where Hanno's Numidian cavalry are coming on, near naked, the only colour the leopard-skin cloaks they wear across their shoulders like a sash. The best cavalry in the world apart from their own.

The line is thin on their left. If the Numidians break it and get in behind them, they will be cut off and slaughtered, man and beast.

Gajendra is shaking so hard he thinks he will drop his *ankus*. His throat is parched. What he wouldn't give for a flask of water right now.

The Carthage line glitters in the sun. Colossus throws up his trunk and bellows, staggers to the side, rocking the *howdah*. The bowman inside it screams curses at him. Not his fault, Gajendra wants to shout at them. He's hot! He needs to move or get out of the sun.

He can hear the muted roar of the battle far along the left flank. The dust obscures everything now.

Gajendra looks over his shoulder, looking for a rider, hoping for the order to withdraw. Colossus is eager to move. The bronze face plate and the massive chest protector are heating up and he bellows again in protest.

The brigade commanders have rallied to the colours to receive their orders; behind them the master sergeants are reconfiguring their line. The order finally comes – advance on the palisade.

They start to beat the drum. Sergeants bawl out their orders. Colossus curls up his trunk and flaps out his ears as he lumbers forward, gaining speed with every stride. Gajendra looks over his shoulder again. The archer in the howdah shouts out in alarm. The peculiar character of the elephant's gait makes a ride in the *howdah* an unsettling experience. An elephant will raise just one foot off the ground at a time and puts it down before raising the next. Anyone riding on its back receives four separate shocks with each stride, and when this happens at speed it is as much as a man can do to keep from toppling out.

The infantry follows behind, a terrifying sight. They have formed into a square, marching in locked step. The long spears they call *sarissas* are sitting upright, twenty feet in the air, shafts swaying, a bristled row of serried steel points.

Then the dust obscures them too.

Arrows rain in from the other side of the palisade. Gajendra holds his shield above his head and arrows thud into it, one after the other. He sees them bounce off Colossus's front corselets.

The elephant ignores them and sets to work ripping out the stakes from the ground in front of him. If Colossus is hurt or frightened he knows only one way to react. Should he get through this barricade, someone is going to pay.

The noise hurts the ears: the horns, the drums, the screaming of wounded men. Already Colossus's armour is bristling with arrows. Gajendra sees the Agrianians running back to their own lines, their ammunition spent.

What was easy on the drill ground is now a blur. It is hard even to think. Everything is instinct. He hunkers behind his shield, he prays, he urges Colossus on. He is convinced he is about to die.

CHAPTER 13

'*Deri, deri!*' Gajendra screams. *Hurry.*

Colossus needs little urging. He hurls the stakes from the palisade aside as if he is stripping leaves off a branch. Soon there is a gap, and he charges through it, the infantry following. A few brave men rush out to meet them.

Their best tactic would be to attack me, Gajendra thinks. Colossus is dead and blind without me. Instead they concentrate their attacks on Colossus's legs. He knocks them aside.

Two more men dash out, both looking like Zeus himself. They have gold shields and the cheek pieces on their helmets are embossed with stylised curls, like a metal beard and moustache. They look utterly magnificent until they disappear without fuss beneath Colossus's charge. His tusks have been sheathed with razor sharp iron. It makes him difficult to resist.

When the men from Carthage see a score or more of their fellow gutted like goats, they lose appetite for the fight. One thing to see your comrade fall with an arrow, another thing to see his limbs torn off by a wild beast.

To battle elephants takes discipline and icy nerve and the fellow at your shoulder must stand firm. These boys are amateurs from the middle class. They aren't up for it.

The line shivers and breaks. What starts as retreat soon turns into a rout.

Gajendra's instinct is to follow, and it is Colossus's instinct too. But without infantry an elephant is too vulnerable and so he signals Colossus to stop, even though the big fellow has worked himself into a rage and is eager to go on with it.

Moments later, Alexander rides past them in his golden armour with his cavalry close behind. It is the very moment their general has waited for. He will hit the Carthage centre and drive a hole right through it.

By the time the phalanx comes up behind them, Alexander is already lost in the dust. The moves and counter moves are done. It was a gamble, but it has paid off. Alexander sacrificed his flank, trusting the tuskers to deliver a swift victory. Hanno's committed his Numidians too early, and they cannot now cover the break in the line.

It is then that Niarchos appears. He rides across their front with his spear held at the level to signal that the elephants are to desist. More cavalry thunders past them, followed by the elite infantry, the Silver Shields.

Suddenly, they are like starfish stranded by the tide. The battle has swept over them. Gajendra can hear it raging on either side but can see nothing through the dust haze. He feels Colossus beneath him, trembling.

As the murk clears, Gajendra sees that there are only a dozen elephants alongside him; the rest have run to the rear. He stares at the litter of bodies and wonders that he is not one of them.

He is at last a soldier. He feels more like a god.

His mouth tastes foul. He suddenly realizes, with astonishment, that there is an arrow in his arm. How long has it been there?

Gajendra heard one of the Macks talking about wounds once. He said that any wound that did not kill or maim you was something to be cherished. Scars earned you respect and set you apart from other men.

Ravi appears alongside him, on Ran Bagha.

'Look,' Gajendra says, laughing, and shows him the arrow in his shoulder. And then he faints, sprawling across Colossus's neck.

If Colossus had not felt him start to fall and immediately dropped to his knees, Gajendra would have broken his neck.

CHAPTER 14

Carthage bakes. In Megara, a palm tree lies where it has fallen across a stone staircase, lizards sun themselves in the dried fountains, and from his window Hanno can see obscenities scrawled in dried excrement on the walls of his neighbour's villa.

Even after the army's defeat, the Council thought themselves secure behind their triple walls. But Alexander did not attempt a frontal assault. Instead, he encamped his army around the city, cutting off the city's land route and crucifying anyone who tried to break the blockade.

He then secured the isthmus to the south and began construction of a mole across the harbour mouth to cut off their sea route as well.

At first, the idea of building such a barrier seemed impossible. It was two hundred paces from the beach to the harbour walls and Tyrian galleys could pass each other abreast. The channel was too deep and too wide to ford, or so it seemed. Their mathematicians calculated that it would take ten years to fill it.

Six weeks after he started building, Alexander is already halfway there.

'Impossible' is not a word that Alexander knows. Certainly, it has never been successfully translated for him in any language from the Indus to Africa.

Carthage was once the busiest port in the world, a forest of masts, three-deep with corn ships. Now, look what one man has done. Grass seeds drift across the inner harbour. Rubbish is piled in huge mounds along the docks. A green slime has attached itself to the sea wall.

The last of the blockade runners are long gone. The masts and sternposts of sunken ships rise above the water. Even the fishermen have left; it is safer and more profitable for them to sell their fish to the soldiers in Alexander's camps on the other shore.

Today, a mirage makes it appear that Alexander's navy is floating in the sky. Another miracle. The damned man has one for every day of the week.

A line of ox carts, laden with stone, trundles out to the deep-water channel. Another load crashes into the water. Alexander has almost completed the causeway along which he can bring his troops and siege equipment to batter the harbour fortifications.

Huge wooden towers edge out, taller than the city walls. Alexander's bowmen and Agrianian slingers are hidden inside them so that if you so much as raise a helmet on a stick above the parapet wall, it invites a hail of stones and bolts. The helmet will be sent spinning across the barbican in a shower of sparks.

The Macedonian *onagers* – huge stone throwers – have left the ancient wooden lighthouse a sprawled ruin. Round artillery stones as large as a man lie everywhere. One monstrous boulder is embedded in the paving outside the corn warehouse, some poor wretch leaking from under it.

The rolling siege towers loom larger every day. Men crawl across them like ants. They have started hurling boiling pitch over the walls.

The city is full to bursting with refugees swarming in from the countryside. Alexander is burning all the coastal towns, murdering as he goes. The man is pitiless.

Everyone is blaming each other for the defeat. In the Parliament, the Hundred howl at each other like dogs across the speaker's staff. Dignitaries with oiled beards and long ringlets curse each other for fools.

Hanno knows the city can no longer be saved. He has packed his crate of dress uniforms ready to depart. If he can find a way through the blockade, he might yet live to fight another day.

Xatharo walks in and stands in the middle of the room, looking around as if he is expecting a fight. He doesn't look much like a brawler, for he is scarcely taller than a child. But look closer, and a stranger soon revises their opinion.

He has so many tattoos on his face that on first meeting, most people think he is black. The only part of his face not inked are his eyeballs. His head is so misshapen, he looks as if it's been kicked about in the yard by small boys. Terrifying.

He waits for his orders. Get a goat from the market, strangle someone. It's all the same to him.

Hanno goes to the window. Those who can get out are already gone, the city fathers among them. They left soon after they expressed full confidence in Hanno's ability to save Carthage.

'We'll organize a great ceremony for you when you have thrown that cur out of Africanus. Where's my slave with the baggage and the boats?'

Xatharo has been Hanno's creature for many years now. Every general needs men like this, someone they can trust with the sordid details of getting certain things done. Xatharo has proved unswervingly loyal; a rare thing to come by in any age.

Now he peers at the chart spread open on the table and makes a face. 'Is this your battle plan?'

Anyone else and Hanno would have them tied to a cartwheel and whipped for their insolence. Instead he joins him at the table.

'What's this?' Xatharo says. 'And this? And this?'

'This is Alexander's army. This is the isthmus. This is Carthage. Right here is the Coton.'

Xatharo frowns. He has never seen a map before.

'It is what you would see if you were a bird,' Hanno says, 'and could fly above the city and the Macedonian encampment.'

'If I were a bird and could fly above their encampment, I'd shit on Alexander's head.'

'We need more than bird shit to save us now.'

Xatharo peers closer at the map. 'There's the temple. There's the Parliament.' He has the delight of a child in finding things for himself. Finally: 'What's this square here? In Alexander's camp?'

'His war elephants.'

'Where did he get those?'

'From India. He brought a squadron back with him. I hear he has been training with them all through the last winter in Babylon.'

'I have never fought elephants.'

'Nor will you now. I have a different job for you. One that is much more important. It will require all of your ingenuity. It concerns my daughter.'

'She's become a priestess.'

'She has dedicated her life to the goddess Tanith. She refuses to leave the temple, even though I have told her she is not safe there.'

'You want me to get her out?'

'Not yet. For now, you are to go there and watch over her. Perhaps fortune will smile on me, and I will find a way out of this mess. Who knows? If not, then you are to save her life any way that is necessary. Nothing is to stop you.'

'It will be done.'

'I will be frank with you. When you leave here today, we may not see each other again.'

'So when should my orders terminate?'

'When your last breath leaves your body. Until then, I charge you with her life.' He gives him a purse containing a fortune in gold. Enough to tempt a lesser man to abscond, buy himself a fine house in Syracuse and live out the rest of his days in reasonable comfort, away from the hurly-burly.

Xatharo bows and leaves. Another man might wait to see which way the wind blows before deciding whether to risk his life.

Not this one.

CHAPTER 15

There is no race in the world that can drink like these Macedonians. They slop around in Alexander's pavilion ankle deep in wine. They remind Gajendra of his tuskers, standing in the river spraying water over each other, trumpeting and barging everyone else aside.

Alexander does not look like the conqueror of the world when he is in his cups, except there is always such a fierce cunning in his eyes. When he laughs it sends a chill through the room.

No one can ever truly relax in his company. He killed one of his childhood friends, Black Cleitus, at a gathering like this. Took a spear from one of the guards. 'May I borrow this?' Put it straight through his friend's guts. He was grief stricken the next morning, when he sobered up and they told him what he'd done. Black Cleitus was still dead, though, for all Alexander's sorry looks afterwards.

Tonight, his Companions crowd round him, laughing too loud, spilling wine, telling war stories. But for all their high spirits, there is a shadow over proceedings. There is news from Greece: Antipater has made a treaty with Athens, has allied with them against Alexander. He has offered them autonomy if they help him keep Kraterus out of Macedon and secure him the throne. He has dragged Corinth into his little war as well.

Alexander will soon be fighting on two fronts. He appears unconcerned, even jovial. He reclines at the centre of a half circle of couches, holds out his arm and a cringing cupbearer hands him another wine. Then he stands and declares lifelong friendship to Niarchos and gratitude for his valour at Carthage.

Gajendra seethes. What did Niarchos do to earn such plaudits? He spent the entire battle astride his horse, somewhere in the rear.

Everyone is laughing and slapping each other on the back but Gajendra sees the looks every time one of the Persians goes near their king. The Macks don't like it when they get on the ground and bow to him.

The old timers will have none of that. They still call him plain Alexander and there's no grovelling, King of Kings or not. Alexander bears their informality, but anyone can see he's getting to like all this toadying. It is only a matter of time before he takes issue with the old men.

The Gentlemen of the Bodyguard have prudently removed his sword in case there is a reprise of the Black Cleitus episode.

Gajendra slips away, unnoticed. He is staggering from the wine. He smells perfume on the wind. Alexander has brought with him the great pavilion that once belonged to Darius, and he uses part of it to house his seraglio. Gajendra knows Zahara will be in there somewhere.

Soldiers are silhouetted against the rubbish-fires on the beach. Gusts of sparks are driven on the night wind. He hears two guards grumbling; they are cold and tired and waiting for their relief to arrive.

He goes over to see what it is they are guarding. It is a cage. At first, he thinks by the stench it is a wild animal they have in there, but it is too dark to tell for certain.

'What is that?' he says.

'Better not to ask,' one of the men grunts. Something in the way he says it tells him what he needs to know. Alexander has brought Kassander all the way from Babylon in that iron crate. Gajendra cannot believe the poor wretch is still alive. How much more torture will Alexander put him through before it is enough?

Gajendra seeks out Colossus. During the battle, an arrow had found its way through his quilted armour and lodged in the big fellow's shoulder.

'Even your wounds are the same!' Ravi had said, after they removed the bolt and dressed Gajendra's arm.

Colossus shifts in the dark, makes his usual rumbles and squeaks. Gajendra feels the ache in his own shoulder. He had not felt any pain at all on the battlefield, but every night since the wound has left him in a lather of sweat. The joint has seized, and he can barely raise his hand above his shoulder. He has told no one about this, for fear they will not let him fight again.

After tending to Colossus, he goes off to find Ravi, who is bundled by the fire.

'You still sleep with us mere mortals then, general?' Ravi says.

'Don't mock me. You never thought I'd even be a captain, did you? Maybe I will be a general one day.'

Ravi chuckles. 'How was it, carousing with the mighty.'

'Horrible. All the talk was of Niarchos and what a hero he was at Carthage. It was nauseating. I was the one who led the charge!'

'No, Colossus was. They should make him the new Elephantarch, not you. Look, Gaji, Niarchos is one of them, a Mack. You're an elephant boy. What did you expect?'

'I expect to be as treated the same as any of them. I have Colossus and I have courage and my will. All I need is one good battle, and I shall be standing next to Alexander at the next feast. He will be lauding me, not that arrogant Greek!'

'You had one good battle. A good battle is one that you live through and don't lose an eye or an arm or your balls. You can be as brave as a tiger but it's always the generals who get the credit. That's the way it is.'

'I will not be nothing all my life.'

'Oh, Gaji!' Ravi sighs and rolls over. Soon he is snoring, but Gajendra stays awake staring at the stars.

Mara is lighting copal at the feet of the goddess. Tanith has been fashioned from a single piece of black onyx. Her eyes, which are made from sapphires, are a startling blue.

Lamps flicker in the notches on the walls. The massive mahogany beams in the vaulted ceiling have been blackened by hundreds of years of incense smoke.

She hears the high priestess approach, her bare feet shuffling on the marble. 'Our temple has been outraged.'

She looks around in confusion. Alexander is not even within sight of the walls.

'It is your father's doing.'

'I don't understand' Mara says.

'He is a barbarian!'

'What has he done?'

'Men are not allowed inside the sacred temple.'

'My father is here?'

'Worse. He has sent one of his villains.'

Mara follows the high priestess out of the sanctum. Outside, the temple entrance is flanked with huge pilasters, the courtyard divided by an altar and podium. Xatharo is lounging in the centre, on the rim of a marble fountain, as if it were a public seat in the forum.

'My getter,' her father calls him, the one who gets things done. She has seen him coming and going by her father's back door all her life, but she has never spoken to him. He frightens her. Though he is short, he looks the sort of man who would enjoy breaking someone's arm.

'How did the guards let him past?'

'The guards are your father's men,' the high priestess says.

Mara turns to the getter. 'What are you doing here, Xatharo?'

'You know who I am, then?'

'I have seen you. I have heard of you.'

'No man is allowed in these gates,' the high priestess tells him.

He gets to his feet, leisurely as you like, and stands with his legs apart daring anyone to move him. 'Tell that to Alexander when he comes.'

'My father will stop him.'

'If he does, I'll leave.'

She spares a glance towards the temple gates, to the Agora just beyond. Carthage conducts its commerce there; it is always full of melon sellers, crowds of pigeons, money changers and prostitutes. There are often long files of priests making their way to the temple of Baal-Ammon, tinkling bells.

But today the square is empty. The silence is somehow more frightening than the roar of a rampaging mob.

'You have to leave.'

Xatharo sits back down on the edge of the fountain and shakes his head.

'Why are you here?'

'Your father worries for you, as fathers must, I suppose.'

'You are breaking the sanctity of the temple.'

'Better than someone breaks your sanctity.'

'You think that if my father cannot stop Alexander with all his army, then you will save me on your own?'

'Yes.'

He sits there, unshakeable, immoveable. Xatharo is not a man, he is a fact. If he is there, you cannot budge him; if he comes for you, you cannot stop him. That is what they say.

She looks at the high priestess and shrugs.

CHAPTER 16

'You have to hurry, sir.'

Hanno's lieutenant stands in the doorway, agitated. The Councillors have decided to give Alexander his head on a pike and sue for peace. They think to blame all on their general and come to an arrangement with the lord of war.

Well, it's too late for all that. Alexander has his war won; he has no need for treaties. He will happily accept any part of Hanno's sectioned anatomy and carry on his war as though nothing had happened. The walls will be down in a day or two. Why accommodate when he can crash in and take what he wants anyway?

Hanno feels the floor shake under him as another great stone hurtles into the city from one of Alexander's catapults on the causeway. His bodyguard insists that he leave. He thinks about going back for Mara, but it is too late for that now. They simply don't have the time. He hopes that Xatharo can keep his commission. He has never failed him in anything before.

He turns to the window. Alexander's army appears as countless needle points of torchlight in the darkness. He sees something flash on the platform of a siege tower. An *onager* lobs a phosphorus flare over the harbour wall and the night explodes in a green dazzle.

His bodyguards have made plans to smuggle him out through the Macedonian lines in the back of a handcart. It is one final humiliation. But Hanno promises himself that, if he lives through this night, he will settle with Alexander one day.

This is not over.

Gajendra leads the column of elephants towards the causeway, past the lines of siege engines, stone throwers and assault towers. They pass last night's assault troops as they head back to the camp to rest. Their faces are white from stone dust and exhaustion.

Look behind you and all is peace; smoke from a thousand breakfast fires drifts to the south, carried on the morning's zephyr. It is pleasantly rural; a patchwork of walled estates and paddocks for sheep, goats and cattle, though the animals have long gone to feed Alexander's army. Camel trains move in from the desert, an endless line of them with supplies for the army. His ships ripple in the heat haze. Gulls fight over the scraps on the beach.

But look ahead and you are afforded a vision of hell.

Black smoke blocks out the horned mountain behind the city, even blocks out the sun; infantry swarm up fixed banks of ladders in columns of four; the whole city is aflame. The air is acrid from last night's incendiaries and the charnel house stench on the wind leaves an acid taste at the back of the throat. He hears the inhabitants singing to Melchert, son of Baal, for salvation. Olive oil is burning in the warehouses.

He wouldn't like to be a citizen of Carthage right now.

The priestess is trembling, outraged and afraid. Xatharo ignores her and stretches himself on an altar, like a cat claiming a warm spot. When he hears Mara's voice, he opens his eyes and sits up.

He says, in a voice that is supposed to be respectful, 'Has my lady changed her mind?'

'Has it occurred to my father that I am happy to die here?'

He gives her a brutish shrug.

'I do not want you here.'

'But I am here.'

'You must go.'

He shakes his head.

She stabs her finger into his chest. It is hard and unyielding. 'I will not leave.'

They hear a noise carried on the wind. It is the sound of the battering rams at the city gates, a double heartbeat that sends a concussion through the body. With each blow the walls of the temple blur and white dust trembles from the joining in the stones.

Alexander is on his way. Outside, men are dying in the city square.

'You don't have a choice,' Xatharo says.

CHAPTER 17

Colossus lends his shoulder to the gate, testing its strength with his head. It bends. He puts his shoulder to it, rocking it back and forth, but it is iron and though the hinges creak, they do not break.

His pride is wounded by its intransigence, for suddenly he goes up on his back legs and pounds it with his forefeet. The archer in the *howdah* shrieks, thinking he is about to topple off. But the strappings hold, the doorway gives way with a crash and the soldiers stream past them and into the city.

His job done, Colossus shows no sign of wishing to contribute further to the cause. He saunters inside the gate, finds an acacia tree, and helps himself to breakfast.

Gajendra might order him to continue into the city but decides against it. There is no glory to be had in a street fight. Colossus strips the tree and then sets about the roof of an empty melon stall, which has been thatched with palm fronds.

The gateway is set into the city's defensive wall and is topped with a walkway. A guard lies with his head on the stairs, his brains bleeding down the stone. Why didn't he surrender? Perhaps he did. Alexander's men have been three months besieging this city. They are in no mood for mercy.

The soldiers are flooding through the gate, eager for women, gold, anything they can get their hands on. The city is alive with screams. But he and Colossus have found a private oasis away from the looting and killing, which Gajendra wants no part of.

Neither does Colossus. He lumbers around the square looking for something else to eat. But if there were anything to eat in this city,

Carthage would have eaten it. They have been starving for weeks now.

There are sparks in the air and ash falls like snow. Who has set light to the city, the defenders or Alexander's storm troops? Perhaps both.

There is no glory here, his fellow soldiers are acting like bandits. He does not like to hear women and children scream. But after the battle, when men have their blood up, who is to stop them?

Mara is standing by the pit where she gave her baby up to Tanith.

Xatharo walks in. The city is lost, he tells her. You must come with me.

'Is my father slain?'

'I don't know.'

'I would rather the truth.'

He draws a breath. 'And if I knew it, I would give it to you.' He is a sullen fellow, even on his best form and not given to emotion, but the licence on his patience has expired. 'The time has come. You are to come with me now, and if you obstruct my purpose I shall as soon drag you out of here by whatever means necessary.'

She stares at him, astonished not as much by what he says as the length of this speech. She had not thought him capable of putting more than three words together.

She hesitates so he grabs her by the wrists and pulls her out of the shrine.

Outside, the square is clogged with starved skeletons headed for the docks or the gates, clambering over and around the broken carts and debris of discarded furniture that others have left behind. People claw at each other. She sees a woman fall screaming under the feet of the mob. Men are elbowing old women in the press, even children are trampled. Militia push through the crowd, the last brave men in Carthage determinedly making their way to the walls and their own deaths.

Xatharo surveys the chaos and drags her back inside the temple. They run across the courtyard to the back gate. She hears war drums and then a shuddering boom from the other side of the city.

'What was that?'

'The elephants are breaking down the gates. The soldiers are coming.'

He leads her down narrow alleys, his fist locked around her wrist. He is so strong she thinks he will pull her arm out of its socket. He ignores her protests.

The streets between the Byrsa and the hill of Tanith are a warren, but he knows his way around like a cockroach, every crack and byway. She looks up at the bleached colonnades of the palace. The gilded rooftops of the Parliament shiver in the heat mirage of the fires burning below. She thinks she sees the glint of iron helmets.

She and Xatharo come out at the docks, but it seems everyone in Carthage is there.

'What now?' she asks him. There are boats but not enough for everyone that wants to leave. Some are already heading out to sea, people lunging to get on board, the crews fending them off with gaffes. One is overloaded and capsizes in the harbour blocking the channel.

'I had a boat waiting,' Xatharo says.

'Where is it then?'

He points. 'Over there, that skiff heading out past the breakwater. He must have thought we were not coming.'

There is no way through the crush. There are only a handful of boats left at the dock anyway, and those that have not pushed away are dangerously overcrowded. The people of Carthage have turned into wild animals. A woman goes down right in front of them, with blood streaming from her nose. Even while she is on her knees, men trample her as if she isn't there.

'We will try the west gate,' Xatharo says but when they get there, it is worse. The militia have lost control and there is nothing passing through or around it. An ox cart has turned on its side, blocking the road and there are shops burning.

Xatharo turns and runs back the way they have come, pulls her along another alley. A child is sitting on the cobblestones crying and she wants to pick him up and bring him with them, but Xatharo shouts, 'Leave him!' He rushes her past.

They hear horses in the street. She looks back and sees Alexander's cavalry streaming past, their swords drawn.

'Don't worry about them. It's the infantry you have to watch for. Those cocksuckers won't leave anything standing.'

He kicks in the door of a shop. It is a tailors, and there are bolts of cloth and scissors lying around on the benches. He shuts the door behind them and bars it. He picks up the scissors.

'Come here.'

'What are you going to do?'

'Your hair's got to come off.'

'What?'

'You want to be raped? I mean, not just once. You'll get passed around an entire regiment looking like that.'

She knows there is no point in resisting. He grabs handfuls of her hair and chops through it with the scissors. In moments it is on the floor at her feet, but he still isn't satisfied, keeps cutting until it is shorter than his. When he has finished, she runs her hand across her scalp. She isn't a woman anymore.

He rummages through the benches, finds a tunic and throws it at her. 'Put it on.'

She hesitates.

'What are you waiting for, a servant to do it for you? I won't look, don't worry. I have to find you something for your feet.'

And he disappears into the back of the shop.

He comes back with a pair of boy's tough leather sandals. 'They'll fit you near enough. You're lucky the tailor had sons.'

He looks her up and down. 'I don't know if I've done you a favour. You look like one of those dancing boys they pay double for down at the docks. We'll hide upstairs. We have to stay out of the way until the bloodlust is over.'

He leads her up the stairs onto the roof. They crouch down under the parapet, listening as the screaming gets closer.

Xatharo peers over it to look down into the street. 'They're coming! Don't make a sound. Pray to that goddess of yours. We're going to need all the help we can get.'

CHAPTER 18

The warehouses down at the docks have been burning for days. Sometimes their quarter of the city is quiet, at other times they can hear Alexander's soldiers laughing and shouting right next door.

They sleep on steps or on rooftops during lulls in the fighting, leaping over parapets to move on when the soldiers get closer. Mara is hungry. She is thirsty. There are times she wishes she had jumped into the black arms of Tanith when she had the chance.

It is growing towards evening on the second day, and above her the Byrsa is mostly in shadow. She hears the tramp of hobnailed boots and peers into the narrow street below. She sees a three-storey building shimmer and tumble in a cloud of dust. The soldiers are clearing the tenements as they advance. They will not contest Carthage; they would rather pull it down, brick by brick.

The alley below has been barricaded with ceiling joists and hunks of limestone. The soldiers scramble over them while women and children hurl capstones and pans of boiling water from the roofs. The soldiers hold shields over their heads as they batter down doors, prising away shutters with their swords and then scrambling into the dark interiors to dispute with angry skeletons who fight back with chair legs and kitchen knives.

Xatharo nudges her urgently. He points. Two sappers have levered away the main doorframe downstairs. She feels the tremor through the roof. He grabs the wooden plank that has become their lifeline, throws it over the alleyway to the next building and they scramble across.

Moments later the tenement they had been hiding in comes down in a choking cloud of dust.

When it clears, she sees more soldiers moving up the street through a mirage of heat. A catapult bolt deflects off the parapet in a shower of sparks. She screams and leaps back.

Below her an old man runs into the street on fire.

Xatharo pulls her away. He says he will get them out of this, but she doesn't see how.

Torches move along the black defiles of the city. Gajendra supposes that he should be used to the smell of death by now, but he isn't. It is making him nauseous. The elephants don't like it much either. Colossus trumpets in protest.

The streets are full of bodies, charred and crushed, some still moving or moaning. The street cleaners are dragging them out of the way of the cavalry with their hooked steel poles, without bothering to check if any are still alive.

He sees two young boys crouching in the moon shadow. They have been cornered by four infantrymen. The soldiers are laughing, having a fine time. One of the boys has a dagger out and the bigger one has taken shelter behind him.

Finally, one of the soldiers decides it's time to be about their business and draws his sword. He lazily chops at the boy's head. The boy darts inside the blow and slices the man's neck, taking the sword from his hand before he is even dead. It is so quick the other three stand there astonished, and while they are busy being surprised he goes after the one nearest him, slashing his hamstring and putting him down.

The other two rouse themselves. They have armour and he has none. They back him against the wall. Gajendra wills the bigger boy to grab a sword and help his companion, but he doesn't move.

This is no good, Gajendra thinks, and goes over.

The boy is on the ground now, still parrying blows with the sword, but there is blood leaking out of him everywhere and, strong as he is, he looks beaten.

'Stop!' Gajendra shouts.

One of the attackers turns around. He is an ugly veteran, with a scar on his nose and sprays of fresh blood across his face. In his present mood it's clear he would as happily put his sword in Gajendra as in the boy on the ground.

'Who are you, dog breath?'

'I'm the man with four bowmen behind him keeping him from harm. Who are you?'

Gajendra is hoping his archer is still with him, but he cannot afford to turn around and check. Anyway, judging by the looks on the soldier's faces someone or something is backing him up. He hears the tinkling of a bell. It is Colossus.

'Leave them, they're my prisoners now.'

'He killed our comrades!'

'No, he killed one of them. The other's one's still alive, I can hear him bleating. When I tell Alexander, he will not be pleased. Four of you against one boy and you couldn't dispatch him? What are your names?'

He looks over his shoulder. Colossus has flared his ears in warning.

They think better of tangling with an elephant. One of them says something, a curse most likely. They walk away, dragging the other two with them, leaving smears of gore in the dirt.

Gajendra goes to the boy, who is still reaching for his sword. He kicks it out of his reach. He bends down and is astonished to discover that it is not a boy at all. It is a man with a nasty attitude. He slashes at Gajendra with his dagger and then passes out.

CHAPTER 19

They are not much to look at, as prisoners go. The smaller one is an uncommon fellow; a crooked little man with a tattooed face, as wide as he is high, but what there is of him is all muscle. He lies there, spread-eagled like a sacrifice, his head half stove-in. He has a wound the width of four fingers in his shoulder and down into his chest.

Not much on an ordinary man, Ravi says, but he's only ten fingers high to start with.

The boy with him is not much bigger. He is a delicate thing with snake hips, looks as if the next strong wind will blow him away. He would fetch a good price on the auctioneer's block as a rich man's private pet. There is high colour in his cheeks. The Macks would pass him around like a wine jug if they got hold of him.

He is huddled against the wall, one hand laid on the bloodied dwarf. He is trembling.

'Who are you?' Gajendra asks him.

The boy vomits on the ground. Ravi makes a face. 'Oh, that's it,' he says. 'Spew everywhere. We find one good place to sleep and now he's filled it with his stink.'

'He can't help it. We shouldn't have given him so much food. He probably hasn't eaten anything for days.'

Ravi sighs. For all his truculence he was the one who walked through the dark to get the plate of stew for him.

The boy wipes his mouth with the back of his hand. 'My name's Mara.'

'And who's he?' Gajendra asks, pointing at the little fellow.

'That's my uncle. He's called Xatharo.'

'Your uncle's a dwarf?'

'Don't call him that. He won't like it if he hears you use that word.'

'Well, he's mine now so I'll call him what I want. And a "thank you" would not go amiss.'

'What do you wish me to thank you for?'

He hears Ravi take a breath at his insolence.

'For saving your lives,' Gajendra says.

Gajendra has been inclined to make allowance for the boy's situation but now he wishes he had left them both to the mercenaries. This one could have been buggered by half the irregulars already. That might have better instructed his attitude.

'What were you doing there?'

'My uncle is a merchant. We were running away from the soldiers.'

'What are these tattoos on his face?' Gajendra says. 'He looks more like a bandit.'

'It is a custom where he is from.'

'So why do you not have them?' Ravi says and then he looks at Gajendra. 'He's the worst liar I have ever met, worse than the carpet salesmen in the Babylon market.'

Gajendra squats down. 'You know we could give you to the slavers. I would turn a tidy profit... for you, anyway.'

'Do whatever you wish.'

Ravi is disgusted. 'Get rid of them,' he says, over Gajendra's shoulder. 'They're not worth the trouble.'

What is it that stays him? He should be dismissive of the boy's arrogance, yet there is something admirable about this show of defiance from a boy with arms like twigs.

'You could sell the other one to a circus,' Ravi says.

'If he lives.'

'Which he won't. Look at him. Can't take more than a jug of blood to fill him up and he's leaked all of that over the straw.'

Gajendra stands up and sighs. Ravi is older and wiser and probably a better judge. But he isn't the new captain of the elephants. 'No, I'll keep them for dung larks.'

Ravi doesn't approve. 'That's just what we need. Two more elephant boys. Even the tuskers can't shit fast enough to keep them all busy.'

'What would you have me do? The ugly one is dying and the other one's just a boy. Someone has to help them.' Gajendra coughs; the air reeks of blood and smoke. 'Besides, did you see the dwarf fight?'

'He'll be dead by morning just the same,' Ravi says.

Gajendra bends down to examine him. He remembers the first time he saw such wounds after the battle against Alexander at the Jhellum River. He had thought he would never get accustomed to seeing men with arms torn off and their guts out. But he has.

A man can get accustomed to anything, given practice.

Later that night, Mara finds a bucket and goes off to fetch water. She brings it back, wets a cloth, and wipes Xatharo's face with it. It's the least she can do for him. She doubts he will still be alive by morning.

The whole square is filled with sleeping soldiers. Men are whimpering in their sleep all around her, even the ones who aren't wounded. The stench is unbearable. She wraps a scarf around her face and tries to take shallow breaths through her mouth. The fires are still burning down at the wharves.

Xatharo's eyes blink open. 'Don't tell them who you are,' he whispers.

Sometime during the night she falls asleep. She dreams she is in her husband's house. Her baby stares at her with unseeing eyes. Mara holds out her arms to her. But then the child falls and she cannot catch her. She disappears into the Tophet in Tanith's temple.

The dream wakes her. Her heart is racing, and she is sweating. For a moment she does not remember where she is. She looks up. She is lying under one of the arcades around the market square. There is a red glow in the sky over the docks where Alexander's men have torched the granary. The Agora is full of drunks, toasting their victory. Shadows dance around the walls. The whole city reeks of death and smoke.

Someone is screaming and she can hear the ring of horses' hooves and the clash of iron swords. The fighting must still be going on somewhere. They are bringing more wounded into the square. They lie moaning and shouting, but there is no one to tend to them.

Beside her Xatharo lies quite still and she puts out a hand to check for breath on his lips. He is alive, but barely.

She wonders what has happened to her father. Did he escape the city, or have they captured him? Her captors do not seem to know or care.

She closes her eyes and puts her face against the brick wall.

CHAPTER 20

Gajendra watches women and children being herded into the square, ready for the day's slave auction. Their captors' names have been scrawled on their bodies in blood so they can get paid. It's good business and lines of them stretch right the way to the docks.

He trips on a severed limb. The air stinks of charred flesh. He wants to get out of the city and back onto the plain so he can breathe again.

He has put his two prisoners with the elephant boys. Not much they can do for the one with the tattoos. They have soaked the worst of the wounds in honey, bandaged him as best they can. The rest is up to him. He hopes he doesn't die; a man like that, he could have his uses.

The pretty boy is a strange one. If it had been Gajendra's own uncle, skewered like that, he would have wept buckets and talked to him, tried to coax him back to the living. This one just sits there staring at the sky.

He goes over. The boy gives him a look, like Gajendra is a slave who has walked into his bedchamber without begging leave. In the daylight he looks even worse than he did last night. His skin is white as milk, and he is as skinny as a twig.

The little ugly fellow appears dead, then lets out a snore to prove he's not. But his condition does not inspire confidence. Gajendra remembers how his father died, the smell of rot, the reeking sheets, shouting nonsense. But death is an unpredictable fellow; you never know what he will do next.

Gajendra crouches down. 'If this one's your uncle, as you say, where's your mother and father?'

'They are both dead.'

'How?'

'My mother of a fever. My father – Alexander's men killed him.'

'Well, you're lucky. If it weren't for this uncle of yours, you'd be on the slave blocks over there.' He pinches the skin on the little fellow's face, and he groans and twists. A good sign if he can still feel pain. Gajendra stands up and throws the boy a shovel.

'What is this?'

'The boys will show you. It's not difficult. You muck out the elephant dung and shovel it into that cart over there. When it's full you take it and dump it somewhere.'

The new boy drops the spade on the ground.

Gajendra grabs the boy's hands. They are soft like a girl's. 'You've not done a day's work in your life, have you?'

He doesn't answer.

'How did they let you get this way?' He picks up the shovel and hurls it at him. 'Do it or I'll give you to the Greeks. You're going to have blisters somewhere by the end of this day, and I promise you, you'd rather they were on your hands.'

The boy goes off, surly, then stops and turns around. 'Is the temple burned?'

'Look, you lost the battle. Get used to it. Your city's gone, so is your old life. It's the way of it.'

'What happens to us now?'

'I'll treat you well enough if you don't give me any trouble. Learn to look after the elephants and the rest of the time just stay out of the way. That's all you need to know.'

'We're slaves?'

'Of course. What did you think, I'd make you captain of the infantry?'

'What if I try to escape?'

'I don't care what you do. Run away if you like. I'll give you five minutes on your own out there. You'd better pray your uncle gets better, son, you've got some growing up to do.'

CHAPTER 21

She has never been around animals much, unless you count the peacocks in her father's garden. She has certainly never seen an elephant close up before and she is appalled. The noise they make is terrifying, they all stink and every one of them is the size of a house.

Ravi watches her, slapping the elephant hook against his thigh. 'What are you doing?'

'Mucking out.'

'You don't look like you know which end of the shovel to hold. What's wrong with you, boy?' He pinches the flesh of her arm. 'Look at you. You need to toughen up.'

She would hit him with the shovel if she knew which end to hold, she thinks. Damn these people.

'Don't stand there,' Ravi says and shoves her to the side. 'You stand behind him and he can't see you. He'll squash you like an ant.'

'I can't do this.'

'Why not?'

'Look at me! I'm not used to this kind of work.'

He slaps his knee and laughs so hard she thinks he is going to fall over. When he's done, Ravi grabs her hands and examines them. They are raw and blisters are starting to form already. It's only the first morning.

'Piss on them,' he says. 'It will harden them up.'

My father would have you horsewhipped if he heard you, she thinks. He'd as likely piss on you.

'How old are you?'

She hesitates. 'Fourteen.'

'No wonder you look like a girl. Maybe you'll get some muscle when your balls drop.'

'When can we rest?'

'That's just one elephant. You haven't even started yet. Gaji's soft, he should take the whip to you.'

'How is Xatharo?' she asks him.

'He's alive. He's a tough little fellow.'

Later that day the order comes to get the elephants out of the city. She straggles behind as they march them over Alexander's causeway. She cannot believe it has come to this. The other dung larks, as this Ravi calls them, push her around and taunt her in a language she does not even know.

If Xatharo dies, she will be on her own. There must be a way out of this.

They take the elephants down to the lake for their bath. The elephants love the water, Ravi tells her. When we can, we bath them at least once a day.

They form them up in a procession, each elephant holding the tail of the one before. The water is torpid and brown. The elephants plunge in, and the boys set to work with the pumice, scrubbing them like naughty children.

The one they call Colossus is a massive beast with ragged ears and a scarred hide. He makes a great trumpeting as he sinks to his haunches in the river, spraying water joyously in the air with his trunk. Up close his skin does not even look alive; it is so grey and withered it is like something you might find hanging cured upon a wall.

He is enormous; the height of two men and the size of a small palace. But it is his eyes that astonish her. They watch her intently, not with the brute indifference of a beast of the field but as if he knows what she is thinking.

She stands exhausted, knee deep in the water, every bone and sinew creaking. Colossus reaches out for her with his trunk.

She is too frightened to move. He trails his trunk over her face and body, leaving her covered in slime. She thinks he will pick her up and throw her if she makes even a sound.

But he doesn't. She feels the rubbery trunk curl around her body and pick her up. He deposits her on the river sand and stands over her, staring at her with one sad pink eye.

She notices his eyelashes for the first time, how thick and wiry they are, and how his wrinkles criss-cross his skin. She reaches out to touch him, but he turns and wades away in the direction of his fellows, blasting water over his back as he goes.

It is a dull morning, grey and hot. The clouds suffocate and are greasy pale like the dead. But how brightly Alexander shines; how eager his blue eyes. He glitters like a newly minted coin.

There is a huddle around him. He is the air that others breathe. Niarchos is there, like a hawk with that beak of his and hunter's eyes, hazel and vicious.

At his signal they all retire a step, their heads craning. Alexander is praying in front of a statue, making an offering of a skinned beast. He turns and smiles as Gajendra enters.

'Ah, elephant boy! Do you know this god? His name is Baal. My advisers tell me that he is really Zeus, but in another form. He is the god of the thunderstorm.'

Baal stands, arms outstretched, pointing to the pit where sacrificial victims are burned. The temple is strangely empty. It has been looted. All that is left are a few benches, and a gorilla skin hanging on the wall. Frankincense burns in mounds as big as ox carts.

Baal makes the generals look small and peevish. He has a thunderous expression, while these men look like schoolboys who cannot get what they want.

'They give their firstborn to the gods in times of war and famine,' Alexander is saying. 'I wonder how many firstborns gave their lives needlessly to stay me. If they had but known. You cannot ask a god to work against his own son.'

He gets to his feet, jumps up on the plinth beside Baal to mimic his frown. There is a shudder through the corps of those who attend him. This blasphemy shocks them. You should not even mock a god you do not believe in, for you never know.

'Do you not think I should make a very fine god, elephant boy? I should like to be asked for my favour a hundred years from now. To have someone pray to my statue, now that is something to be wished for, isn't it? We are only here for a short time but may be remembered forever if we live with courage and ambition.'

Alexander laughs and jumps down to the marble. There is such restlessness about him today, he cannot stay still for a moment. He takes out his knife and stirs the incense coals with the edge of the blade, breathing it in.

'Men say that I am Hercules brought back to life. What do you think?'

'I don't know much about him.'

'He was a god. Do you think I'm a god?'

Gajendra can feel the other generals' eyes on him. If he says yes, they will set on him like a pack of wolves. If he says no, Alexander may take it as an insult. He seems to be the only one who cannot feel the tension.

'Come on now, answer. I rule half the world. I am invincible in battle. Is that not godlike?'

'But are gods not immortal?'

'Perhaps I am immortal. Until a man dies how can anyone be truly sure?' His flatterers laugh. No one else. 'My father saw my mother consorting with Zeus, did you know that? In the form of a serpent. Gods are shape shifters, elephant boy, or they are in our world. So, if my father was right, I'm the son of a god. And the son of a god is a god.' He beams at them all, his point proven. Then he pats Gajendra on the shoulder, steers him away from his generals and lowers his voice, so they cannot hear. 'Niarchos wants your head, you know. He says you are uppity. An uppity Indian.' He laughs. 'Nothing worse.'

'Why would he say that?' Gajendra says, staring at Niarchos.

'Oh, he means nothing by it. You should congratulate him. He is to be married. I am giving him one of my harem, as thanks for his steadfast duty. Zahara is one of the most beautiful women I have.'

Gajendra feels the blood drain from his face.

'There is news of more import. Antipater has bought off Athens and Corinth. He is gathering an army against me. He plans to go against me at Sicily.'

'I have heard these rumours,' Gajendra says. But he is not really listening. Alexander is marrying Zahara to Niarchos?

'What do you think of Antipater's plans?'

Gajendra tries to concentrate his mind but all he can think of is standing in the orange grove by Astarte's temple in Babylon, promising Zahara that one day she would be his.

He turns back to the generals. 'There has been talk about the camp,' Alexander says to him. 'They say it is all your fault.'

'How is it my fault?'

'For making Antipater my enemy. If you had not informed me of the plan to poison me, I should not have crucified Iolaus and had Kassander put in a cage.'

'But then you would have been dead.'

'Is that all you can say in your defence?' he says and laughs. The corps join in, dutifully. 'I suppose you wish me to reward you. Did you like the way they died?'

'Who, lord?'

'Come on, elephant boy, keep up. Iolaus and the captain of the elephants! What was his name?' He snaps his fingers for memory.

'Oxathres,' one of the generals says.

'Yes. Oxathres. You never liked him, did you?'

'I hated him.'

'Well, there you are then. He took two days to die. A long time. He did not look as strong. I should have wagered three hours, the most. You?'

'I thought he suffered overmuch.'

'Overmuch? But he wanted to leave me to die by inches. He set the stakes, not I. How did you feel seeing your captain wriggling like that? They die of suffocation, you know. The pain is secondary.'

'I should hate to die that way.'

'A man should never be afraid of death. Look it in the eye, stare it down, invite it in for wine and welcome. Pain is nothing. Are you scared of pain?'

'I am scared that I will fail you.'

He claps his hands. 'An excellent answer.' He turns to his Companions. 'Listen and learn.'

'I only wish to be recognised for my efforts.'

'Ah, but you are. You have many talents. I cannot turn my back on you for a moment. If you are not taming wild elephants, you are discovering plots against me. A question for you. We leave for Sicily within the week to face Antipater and his Greeks. My generals say that we should leave the elephants behind, that they are too expensive to feed and too difficult to transport. What do you say to that?'

'I say that if you have a weapon that is certain to confound and defeat your enemy, then you should use it.'

'Ah, but they do not think so. They say we won here because Hanno had never faced elephants before. Next time our enemies will be ready. Antipater is not stupid; he will have reports of my campaigns in India. He will know what to do.'

Colossus still has scars on his legs and flank from wounds he received at the Jhellum river, the battle where Alexander finally discovered how to defeat elephants. The Macedonians had encircled them first, using archers to pick off their mahavats, and then Alexander's slingers attacked the elephants' eyes with a volley of darts. When the tuskers were half blinded and had no mahavat to guide them, the infantry worked as a team, the bravest distracting the elephants by chopping at their trunks with a scimitar while their comrades hacked at the hams at the backs of their legs with axes.

It was brutal but effective. Gajendra doubts that any army but Alexander's might be as successful. It took iron discipline to do what they did. As it was, the Silver Shields had taken frightening losses.

'Do you have a remedy to this battle plan? Could you save our tuskers from a similar tactic?'

Gajendra looks him in the eye. 'Yes.'

'We are eager to hear it.'

The generals fold their arms. This Indian is going to tell them how to make war? This should be good.

'I would not use elephants against infantry. As you say, a well-trained phalanx will not be as easy to frighten as the Celts and Gauls we fought outside Carthage.'

'What then?'

'I would put them on the flanks and pit them against cavalry. Horses are terrified of elephants. They cannot make a successful charge against them. But I would disguise the move. I would make an oblique attack from the centre across the enemy's front.'

Alexander stares at him for a long moment, then laughs and punches his shoulder. 'My little elephant boy is a student of war!' He turns to his commanders. 'Who would have thought?' He laughs again. 'What else would you do, my little general? Show me.'

He grabs Ptolemy and Perdiccas and his other generals, pushes them around like counters on a money changer's table. They flush, appalled, but they can hardly protest.

'Here, you are my new Elephantarch for the day,' Alexander says. 'Tell me who should go where.'

'What are the forces ranged against me?'

'Kraterus has the veterans who have deserted to his cause, as well as Leosthenes' men.'

'Leosthenes?'

'He commands the largest army of mercenaries in the world. He put himself out for bids. I would not stoop so I left the auction to Antipater.'

'So how many infantry?'

'Forty thousand. Perhaps fifty.'

'Cavalry?'

A casual shrug. 'Five thousand. But Greek cavalry. We shall have four thousand, my new phalanx and my Silver Shields. Twenty-five thousand, plus our irregulars.'

Alexander pushes Ptolemy to the centre. 'Be Antipater's phalanx.' He grabs Perdiccas and pushes him in front of Ptolemy. 'And here, Perdiccas, be the archers. Where shall Antipater place his bowmen?'

'They will be with the infantry,' Gajendra says. 'Archers are worthless against heavy cavalry. No bow is effective beyond a hundred paces, twenty-five if the wind is off the sea. I should use my own archers on the backs of the elephants where they are not nullified by speed.'

'An elephant can only carry one archer.'

'An elephant should carry at least four or five.'

The generals shake their heads and mutter. They don't like this; they want to keep to the old ways.

Perdiccas says, 'Four archers will slow the elephants down.'

'How?' Gajendra says.

'The extra weight.'

'Do you know how many men an elephant can carry on its back?'

Perdiccas doesn't. Gajendra sees by his face that he would like to thrash him. A gyppo talking back! Alexander beams. He thrives on conflict, even amongst his own.

'If you don't know how many, then how do you know it will slow him down?' Gajendra says. He turns to Alexander. 'The *howdahs* need to be bigger, so you can have four archers or slingers in there. Instead of wood, you use hardened leather, to make it lighter and you give the archers lighter armour too. Then you have something no other army has – a mobile artillery.'

Alexander turns to Niarchos. 'You hear that, my friend? What a lieutenant you have here!' He shoves Lysimachus out next to Perdiccas, as Antipater's cavalry. 'Seleucus, you shall be the right wing. And Niarchos is Antipater. There, you have your enemy. You are outnumbered two to one. What shall you do now?'

'First I should better armour my elephants.'

'Better armour them?'

'To protect their legs against infantry. I can design the plates for you and your smithies can make them. It is not difficult. It's hooped iron tied together with leather thongs. You need heavier trunk and face armour, also.'

'Why are we talking so much about elephants?' Lysimachus grumbles. 'We know what they can do.'

'But they can do much more,' Gajendra says. 'If I were Alexander, I should use my elephants as a shield.' He walks up to Ptolemy but then turns towards Lysimachus. 'If your enemy sees the elephants, he is focused on the elephants. He may not think there are also several squadrons of cavalry behind them. He will not think you will go against his own cavalry because horses are too quick. But horses don't know that. They will turn.'

'Stand back, Lysimachus,' Alexander says, and he does as he is commanded.

'I should halt my elephants here, for the job is done,' Gajendra says. 'There is a break in the line. You are behind me with your Companion Cavalry. The mass of infantry is to our left. But if I am Alexander, I should ignore them.' He steps past Perdiccas and Ptolemy, stands nose to nose with Niarchos. 'Here is Antipater at the rear. This is where I should apply my violence.'

Niarchos and Gajendra stare at each other.

Alexander claps his hands. 'An excellent discourse. My elephant boy may make a fine general one day. It is decided, then, the elephants come with us. Can your beasts travel by ship?'

'It is difficult.'

'How difficult?'

'They must be manoeuvred up a plank to the ship's deck. They will be unhappy about it.'

'But you can do it?'

'I can do it.'

'You have managed elephants on a ship before?'

'Of course.' A lie.

'Good. Give me the details of what you need for the new armour, and we shall set to work on it, as well as new *howdahs*. We shall have more archers on each beast. Gentlemen, we are going to Sicily!'

They are not all as enthusiastic as Alexander. As Gajendra leaves, the other generals position themselves so that he must squeeze through or else shove them aside. They look like lions hungry for supper.

'Jumbo fucker,' one of them murmurs as he passes.

CHAPTER 22

Zahara passes, a covered wagon taking her and the rest of Alexander's harem along the waterfront to one of the *triremes*. He can only see her eyes; the rest of her face is hidden behind a veil as she sits huddled in the back with the other girls. There is an escort of cavalry, so it is barely a glimpse.

'In bed she'll just lie there.'

He looks around sharply to see who has spoken. It is Mara.

'What are you talking about, cherry boy?'

'It's the trouble with beautiful women. They think if they lie back and sigh it's all a man deserves. She'll want a ruby for every kiss and a diamond for every entry.'

Gajendra cannot believe a slave would address him like this. He sees the other dung larks look at him to see what he will do. It sets a bad example, this. One of the water boys answered back to him yesterday and he had to thrash him to keep the rest of them in line. So why does this fresh-faced little mucker have special privileges?

Two other boys wheel away their handcarts filled with elephant dung. He pushes Mara in their direction. 'Get back to work.'

If this continues, he shall have to start carrying a whip.

He's too soft with these lads. He looks for the women, but they have passed and are already down at the dock boarding Alexander's *trireme*. There is an ache in his chest.

He wonders again why he did what he did. The boy has stirred a doubt in his mind. It has ruined his day.

They are trying to get the elephants on the ships. Mara watches Gajendra coax them down to the dock one at a time. He uses the bull hook to guide them, touching their trunk now one side, then the other, talking to them all the time in a language she has never heard before.

Colossus is the last in line and is more tentative than his fellows. She can see that Gajendra is worried about him. Ravi goes to help him. It seems that Colossus will tolerate men throwing spears at him, but he doesn't like the look of Alexanders' ships one bit.

There is a sharp wind, raising waves on the inner harbour and unsettling the animals. Elephants may like the water, but the sea is a different proposition.

Gajendra climbs on Colossus's back and coaxes him forward. It is not one movement but a series of clicks with his tongue and nudges with his knees and feet, as well as taps with the hook. Mara allows herself to admire him. It is every bit as skilful as the best riders in her father's cavalry.

They have constructed a stout walkway of flat beams between the dock and the ship. Colossus eyes it suspiciously, flares his ears in alarm and turns away. Gajendra is patient. He leads him back. Colossus trumpets and circles. At the last moment he turns away again.

'This is impossible,' one of the water boys mutters at her shoulder. 'They will never get that stupid beast on the ship!'

'He's not stupid!' Mara snaps at him. The boy takes a step back, astounded that the new dung lark should talk to him that way.

Colossus circles again and Ravi is almost trampled under his hind legs. After five attempts everyone is cursing and covered in dust. They all stink of sweat and elephant.

Alexander appears on the wharf, with his usual *coterie* of staff officers, hangers-on and yes-men. 'Having trouble, elephant boy?'

'It will be all right, my lord.'

'What's going on here?' Niarchos shouts. 'What's the delay?'

'Colossus is a little anxious today, that's all.'

'Well, what are you going to do about it?' Alexander says.

'We'll get him there.'

'You'd better. We have to be under sail tomorrow night. I want the army landed in Sicily within the week.' He rides off, leaving Niarchos behind in charge of things.

There is a hole smashed in the jetty where Colossus has stomped his foot. They try to control him with long pikes and ropes, but it does no good either. The big fellow is getting angry with them. He yanks on one of the dock stanchions with his trunk then butts it with his enormous head. The whole dock starts to sway.

Mara looks at Gajendra. He is sweating. Even he looks frightened now. Niarchos has lined the docks with soldiers carrying javelins, bows and axes. If Colossus does too much damage, they mean to take him down.

Mara has no experience with elephants but the answer to the problem seems clear to her. If the beast is frightened of the sea, then make him think he is still in the forest.

She steps forward. 'You cannot do it this way!'

Gajendra looks at her, wide-eyed. 'You have a better idea, boy?'

'Yes, I do.'

Gajendra has Colossus let him down. He grabs her by the arm and leads her away, out of earshot of the others. 'Tell me.'

'He's afraid of the water. So don't let him see it. Cover his eyes. Then hang awnings on the ship so he can't see the water even when he's on board. Cover the deck. Use bushes, trees and dirt. And reinforce these boards,' she says, hammering her heel on the jetty. 'A big animal like that needs to feel solid earth under its feet.'

He hesitates. He follows the reasoning but frets over the delay such precautions will take. Yet what choice do they have?

It takes another half a day to cart in enough dirt to throw on the *trireme*, shroud it with canvas awnings, then have a detail of slaves carry bushes and small trees down to the dock. The soldiers stand around, laughing and making ribald comments.

The carpenters· have strengthened the jetty and covered it with dirt, like the ships. Gajendra looks on, his face a mask. He has staked his pride and his position on this. If he cannot get these elephants on the ships, and Alexander leaves without them, he will be just another shitkicker the rest of his life.

He drapes silk curtains from Colossus' headdress and lets them fall, so his eyes are covered. Then he leads him back down to the dock, tapping behind his ears with his hook to guide him.

Colossus sniffs the air with his trunk and moves slowly, not trusting the ground underneath him, but when he feels the dirt and bushes either side of him, he gains confidence.

Mara silently wills Colossus onto the ship, prays that he does not stumble or baulk. She feels an affinity with him now.

Gajendra appears calm, but the sweat gleams on his face. He walks beside Colossus's head, singing to him. Ravi sets his own elephant to follow, and the two tuskers go tamely along the gangplank and onto the *trireme*. There is a cheer from the water boys. Even the soldiers applaud, the same ones that had been mocking them all morning.

Mara catches Gajendra's eye. She does not expect effusive thanks. Just as well, for all she gets is a slight nod of the head.

The boys jump onto the ship and use pitchforks to pile the hay in front of Colossus. He is content enough now. Then they load the rest of the tuskers on the same way. There, it is done. Soon they will be on their way to Sicily.

CHAPTER 23

They take Xatharo below decks, throw him in a corner and leave him to it. He lies there like a bundle of bloodied rags. You could pass him in the dank corridor and not even know there was a man lying there. Mara cannot wake him. She checks for his pulse and his breathing, is surprised to find him still alive. She wraps him in her cloak, finds some water and dribbles it on his lips. He hardly stirs.

A fair wind snaps the rigging and sends a thrill through the canvas. There are rain squalls out on the ocean. Gulls wheel in the air, hurled about by the wind.

The elephants stagger as the ship see-saws on the swell. Colossus and Ran Bagha trumpet pitifully. Mara is afraid they will snap their chains. There is no one to tend them as all the water boys are clinging wretchedly to the side, seasick themselves.

Dark clouds scurry across the face of the moon. The plaintive trumpeting of the elephants makes her forget her own misery. She leaves Xatharo and makes her way up to the deck to their enclosure. She has never seen two more thoroughly miserable animals.

She starts to talk to them. She knows they cannot understand, but if you can talk to a horse, you can talk to an elephant is how she reasons it, and she has seen her father talk to his horse more tenderly than he ever talked to her or her mother.

She goes to Colossus and rubs the widest part of his peculiar long nose. It is like rubbing sandstone. She tells him it will soon be over and what a brave lad he is.

After a while Colossus stops his trumpeting and the other beast follows his lead. They put their trunks in each other's mouths for comfort. They are even stranger creatures in the dark, when all you know of them is the smell and that curious rumbling they make.

'There, my big man, don't be afraid. It's going to be all right. The captain just calls it a fair wind. Soon you will be on dry land, and we will find you some trees to eat.'

Colossus seeks her out with his trunk. After he is done she is covered in slime, but she is too wet and too seasick to care.

Gajendra staggers across the deck. It is his first time on the sea. He needs to go to his elephants, but another spasm of retching sends him rushing for the side. The sea spray on his face feels cool. He wipes the bile from his mouth, and makes his way towards the stern, where Colossus and Ran Bagha are riding out the storm in their chains. He sees the new dung lark standing under Colossus's front legs, rubbing his trunk. What does he think he's doing?

One big wave and Colossus will crush him against the gunwale. He'll pop like overripe fruit.

'Get away from him!' he shouts at the boy.

'Someone has to keep them calm.'

'That's my job.'

'Last time I saw you, you had your head over the side crying for your mother.'

Gajendra drags him away from the elephants. But then the ship pitches on another wave, and they are thrown together. Mara holds on to him long enough to confirm his suspicions about the boy's nature. A catamite.

He shrugs him off. 'Don't touch me.'

'I'm sorry.'

'I'm sorry, *lord*.'

The boy hesitates. 'I'm sorry – lord.'

Gajendra nods towards Colossus, who is watching this exchange with unnatural interest. 'You have a way with the tuskers. I haven't thanked you for helping me get Colossus onto the ship.'

'I wasn't sure that you would.'

'I'll make sure you get extra rations when we get to where we're going. You and your uncle. Xatharo,' he adds when he sees the blank look on his face.

He has caught him out, but before he can make more of it his stomach rebels again and he rushes for the side. When he is done, he looks back and sees Mara there again, gripping the rail, whispering to Colossus, telling him everything is going to be all right.

Whoever he is, Gajendra thinks, he's as mad as I am.

Gela, Sicily

The infantry goes ashore in boats. They form up, march into town and overwhelm a small garrison of Greeks after a short skirmish.

The navy lands the rest of the horses and supplies. The elephants take a little longer, but finally the army is encamped outside the town. Alexander is everywhere; supervising, sending out scouts, ordering the Silver Shields into a defensive perimeter. He holds his first war council in a small fort overlooking the harbour. When Gajendra arrives, a goat-skin vellum map has been placed on a trestle table in the middle of the room.

Gajendra stands at the back, as Alexander goes through his battle plans. He shows them all the route they will take through the mountains to Syracuse. He wishes to come upon Antipater and surprise him. It is as if the more he is outnumbered, the more eager he is to start the fight.

Antipater and the tyrant of Syracuse, Sostratus, have discovered a firm friendship, united in their disregard for Alexander. Antipater has brought with him an army of Greeks from Corinth and Athens. They are good for disporting with little boys, Alexander tells them, but hopeless in a fight. Forty thousand of these men are infantry, so he claims it will just make more corpses, for numbers do not matter against a well-drilled army.

'And after we have won, I will take back my Empire, and Corinth and Athens will have to answer to me.'

Alexander's navy will establish a blockade. Antipater and Sostratus will have to treat or fight.

Niarchos walks in, stamps to the water pitcher and splashes water on his face. He scowls when he sees Gajendra. 'What is he doing here?'

Alexander is amused by his irritation. 'I asked him to attend,' he says, mildly. 'He is your second-in-command and understands the elephants better than you or I. It may serve us to listen to him.'

Niarchos is thus reprimanded. 'Are all your beasts landed safely?' he growls.

'They are,' Gajendra answers.

'I still say we hardly need them,' Niarchos says to Alexander. 'Our cavalry is enough for this rabble we're against.'

'I made you Elephantarch because I thought you would appreciate their unique abilities. Gajendra has suggested that you might even take command of them from a *howdah*. It would give you a better view of the battlefield and you could use drums and flags to signal your intentions. It is how the Rajah of Taxila does things, apparently.'

Niarchos looks as if he will have apoplexy. He may be general of the elephants, but he does not intend to go near one.

'If these elephants are not such a formidable weapon,' Alexander says to him, 'why did you have me turn back after the Jhellum River? We would be at the end of the world by now and ruler of it. But you and the rest of the Companions said the next king had four thousand elephants and we would be no match.'

It still rankles with Alexander, Gajendra thinks, what happened in India. He will get his revenge on all of them for stopping his inexorable advance on the unknown. The generals look accusingly at each other. Alexander feigns not to notice. Divide and conquer, that is his way.

He stabs a finger on the chart. 'Antipater is disembarking his army at Syracuse as we speak. I should like to join battle with him before he has had a chance to choose his battleground. He will think the elephants will slow us. I should like to prove him wrong.'

'Should we not wait for our blockade to take effect?' Perdiccas says. 'If we draw his navy out to sea and destroy it, Antipater is finished anyway.'

Alexander looks at him as if he has stepped into something foul. 'Where is the glory in that?'

'But you have spent half your treasury on the new fleet,' Ptolemy reminds him.

'So that I should not be at a disadvantage when I am on the land.'

'But what if Antipater will not leave Syracuse?' Niarchos says. 'Must we embark on another long siege?'

'Antipater knows that if he wants Macedon to accept him as king, then he must defeat me in open battle.' He smiles. 'Besides, I have his son.'

There are nods around the table. They are agreed.

Gajendra is eager to begin. This is his chance.

CHAPTER 24

Alexander sends for him. The guard escorts him through the camp and past the general's fine pavilion to a field a *stade* away. He is there with his Persians, all oiled ringlets and muttered sniggerings. At first, Gajendra thinks his general is feeding a wild pet, the way he teases and coos before dropping a well-gnawed bone into a cage.

Gajendra's nose twitches. It is not an animal he has in there; it is Kassander. He has kept him alive for four seasons, somehow the poor wretch survived the long journey from Babylon and the sea crossing. He is still in the same sturdy, iron cage.

Kassander is not in the fettle he once was. Rolling around half-starved in his own excrement has taken a toll on his good looks.

Gajendra thinks about the man he saw striding so defiantly to his execution that morning in Babylon. How he must have wished for the genteel mercy of a crucifixion these last months. His clothes have rotted off him and the smell would stun a hyena. He is skin and bone, a skeleton with sores.

'Ah, elephant boy!' Alexander says when he looks up and sees Gajendra.

'My lord.'

'Tell me, how are my elephants?'

Gajendra forces himself to look away; he can feel his gorge rising at the back of his throat. 'They are well now they are back on dry land.'

'Niarchos told me how you were finally able to get them aboard. You made the ships look like a jungle! That was inspired. He says the idea was of his own invention, is this so?'

So, the bastard intends to garner all the credit for himself. It makes him want to spit. If anyone should get the plaudits, it should be the catamite from Carthage.

'You hesitate. Don't tell me a Macedonian general would try to take credit for another's deeds?' He laughs and his crowd laughs along with him. Here is a man with ten shadows and ten echoes.

Kassander is howling and clawing at the bars of his confinement. It seems a bone and a piece of gristle is not enough for his dinner, after so long a fast.

'I had a tutor once,' Alexander says. 'He caught me burning incense in my room while I studied my books. He thrashed me for it, told me I was being wasteful. "When you conquer the spice regions you can have all the incense you like," he said. When I conquered Gaza I sent him eighteen tons of frankincense and myrrh. Do you think I made my point?'

'And you made him a very rich man.'

'Well, I didn't want to be vindictive. But you see what I'm saying. Nothing is ever in the past. Whatever is done to us, is with us forever. It speaks to us always and urges us to present action.' He smiles, as if he can see into Gajendra's soul. 'They don't like you.'

'Who, my lord?'

'The other generals.'

'What have I done to them?'

'You breathe.'

'I shall try to do it less, and more quietly.'

'That won't be enough, it will never be enough. Your crime is you were not born in Macedon, a grave error for one so young and ambitious. And you are ambitious, aren't you?'

'I want to be like you.'

'Every man wants to be like me. But that's only part of it. There's something more, isn't there?' He throws Kassander another piece of gristle. He leaps upon it like a starving dog. 'What do you want, elephant boy?'

'I want to be a general. I want to ride at your side when you conquer the world.'

Several of his sycophants find this amusing. He silences them with a glance. 'Ride at my side? On an elephant? You should hardly keep up.'

'The elephants are a means to an end.'

'Go on.'

'I want a horse like yours, a white stallion, Arab, pure bred. I want a beautiful woman in my bed.' Alexander, at least, does not seem to think his ambitions are either shallow or stupid.

'What should you give for such an embarrassment of riches?'

'Loyalty.'

'I can have loyalty at the cost of a few nails and some pieces of wood. Fear makes men loyal. That is why I had your captain crucified. I didn't make him suffer out of ill will. It was tactics. You understand that word, don't you?'

Alexander stands very close, holding his gaze. 'You can lead elephants, but can you lead men?'

'I know that you have to understand the nature of both before you can get them to do what you want.'

'There was a look on your face when you heard I had promised Zahara to Niarchos. What is she to you?'

Gajendra does not answer.

'You like them, do you? Women? I mean, apart from breeding.'

He nods. Alexander's lip curls in disappointment. Gajendra feels he has given the wrong answer.

'Well, there is nothing to be done. She is a princess, and you are an elephant boy. It was foolish of you to dream.'

Alexander returns to Kassander. He picks up a hock of beef that a servant holds out to him on a silver tray and starts to chew it. The thing in the cage thrashes and howls, tries to grab it from between the bars, but Alexander stays a finger's breadth out of range. The crowd snicker, amused.

'I remember once going into my father's study as he was writing a letter to an ally of his. The man who was to take the missive for him was waiting in an anteroom. Do you know what the letter said? It said: *Kill the man who brings you this missive.*'

'Why?' Gajendra says.

'I never discovered the reason. All I know is that after he had sealed the letter, I watched him go outside, put his arm around the fellow and invite him to stay for dinner. They were up all night, drinking wine and telling jokes. They parted on the best of terms.'

'Why are you telling me this?'

Alexander beckons him closer. 'A lesson for you elephant boy. Never tell anyone what it is you really want.'

They have roped the elephants together, under some trees. Mara and Xatharo are sitting close by with the other water boys. A strip of linen supports Xatharo's left arm.

Two days ago she thought he would die, but already he is walking again. One arm is useless, and he is as weak as a new-born lamb, but somehow he is alive. You cannot kill this man even if you cut him in half. Should you try to drown him, the sea would choke on the bones and spit him back.

Xatharo may still have one foot in the Shades, but the elephant boys are wary of him. The tattoos on his face scare them and he snarls at anyone who comes close. No one expects such belligerence from a little fellow. Even Gajendra lets him be.

Mara wonders how old he is. It is impossible to tell. She has seen him slipping in and out of her father's private study since she was a little girl. His size deceives. Any man that calls him a midget finds himself on his back with his teeth scattered and his nose broken. He is like one of those dogs that hunt lion. He goes for the belly first and then, when the entrails are out, he goes for the throat.

She has asked him many times what the tattoos on his face mean and he always has a different answer. There are thick rings on his fingers. She suspects this is not vanity but for fighting, the quicker to gouge out an eye.

He needs to get his strength back, and she has saved some of her dinner for him so he can have the extra ration. He tears at a hunk of bread with his teeth and tips back a waterskin so that the water runs into his beard. Then he leans toward her and touches her knee, as if he is about to impart a gentle word. 'We have to escape.'

'What's the point?'

'You are not going to last long here. Someone will find us out eventually. I promised your father I would keep you alive.'

She is quiet for a time and then takes a deep breath. 'I don't want to escape. I want to stay and avenge him.'

'What?'

'You can do it if any man can. Let me help you. This way we do something for Carthage and for my father.'

'My charter is to keep you alive, no more than that.'

'For what purpose? My father is dead, and Carthage is destroyed.' She leans in. 'Let's kill Alexander.'

He roars with laughter.

'I'm serious.'

'I know you are. That's what's so funny.'

'We just have to get close enough.'

'No one comes close to him except the Companions, and he doesn't even trust them that well anymore.

'We will use Gajendra.'

Xatharo shakes his head. 'It's a worthy notion but a ridiculous idea. Besides, I told you. I gave my oath to your father. I never break an oath and especially not to him.'

'My father could not have known that one day we would be in a position to avenge him, avenge all Carthage! Do you not listen to the water boys? Alexander has taken the elephant talker under his wing. He nurtures him like a favoured nephew. There have even been personal audiences. Fortune has given us opportunity. If I befriend him, I might get close to Alexander.'

'Befriend? I won't let you whore yourself to that Indian!'

'Would it not be worth it to kill Alexander?'

'Killing is not a job for a woman, especially one as high born as you. Forget this madness. I gave my word to your father to protect you to my last breath, not let you throw away your life. Go to sleep.'

He lies down in the straw and rolls over.

She looks at her hands. They are raw and bleeding from the work. There is dirt under her fingernails, and it is ingrained in her skin. She stinks of elephant and their droppings. She has never felt so tired in her life.

Is this all for nothing, too?

She listens to men snoring and calling out in their sleep. The few still awake talk of camp followers and wives and swap whoring stories. Some young fellow is speaking about a goat, another one about a whore with no legs in Alexandria. He paid extra. One goes to it with his sister, one with a midget in Babylon. He claims he himself is so well-favoured in nature that he had three of them at once, end to end.

If her father could see her now. All her life she has been cosseted and protected. Now she is sitting in a field listening to soldiers boast about their carnal exploits while she talks about assassinating a Macedonian general.

She closes her eyes and hears her husband laugh as he plays dice in the courtyard with his brothers. How she misses him. They must be loving his company, the gods. He would take all their money at a game of chance, but he'd shout them wine afterwards.

The next morning Xatharo insists on chopping her hair again. From everything she heard the night before, she wonders if it will make any difference. It seems to her, men who will have intercourse with cripples and goats will not play favourites when it comes to gender.

But Xatharo worries that if Gajendra discovers her true identity he will give her to the auctioneer and turn a profit. If one of them sees you can't pass your water standing up it will be all over, he tells her. Be careful until I work out a way to get us away from here.

He worries night and day about how to keep her alive; all she can think about is killing Alexander.

CHAPTER 25

They drill the elephants all morning. There is *upasthana*, teaching the tuskers to rise over small palisades and *samvartana*, getting them to rise on their hind legs and take a giant step over a ditch. But most of their training is designed to get them ready again for pitched battle; to bear the noise of the infantry sounding trumpets and banging swords on shields.

After the drill, the water boys take the elephants to the river to scrub them down with brushes and pumice stones. Mara gives Colossus his bath. He won't let any of the other water boys close.

Gajendra watches. The boy is better at this than he is at shovelling dung.

Ravi comes to stand beside him. 'That lad has a way with our tuskers. It's a rare gift.'

'It's no gift,' Gajendra says. 'It's bribery. Do you know how many times I've caught him feeding him apples instead of mucking out the straw? I've warned him about it enough times. If he keeps this up, I'll send him over to the infantry. They'll soon sort him out.'

'You want to know what I think? The little ugly one is not that boy's uncle. He's a mercenary and he bought the boy from a brothel or an auction block. A freak like that is not going to get a girl or a boy unless he pays for it. Or else he's his pimp. He'll do a fine trade from the Macks if he has the chance.'

Gajendra watches how the boy pulls at the hair at the nape of his neck, as if he is looking for a curl. Does he know he is being provocative? He himself has never been one for splitting the peach but there's something about this one that unsettles him.

Every day Mara pursues him with questions. Why do they turn more slowly to the left than the right? Why do they put their trunks in each other's mouths?

'You are a slave,' Gajendra keeps telling him. 'Learn to keep your peace.'

'I only want to learn.'

'Dung larks only need to learn how to shovel shit. Get on with it.'

Mara watches Gajendra move among the elephants, examining each and every one, as gentle as if he were with his children. They reach out with their trunks and feel for him, like a blind man reading a face. He clicks his fingers for a boy to come and tend to an injury on one of the animals, scolds another for not fetching their food fast enough. He talks to the beasts as if they are babies, cooing and chanting.

Colossus is always the last to leave the water. Mara picks this moment to wander away and find a bush to relieve herself. But when she looks around, she realises that Colossus has followed her.

She hears Gajendra coming.

'Go back,' Mara says and tries to shoo Colossus away. He stops, trunk swaying and trumpets at her.

Gajendra bursts through the bushes. 'Have you taught him a secret signal? Why is he following you?'

'I don't know!'

'An elephant has one mahavat, only one, do you understand?' He taps the hook on the elephant's ear, and Colossus turns reluctantly away.

That night, Alexander orders that the elephants should be suitably prepared to attend Niarchos's wedding feast. Gajendra has a dozen of his tuskers painted in gaudy colours, even their toenails. His boys use reds, ochres and greens. They put circles around the beasts' eyes and geometric patterns over their trunks and bodies. They even put headdresses on them, the same ones they would wear for battle.

When it is done, Gajendra leaves Ravi in charge and retires early to the straw. Later, he wakes to the sound of drums and flutes, and tries not to think about what is happening. Bitterness and jealousy curdle in him like bad milk.

He imagines Zahara beside him. He puts out a hand in the darkness, as if he is resting it on her hip. He feels her sweet breath on his face. The longing is so urgent he groans aloud.

It is no good. He abandons all thoughts of sleep and sits up all night with the elephants, staring at the sea.

CHAPTER 26

Gajendra walks to the riverbank and throws himself down on his haunches. He looks as if he has been told he is to die tomorrow. He scoops water over his head and stares at his reflection.

Mara wonders at him. A good young man, but over fond of melodrama.

He turns and sees her.

'Should I leave you to drown yourself in peace?' she says.

'What are you doing here?'

'I needed privacy.'

'What for? Just find a tree like the other fellows. Have you always been so precious?'

'May I ask what is wrong, lord? Has one of our tuskers died?'

'You heard the celebration last night. Alexander gave our Elephantarch one of his harem.'

'What a fortunate girl.'

Gajendra tosses a stone into the muddy water with great force.

'This cannot be the reason you are here crying into the river?'

'She is too good for him.'

'I think you have things the wrong way round. Niarchos is a Macedonian general. You are just a foreign mercenary. How might a mercenary marry a princess?'

'I am not a mercenary. I am captain of the elephants.'

'A grand title but you have elephant droppings under your fingernails just like the rest of us. That's not going to get a princess into your bed.'

He gets to his feet. 'Have you ever been with a woman?'

Mara shakes her head.

'Do you ever think about a girl and feel like your balls are going to explode if you don't have her?'

'No, that has never happened to me.'

Is that how my husband felt about me when we were married, she thinks. She should like to think so, but this initiation into the rites of men is a little daunting for so early in the morning. In Carthage she might only now be rising from her bed and calling the servants to peel her a peach and pour a warm bath.

'Is that how love feels to you?' she asks him.

He shrugs. 'I suppose all you think about is boys?'

'Who told you that?'

'It's obvious. Ravi thinks you're a dancing boy and your so-called uncle is actually your pimp. Is it true?'

'Does it matter to you what I was?'

'No, you're right, it doesn't.' He gets to his feet. 'What would someone like you know of love, anyway?'

'More than you suspect.'

'I mean, here in the heart.' Gajendra punches himself in the chest to reinforce the impression of strong feeling. 'Not the false show you put on to dupe a customer out of his money.'

'You are the one who thinks I'm a catamite. I didn't say that I was one. I have never given love for money nor shall I ever.'

'What are you then, looking like that?'

It's a question that begs an answer and clearly, she does not have one. Xatharo would have them think anything of her but that she is Hanno's daughter. 'This I know, *lord*. There is more to love than all your lusting and sleeplessness.'

'Like what?'

'Like having someone admire you for all your virtues and love you despite your worst faults. Will she do that for you? All you see is a mysterious object that you want most of all because she is denied you. A trophy, a conquest, like a fort or a palace. Don't call it love. It's nothing like it.'

She can see that Gajendra is startled by her vehemence and does not know what to make of it. None of his other water boys would ever dare speak to him like this. She has gone too far, but now she has started she cannot stop herself.

'Has anyone ever told you that you are kind, arrogant, brave and self-obsessed?'

'Maybe Ravi.'

'Because Ravi loves you. But if you've never had a woman say it, then all your longing and groaning and melancholy means nothing.'

He turns pale. 'It's time for you to muck out the elephants,' he says.

CHAPTER 27

Alexander orders the army to march. He wishes to be at the gates of Syracuse before Antipater has a chance to properly prepare.

The infantrymen break down their eighteen-foot *sarissas* into two pieces, lashing eight of them together in one bundle. Two men will take turns to carry them over their shoulders during the march. They decamp with their iron helmets strapped in front, ox leather shoes hanging by rawhide laces around their necks.

The wagons, the women and traders follow behind as best they can. There will be one pack animal for five men and one servant for ten. His forty elephants will follow single file, with their food and supplies.

It will not be easy. Every day an elephant needs enough fruit and fodder to fill several ox carts as well as enough water to create an inland sea. Somehow, they will have to provide it or let the beasts forage for themselves, which will slow them down even more.

Gajendra remembers a saying he first heard in India: *To take revenge on an enemy, first buy him an elephant.*

He supposes Alexander will learn the truth of it soon enough.

That first afternoon, as they march east from the coast, they see a great mountain looming in the distance. The locals call it Aetna. They march towards it.

An hour before sunset the order comes down the line to make camp. There is a farm nearby. The farmer has been warned of their approach and knows the Macks will steal his pigs, so he hides them as best he can, locking them in a stone barn on the edge of a field. But one of the Macks hears them squealing and calls over his fellows. They smash down the door with an iron ram they have brought with them in case of a siege. The pigs run out across the field and the soldiers run after them, laughing.

It is an hilarious diversion for all save the pigs and the farmer until they reach the road, and the elephants see them. Then the game becomes deadly serious.

Gajendra, walking beside Colossus, is first to see the pigs coming.

He shouts a warning, but he already knows he's too late. Colossus flares his ears and turns to face them, trumpeting. Gajendra grabs Ravi, who is closest to him, and drags him behind a tree. The soldiers are still laughing. They won't think it's funny for much longer.

Colossus throws back his head and screams, ears flared, trunk raised high in the air. He takes off and the rest of the elephants follow. Dozens of water boys go down under their feet, caught up in the charge. Gajendra sees one of the mahavats stand in front of his elephant and order him to turn back with a sharp command and a whack with the bull hook. It is like trying to stop a runaway cart using pure reason. The tusker tramples him underfoot.

Horses shy and run. The baggage trains are upended and tumble down the side of the hill. Carts are turned into lumber, iron-rimmed wheels pulped like twigs. He hears men screaming.

There is nothing he can do about it.

His tuskers take off down the valley. It is chaos: shrieking pigs, shrieking men, shrieking elephants. He waits.

When he finally steps out from behind the tree, all his elephants are gone. Bloodied rags and pieces of meat – once men – lie on the ground. The pigs are still squealing. Will no one shut the pigs up? Most of the carts are firewood. Men are walking around dazed.

He runs back down the column, finds one of the Agrianians, picks him out by his white tunic and tattooed face. 'Get your archers, kill these pigs now!'

The man is startled at having an Indian give him orders but he can see the sense in it and shouts at his fellows to see that it is done.

Meanwhile, Colossus has disappeared into an orange grove. Gajendra can see the treetops trembling. It is not hard to track him. It is like a squadron of cavalry has crashed through.

Finally he stops to help himself to oranges. Gajendra puts his hands on his knees and bends over to catch his breath.

His elephant is a methodical eater. After he has finished stripping the fruit, he removes the leaves from a branch and places them in his mouth. Then he snaps off the branch. After he finishes chewing, the twig is ejected, stripped of the bark. He repeats the procedure several times until the tree is bare.

His trunk angles towards Gajendra, detecting his scent. He continues eating. He stamps his foot occasionally, not completely satisfied that the foul-smelling devils with the curled tails are gone.

There is nothing Gajendra can do now but wait until he is calm again. He talks to him; sings him the song he likes when he is hurt.

Colossus selects another tree, gobbles a few oranges and strips the leaves. He allows Gajendra to move closer. He swings his trunk and sniffs the air again, checking for pig breath and pig smell.

He clearly blames Gajendra for this upset, for he turns and bellows at him.

'Come on,' Gajendra murmurs, 'everything's all right now.' He takes another step closer, and the elephant's trunk curls in defiance. He's not ready to come back just yet. Gajendra stays where he is.

There are footsteps behind him. It is Mara, flushed and sweating. 'What happened? Why did they run?'

'They're scared of pigs.'

Colossus pillages another orange tree; two shakes and it is half out of the ground by its roots. He scoops up the oranges with his trunk and puts them into his mouth very daintily, one at a time. He takes a step towards Gajendra and opens his mouth, as if he is laughing. It is a conciliatory gesture.

Gajendra gathers more oranges from the ground and tosses them into his maw.

'When does an elephant learn to like oranges?' Mara says.

'When there are no watermelons to eat.'

He steps towards him but Colossus steps back again, swinging his trunk, deciding if he will be led. Gajendra hears them shouting up at the column, then the shriek of a pig as an Agrianian archer hunts it down. They will all be eating pork tonight, but it has cost them dear. Alexander will not be pleased when he finds the dead laid out and sees what is left of his baggage carts.

Mara puts a hand on his shoulder as if they are comrades.

Gajendra shrugs him off. Being a fair boss is all very well but this is sheer insolence. 'Can you persuade him back to camp?' Mara asks.

'As soon as he is settled. A big fellow like this, you can't bully him. He'll come when he's ready.'

Finally, Colossus lets him close. He taps him on the trunk with his *ankus*. '*Aana*.'

Colossus reluctantly falls in step behind. 'You see,' he says to Mara. 'He runs from instinct, and he comes back through training. That's your elephant for you. It's no more than that.'

Their part of the column has been decimated. Two men have been dragged to the side of the road, dead. Five others have been badly injured. Siege equipment and sacks of vegetables lie scattered up and down the road.

He finds Ravi. 'Where are the other elephants?'

'We've rounded up about half of them and we're still searching for the rest. Those idiots,' he nods his head at some Macks who are busy gutting one of the sows, 'they think the whole thing is a lark.'

Ravi leads Ran Bagha back up the trail. Colossus is still skittish. He keeps stopping to sniff the air. He can smell the pigs, doesn't hate them less just because they're dead.

Ran Bagha finds Colossus and puts his trunk in his mouth; they huddle for comfort. It is a strange sight, these two mammoth beasts so discomfited by a few porkers.

Someone has already started building a pyre for the two water boys who weren't quick enough getting out of the way.

Finally, Alexander rides back from the van with two of his officers. 'What happened here?' He looks astonished more than angry.

'The elephants took fright,' Gajendra says. 'Your soldiers let some pigs loose among them.'

'They are afraid of pigs?' a Persian says. 'What a wonder our new war machines are!'

Niarchos shakes his head.

'Is there anything else your elephants are frightened of?' Alexander asks him. 'Should we tether all the sheep and mice on the island?'

'Only pigs.'

'Let us hope they can do as much damage to Antipater's army as they have to mine.'

And then Colossus does something Gajendra does not expect; he flaps out his ears and takes a step towards Alexander, his trunk raised. Alexander's Arab shies away, nostrils flared. Even the general is surprised at this. He is not accustomed to belligerence from his own side, even from an elephant.

Gajendra taps him with his *ankus* and Colossus subsides. Beast and man regard each other. Alexander rides on.

The Persians cannot resist one final jibe. One of them leans down from his horse as he rides past, and shouts at Ravi, 'Oink, oink!'

CHAPTER 28

That evening Mara and Xatharo take the elephants down through the sheltering trees to the river. Colossus bellows his approval and wanders downstream. They get to work with the pumice and the brushes. After the disturbing events of the afternoon, he has recovered his temper. He is playful and sprays the thick green water on himself and on them.

He lumbers up to the bank and goes in search of a light meal. Mara follows. For all his size he is a delicate creature. She watches him feed; his trunk encircles a clod of grass, sniffs at it then plucks it out of the ground. He taps it on his foreleg to dislodge the soil, then places it in the side of his mouth, the roots protruding. He devours this morsel thoughtfully, before proceeding to the next.

Some soldiers emerge from the trees on the bank, an ominous presence; they say nothing, just watch. Mara knows what they want. She hopes that if she does not look up, they will move on.

The Macks are twenty- or thirty-year veterans by the look of them, seamed and craggy, with grey in their beards. The leader is a bluff fellow with a scar across his left eye like melted wax. Another is staring at Mara and fingering the blade at his belt as if he cannot decide between buggery and slaughter. There are two others in the shadows of the trees.

Her husband never looked at her this way, even when he had been away for months. She has learned that there are men who hate the very thing they lust for. There's a poison in them and when it runs, it goes straight to their crotch.

'What's your name, boy?' one of them calls out. 'Come on, don't be shy. We won't bite.'

She doesn't look up, hoping it will discourage them and they will tire of their game and go away.

'Come over here. We're not beasts in the field. We'll take nice care of you. Here,' he says, and tosses a coin in the mud. 'Here's a bit of silver for your trouble. You can't say we're not generous men.'

'I'd like to grease him up like a piglet and skewer him up to the lungs,' the one with the knife says. 'Come on, let's stop messing about with this, if he won't show us the proper favour, we'll teach him to bow to Macedon!' He grabs his crotch. 'I've got something right here he can pray to.'

One of them grabs her by the arm and pulls her out of the shallows. Mara puts out a hand to push him away; the smell of him is worse than anything else. She sees Xatharo wading back through the shallows; this cannot end well now.

The Mack laughs when she struggles. It is what he likes. He grabs her in both arms and carries her back to the others.

'Are you looking for a fight, boys?' Xatharo says.

'Who's that?' one of them shouts. 'Is he serious? I shit bigger than him.'

'I shit prettier than him.'

Xatharo smiles. Until now his day has been tiresome. These men have given him hope of proper entertainment. Mara has seen this expression on him before; it is the expression of a child when someone has given him a new toy to play with.

'Now give me back the lad. If he comes to no harm, neither will you.'

This is a huge joke, obviously. The big fellow pushes Mara away. 'And what will you do, you little freak? Bite off my kneecaps?'

Xatharo wades out of the river and strides across the grass. Picking up dung with his bare hands, scrubbing an elephant's back while he pisses on him, putting up with the stench and the disrespect, is all in a day's work. He is accustomed to hardship.

But this, this is what he lives for: call him a freak and challenge him to a fight and you have made everything all right again. His face shines.

The Mack does not even see it coming. Mara almost feels sorry for him. Xatharo is fast and mean. He has the advantage every dog has; he is low to the ground and hard to hit. There is a blur of movement, and the Mack is down, his knee shattered. Xatharo is kneeling on his neck, deciding whether to break it.

Then everything is motion. The other three, appalled by what has happened to their fellow, draw their weapons and move in. These are seasoned professionals; fighting is their business. They all have knives in their belts and know what they are about.

Xatharo has his own knife, hidden in his leather tunic. He stole it from a Bactrian as soon as he had recovered from his wound.

A soldier grows accustomed to fighting men his own size. Fighting someone smaller is not necessarily an advantage; speed and getting underneath is everything. It is over quickly. Two or three swift darting movements and one is down with his hamstrings cut. The other is squealing and clutching at his male parts, which are bleeding profusely.

But the last Mack is quick also and is behind Xatharo with his knife raised. Her protector sees the strike coming but there is nothing he can do to defend himself.

Then a shadow passes across the sun. The man looks up and sees Colossus looming over him. The tusker wraps his trunk around the man's chest and casually dashes him against a tree. There is a dull wet noise, like throwing a watermelon against a wall. The man's head splits open.

Colossus drops him on the ground and stands over him, his trunk swaying, as if daring him to rise once more. But there is little chance of that.

The water boys come crashing through the bushes to see what has happened. They find Xatharo standing there with a knife in his hand and three seasoned infantrymen in the mud, bloody and screaming, the other pulped under a fig tree.

Xatharo wipes the blade of his knife on his tunic and pulls Mara to her feet. Now she knows why her father valued him so highly.

These are four of the finest from Alexander's phalanx, men who can carry an eighteen-foot *sarissa* all day against endless infantry charges, and here they are spread over the riverbank like a hyena's lunch.

When he arrives, Gajendra stares at this scene in confusion. He wants to know how this happened. The water boys mumble and stare at their feet. Xatharo says the four Macks tripped on a rock. Some blame the elephant; others blame Xatharo; one wit claims it is a ritual suicide.

Gajendra looks at Mara and points his finger. 'This is your fault,' he says.

Niarchos finds Gajendra and grabs his elbow. He leads him along Elephant Row, out of earshot of the other mahavats and water boys.

'You heard what happened?' He looks harassed. As Elephantarch he will have to explain this to Alexander. He does not like the idea of some tattooed little Gugga killing good Macedonian soldiers. 'Who is the demon that did this?'

'Those men tried to rape one of my water boys.'

Niarchos is mystified. 'Why, is he good looking?'

'What?'

'Perhaps he provoked it.'

'By appearing handsome?'

'Whoever did this to these men will have to be punished. He cannot get away with it.'

'What will they do to him?'

Again, Niarchos appears confused. He wonders that Gajendra should be so concerned. 'They will crucify him, I suppose.'

'Very well. I'll tell you his name. It was Colossus.'

'An elephant does not slash a man's hams or cut off his balls.'

'That depends on how badly he is provoked.'

'The men say it was a demon the size of a child. He has a tattooed face.'

'The elephant was protecting his mahavat.'

'I don't need this sort of trouble.'

'There won't be any more trouble after this.'

Niarchos shakes his head. 'Get rid of him.'

'Who?'

'The pretty boy. It's only a goad to the others.'

'He's good at his work.'

'At clearing up shit? You don't need to be tutored by Aristotle for that.'

At that moment they both look across and see Mara standing behind Colossus, hands yellow with dung, his mouth hanging open in exhaustion. It's like the boy has never done a day's work before in his life.

'As I said, he's useless and he causes trouble,' Niarchos repeats. 'Get rid of him.'

CHAPTER 29

A mist of cold drizzle descends from the mountains in the west. Xatharo wipes pork grease off his mouth with the back of his hand. Firelight throws shadows on his face. It is suddenly cold. In the distance lightning skims and shimmers over the volcano.

'We have to kill him,' she whispers in the dark.

'We've been through this.'

'I tell you, I can do it. I just have to get close.' She imagines a knife and jerks it upwards with her right fist. 'He will have no armour and no sword. How hard can it be?'

'How many men have you killed, princess?'

'I am not a princess.'

'And you're no assassin either. But I am and let me tell you it is no easy thing. As a rule, I have found that most would prefer to live than not, and they will resist the notion most heartily. Also, you should know where to put the knife; a wounded man will fight like ten men and break your neck while he bleeds.'

'Will you not help me then?'

He sighs. 'I will not consider it for a moment. I will tell you what we are going to do. The first chance we get, we will slip away. It will be easy enough. There are no guards on us. If we can get across those mountains, we can make for the garrison at Panormus. Carthage may be dead but there are still colonies that will welcome us.'

'It won't be quite so easy to slip away if I'm screaming and struggling.'

'Killing Alexander was not what your father charged me to do.'

'My father is dead. He cannot pay your wages anymore.'

'It's not about money. I gave him my word and I will honour it. Now my wound is healed I calculate we could walk to Panormus in twelve days and that is what we are going to do. Forget all this talk about Alexander. I don't want to hear any more about it. We have a plan, and we are going to keep to it. Goodnight, princess. I am going to bed.'

CHAPTER 30

Alexander's army is spread for miles. He is in the vanguard with the cavalry, and the elephants take up the rear. They do not expect to find Antipater until the next day. All the same, Alexander has his scouts sweep the valley ahead.

It is a hot afternoon and some drowse in their saddles. Those walking beside the column have their heads down, shielding their eyes from the bright sun, thinking about water, dinner and rest.

Gajendra feels the ground trembling underfoot and thinks it is an earthquake or the distant volcano. The riders come out of the sun, their first warning when they see sunlight flashing on helmets and swords. They close quickly, like the dead rising out of the earth on phantom horses. He suspects there is a gully that they have used for concealment. Suddenly they are less than two bowshots away and the cavalry at the rear have no time to react. They are too far back.

They are making straight for his elephants.

Colossus smells them. He stops, sticks out his ears and faces the hills, his trunk testing the air. He bellows a warning to the other tuskers.

'Turn them!' Gajendra shouts. 'Get them into battle line. Hurry!'

Suddenly the army is in motion. But it is panic, not orderly movement; no one has expected this. Three of the mahavats, those with presence of mind, scramble onto their elephants' necks and prepare to make a fight of it. The rest just stand there looking stricken. Several tuskers have already bolted.

Gajendra looks up the line. Niarchos is at the van with Alexander, far out of sight. There is no one to save the tuskers except him. He sends a rider to warn Niarchos, but he supposes they will hear the commotion long before he gets there, and by then it will be too late anyway.

The archers are at the rear with the infantry, so he has to hand only a squad of Agrianians that might face the riders, if they can form up in time. The elephants have no armour to protect them from a swift and concerted attack. He could turn them and run, but the horses would easily overtake them.

Most of his mahavats are still milling around in confusion. He grabs one and shouts orders in his face. 'Mount your tusker, tell the others to do the same!'

The man stares at him wide-eyed, but the message gets through. He does as Gajendra tells him. Others follow.

The marauders are now just a bow shot away. Gajendra forms a plan in his mind of how this might go. The key is the horses. How close will they come?

There is a wagon with spears.

He picks up as many as he can carry and runs down the line, throwing them up to his mahavats. 'Do what you can. Keep the tuskers together. Hold them close so the horses can't get inside!'

No one has armour or even a helmet. He looks up to the van. There is movement there. Alexander has seen the danger now, but by the time he arrives, they could lose half their elephants.

The Agrianians, at least, know what they are about. They do not have to be told. They are ready, will have time to get off one dart before the riders are past them. It is going to be difficult, hitting a rider on a fast horse and they have just their shields to protect them. In moments, half these men he is shouting orders at will be dead.

He looks over his shoulder. Ravi has the elephants in a ragged line; Colossus is the only tusker without a rider. Another at the end of the line trumpets and scurries away. Elephants are like men, all the training in the world counts for nothing without valour, without heart.

He can see the riders now. They are Numidians, near naked but for their leopard-skin cloaks. They are riding bareback. Where have they come from?

Not Antipater. But Carthage still has colonies on the north of the island, at Lilybaeum and Panormus. They must have circled behind them; it's how they evaded their scouts.

The Agrianians' wolfhounds are howling, straining at their leashes. A volley of arrows hisses through the air, answered by the flash of their javelins. Some of the horses fall with their riders, not enough to stop the charge. The Agrianians break, run back through the line.

He looks around to mount Colossus, but it is too late.

His tusker is not of a mind to wait for him. He rushes out of the line to meet the threat. This is something the Numidians did not expect and the skirmisher line breaks and flows around him in a wave. The other elephants follow, whether their mahavats like it or not. It panics the horses and some shy on their back legs and bolt, terrified by the smell and size of the elephants.

Gajendra looks around. One rider has got through and is almost on him. He sees him just in time, sways outside the point of the spear and wrenches it out of his grasp. The man screams as he comes out of the saddle, his horse galloping blindly on.

Gajendra is on him instantly, has his knife in his hand and goes for the throat. He has never killed a man before, not close up, but there is no time to think about it. Gore sprays over his face. The man's eyes lock onto his as he dies.

Gajendra freezes.

For the moment he is too stunned by what he has done to get on with the battle. One thing to hurl a spear and not see where it lands; another to have a man's hot blood on your hands.

'Get behind me!' Xatharo shouts at Mara when he sees the riders.

He runs to the wagon and finds a spear and a *falcata*, a hacking sword. He grabs Mara by the arm and drags her clear. 'Stay out of the way! This is their fight, not ours.'

Mara looks around. Colossus has been separated from the rest of the tuskers. He charges at one of the attackers. The rider goes down but scrambles to his feet still holding his spear. Colossus trumpets in outrage as the spear goes into his unprotected shoulder.

Mara twists out of Xatharo's grip and runs towards the fight. She stops to scoop up a short sword from one of the fallen riders, lying twisted and bloody in the grass. Xatharo has no choice but to follow.

Gajendra hears a warning shout, high-pitched. He looks up and sees another of the Numidians coming at him, unhorsed and wielding a sword. The first blow nearly takes off his head, but he staggers back, out of range. The man raises his sword again and Gajendra knows he is going to die.

Suddenly the man screams and falls to his knees. There is a dagger thrust into the back of his neck and as he goes down, Gajendra sees the elephant boy standing behind him.

The light goes out of the man's eyes.

Gajendra scrambles for his weapon and looks around. The attack has been blunted. The Numidians' horses have shied away from the elephants. But his tuskers have lost their line and are milling about without order. Several have taken arrows and have blood streaming down their legs or their flanks.

He admires the courage of the men sent against them; a handful have jumped from their horses and have gone after the elephants on foot. One has darted under the legs of an elephant called Futuh and placed his spear in his belly. Another tusker, Asaman Shukoh, has trampled one of his tormentors under his feet and then tried to run, but another rider has remounted his horse and gone after him.

One of the mahavats has gone down with a spear in him and his elephant is standing over him, protecting him from further outrage, though he is clearly dead. Four of the Numidians have chosen the brave tusker as the likeliest target and are trying to get to his back legs with their spears and short swords.

He is trumpeting and running in circles on the spot, but he finally sets himself, charges one of the men and brings him down. But two others dart in and hack at his hams with their scimitars. Shrieking, he turns on them and throws one aside with his trunk, but the other slices into him with his sword. Yet another hacks again at his hamstrings and the great beast trumpets in agony and falls.

Colossus has trampled one of his own tormentors into the dirt together with his horse. He has a further spear wound in his left foreleg and this infuriates him even more. He captures one of the Numidians with his trunk and kneels on him.

Another has scrambled to his feet and is underneath him with a spear. He is about to thrust it up into his belly it when Mara runs at him screaming. She distracts him long enough that he makes for her instead of the elephant. Xatharo hits him in the back running full tilt and brings him down.

He dispatches him expertly with a knife.

The dead man's compatriot runs at him, takes the little man with a spear. Xatharo goes down clutching his thigh. He clings onto the shaft so his adversary cannot withdraw it. It gives Gajendra time to run him through.

But the man does not die, and Gajendra is unable to finish the job. It is Xatharo who crawls over and concludes the business.

Alexander and his Guardsmen arrive, galloping through the mêlée, and the Numidians bolt towards the mountains. In truth, most have already fled, startled by Colossus's charge.

Niarchos leads the cavalry in pursuit.

Alexander walks his horse along the line of the column. If he is shocked by what has taken place, he does not show it. He leans from the saddle to pat wounded men on the shoulder, laughs with his lieutenants over the bodies of the fallen enemy. The men still cheer him as he rides past.

The sun falls behind the mountains and they light torches and start campfires. No need to disguise their presence now. Someone out there knows precisely where they are.

Gajendra spits the dust out of his mouth. Ravi appears at his side. He points at Mara, who is sitting on his haunches, sobbing. 'Well, a fine hero this one,' he says. 'Kills a man and then sits down to cry about it. They won't be building him a statue on Mount Olympus anytime soon.'

'I have never killed a man before,' Mara says to him.

'Well, you are in an army, and this is a war, so it's inevitable if you think about it.'

'He saved my life,' Gajendra says.

One of the mahavats throws a bucket of water over Xatharo to wake him up. The spear is still in his thigh, and he sits up, grabs it two-handed and tries to pull it out.

'Leave it,' Gajendra tells him. 'You'll need the surgeon to turn it.' He uses his sword to lop off the shaft.

He sees two grey mounds lying in the dust, one of them still, the other shrieking in pain. Colossus stands over the stricken tusker, his head down, blood streaming from the spear wound in his shoulder.

Gajendra goes to him, rubs his trunk, tells him what a brave warrior he is and how well he fought.

Alexander gallops over. 'Did you lose only two?'

'Futuh and Asaman Shukoh,' he says, resenting that Alexander doesn't know their names. Didn't they just bleed and die for him?

'Who organized the defence?'

'I did.'

'You did well. There shall be commendation in this.'

The other elephants, those that did not run, gather around their two fallen companions like mourners at a funeral. They explore them with their trunks, try to comfort Futuh as he screams, then they all set up a bellowing that can be heard all the way to Syracuse.

Alexander turns his back and goes down the line, ordering more cavalry to the rear. The Invincible, King of Asia, has had the tables turned on him. But he appears undaunted, and his concern for the fate of their dead tusker is not all that Gajendra would have wished.

'Get him carved up. We have food enough for the army now. Pork last night, tusker tonight. As long as we have meat, we can march all the way to Rome!'

CHAPTER 31

They have brought the injured to a hastily erected tent and the physicians are at work, stitching wounds and taking out barbs with little ceremony. Men are screaming. It is hard to hear yourself think.

Xatharo lies staring at the roof of the tent, as he waits for someone to attend him. Gajendra studies his body. He has a collection of scars that would not disgrace one of Alexander's oldest veterans. It is clear he has suffered like this often enough that he now thinks nothing of it.

No merchant, no nephew, these two. Whoever they are, he is glad Xatharo is on his side, and he owes the catamite, or whatever he is, his life.

'Another wound, Xatharo, where did they ever find an unscarred place to put the spear?'

He scowls and says nothing.

'You are no merchant, are you? Who are you really?'

'I'm a shitkicker with a spear in his leg. I don't have a past anymore.'

'What do those tattoos on your face say?'

'They say "Mind your own business" in Arabic, Greek and any other language you care to name. Now let me be.' He turns away.

Gajendra knows he will get nothing more out of him. He leaves him there and goes to tend Colossus.

Colossus has rejoined the other elephants. Bales of alfalfa have been stacked in front of him and he is consoling himself with food. The arrow is still in his shoulder. He catches Gajendra's scent but like all elephants he does not see very well and has to confirm who it is with his trunk. He rumbles deep in his belly as he runs its pink tip over his mahavat's face and head. It is both a greeting and a plea for help.

Gajendra gets to work. After a while he can feel someone watching him in the darkness. 'You don't have to be here, boy. Go and have your dinner.'

'Do you know what they're all eating?'

'Well, they couldn't leave him there to rot.'

'Will you eat Colossus when he dies?'

'This one's different.'

'How?'

'He's mine.'

Mara is standing too close, puts a hand on Gajendra's shoulder. He steps away.

'You saved my life today,' he says. 'I didn't think you had it in you.'

'Neither did I.'

'We'll toughen you up yet.'

'That's what I need. Toughening up. My father would be pleased.'

It is a curious remark. Mara stands by the beast's head, whispering to him. There are not many who will even go near him, let alone talk to him like this.

'What's he like?' Mara asks.

'Who?'

'Alexander.'

Gajendra considers. 'One of his guards whispered something to me, on the way from Babylon. He said Alexander sleeps with two things under his pillow: a dagger and *The Iliad*. You know this book?'

Mara nods.

'To him, it's not just a story, it's his family tree. He believes himself descended from Hercules. He doesn't rule other men because of the strength of his army. He conquers by right. He believes himself part god.'

'And the dagger?'

'To protect that part of himself that is not a god.'

'Do you think him divine?'

'He does things that are more than human. His idea of leisure at the end of a long day is a night march. His idea of dinner is a light breakfast.'

'Is that why you adore him?'

'I don't adore him as much as I did.' Gajendra works at the arrowhead, trying to free it with as little fuss as possible.

'How did you learn to be a mahavat?' Mara asks him.

'From Ravi. It's how everyone learns. It's called the *ali baas*. It's usually passed down from father to son, but he doesn't have a son. So I suppose he chose me.'

'What about the language you talk in?'

'It is Ravi's language but all he can remember of it now are the words he uses for the tuskers.'

'And that's the only language they know?'

'It's not like Greek or your jabber. They know what to do when we say certain words, but in a battle they can't hear us, so we do the talking with our feet and with sticks. Or if I'm walking beside him I tap him under the eye to make him kneel, just here to make him stop, the back of his heel here to get him to raise his foot so I can climb up. But it's only an elephant's mahavat that can do it, he won't do it for anyone. He does it because he likes me, and he trusts me.'

'So, it's more like love, then?'

'If you like.' He rubs his hide with his hand and pats him. 'Why do you want to know all this?'

'I want to learn how to be a mahavat.'

'Because one elephant follows you about?'

'Who got him on the ship?'

He pushes Mara playfully aside, not hard, just to let him know he is still the boss. But Mara is only slight, and the push is hard enough that he totters and falls over.

Gajendra yells as Colossus wraps his trunk around him and shoves him out of the way. He has taken sides. Gajendra is astonished. He has never seen an elephant do anything like this before.

'Well, well. He must really like you.' He grabs Mara's hand and pulls him to his feet. 'All right, boy. We'll see what we can do with you. Maybe you do have talent.'

'For what?'

'For this work. At least the big fellow thinks so. Maybe I'll teach you a few things.' Gajendra turns back to his work. The iron arrowhead is almost free. Colossus bellows again but does not move.

'Is Xatharo going to be all right?'

'I don't know. I hope so.'

'It will take more than one javelin to kill him. Some men you can't kill with an axe in both hands. He fought well. A professional soldier could not have done better. For a humble merchant, he knows how to use weapons.'

'I didn't say he was a merchant his *whole* life.'

'I would wager the next time he sees a ledger of accounts it will be the first time.' He works out the arrowhead and a spray of blood splatters over him. Colossus shrieks and takes a step backwards but calms when Mara touches him with her outstretched hand. It is remarkable how she can do this.

'Will my big boy be all right?'

'If you mean the elephant, yes. He'll be sore, but you can't kill an elephant with one dart.'

'You care about him more than you pretend.'

'I need him. He's the biggest and the best. Aren't you, you bristly bastard?' He slathers the wound in honey to keep it clean and looks at Mara. 'You'll have to work twice as hard now; I lost my best shit shovelers today. You're not much good at it, but you're all I've got.'

That night she takes Colossus down to the river with the other tuskers. A storm breaks over the mountains and cloud tumbles down the valley like smoke. Lightning sheets across the horizon. The elephants don't mind the storm; they love the rain.

Colossus is none the worse for his wound. As Gajendra had told her, he's tough.

The other mahavats retreat to the camp. Mara stays behind.

Colossus is an immense presence in the darkness. He is restless though, perhaps because of his wound. He rumbles, he trumpets, he snakes out his trunk and tastes her scent. It is as if he is trying to tell her something.

His affection can be measured in pints of elephant slime. Once she would go nowhere without precious ointments and oils, smelling like summer. Now she reeks of elephant day and night.

If her father could see her now.

'That's right,' she says, 'cover me in slobber. And Xatharo still calls me princess!'

Colossus raises his left foot and stamps it down, the first sign that the stiffness in his shoulder is bothering him. He is still poking her with his trunk. Don't you have a watermelon for me? That's what he's saying.

'What do you make of your Indian? He's a good-looking fellow, isn't he?' She runs a hand along his trunk. It is like stroking a rough stone wall. 'He reminds me of my husband. Did you know I had a husband? He was my mahavat! Everyone needs someone like that, someone to whisper in their ear, someone who knows all about them, someone to take care of them. He's gone now, drowned, so I only have Xatharo to look out for me. But he's in the hospital tent. Perhaps you could do the job for me until he's well again.'

She leads Colossus back to the camp. The elephants have been shepherded into a cypress grove. It is raining harder now and the thunder cracks over the mountains. She throws down her blanket under Colossus.

'If you decide to lie down in the night, remember I am here. Goodnight.'

She falls asleep under her dark and bristled sky, listening to the rumbling of his belly and the swishing of his tail. It is strange, but she feels safer and warmer under a bull elephant with a bad temper than she did in the house of the goddess.

CHAPTER 32

Gajendra cannot sleep. There is something almost divine about thinking you are about to die and then finding yourself alive. He imagines this is why Alexander is as he is. Cheating death is indeed a little like being a god. At night it is as if you can see colours. Even the air tastes sweeter.

Ravi is in the straw, asleep, and he nudges him awake.

'What is it, what's wrong?'

'Niarchos has not come back,' Gajendra says.

'What do I care about that?'

'What if he doesn't return at all?'

'You're thinking Alexander will make you the new Elephantarch, aren't you?'

'I have been, until now, in everything but name.'

'You have to be a Mack to be an officer. You're just an exotic, a foreigner, to them. Don't fool yourself.'

'He has Persians around him. Why not an Indian?'

Ravi sighs in the dark. 'I am older than you. I have seen many men in my time wrestle with their lives, trying to force the gods to submit to them, to arrange their fate so they have things the way they want them. What good does it do? Look at your Alexander. He wants a statue and his name in the histories. Can a statue smile? Can a man be happy after he is dead? Sometimes, the things that make a life worth living can be right under your nose and you don't even see them.'

'I know what I want.'

'Yes, but you're too young to know what you *need*.'

The clouds race across the moon. Rain leaks off the canvas and forms puddles where they sleep. The cured leather tent stinks when it is wet. Men are grumbling and snoring, shifting around in the dark trying to find a dry spot. Gajendra can hear the low rumbling from the tuskers. This is the weather they like. They will be into the puddles like ducks.

He sees one of the Agrianians take off his cloak and wrap it around his javelins to keep the damp from seeping into the doe-skin sleeve and swelling the wood grain. Then the man curls up with his son and his wolfhound under a tree. A strange people, they'll freeze before they let anything happen to their darts.

The storm has flooded the high passes and left everything dripping. It was like this, he remembers, the night the Rajah fought the Macks on the Jhellum River. The river was swollen and fast flowing, and when the soldiers came back they were unrecognizable, covered in mud and blood. He was just a water boy then.

Carthage was his first real battle. He remembers nothing about it now. It was only later that he realised it had lasted from noon till the late afternoon; at the time it had seemed like a brief skirmish.

He had thrown his javelins wildly and not seen where they landed. It was Colossus who had done the work. Gajendra had kicked, nudged and shouted, but the big tusker had done what was needed and carried the day.

Today had been different. It truly was a skirmish, and no matter what Ravi says to him he cannot stop thinking about the man he killed with his knife. Why should it trouble his sleep? It was kill or be killed.

But every time he closes his eyes, he sees the man's eyes.

'How many men have you killed, Ravi?'

'I don't know. You hurl javelins from an elephant's back, sometimes you see men fall. Who is to say if it was your spear that wounded them or how badly they are hurt?'

'I was so close to that Numidian today. I saw the light go out of his eyes.'

'Be grateful the light didn't go out of yours. If it weren't for the catamite you'd be the one lying on the corpse fire tonight. He saved your skin today. I thought he would be hiding behind a bush somewhere. I eat my words. He has fire in his belly, that one, for all his pansy ways.'

'He touched me tonight.'

'What?'

'He's done it before. He... well, it's like he leans his head on my shoulder, or he brushes his hand along my arm.'

Ravi chuckles. 'Did you bend him over?'

'You know I'm not one for that.'

'You can't afford to be fussy, boy. Well, hero or not, he's going to be in trouble now. That tattooed pimp won't be able to help him much from the hospital tent. He's a ripe plum ready for the plucking.'

'Then we should put him in the straw by us. I owe him at least that much.'

Gajendra goes looking for Mara, but he is not easy to find. He can't see a thing. Torches are useless when the rain is this heavy. He kicks the water boys awake but none of them have seen him.

Finally, he gives up and is ready to go back to the straw but while he is up and about and wet through anyway, he decides to check on the tuskers, keep the guards on their mettle. Sure enough one of them is dozing against a tree and he gets a slap around the head for his indolence.

Then Gajendra sees what looks like a pile of rags under Colossus and for a moment he thinks he has massacred another unfortunate in the night, but then the rags sit up and form themselves into the shape of a fool.

'What are you doing there, boy? You cannot lie there. He will squash you flat.'

'Colossus won't hurt me. Will you, old fellow?'

Mara stands up. The boy's head doesn't even touch the tusker's belly. He rubs his eyes, very dainty. A real man would scratch his balls.

'Come away from him. An elephant only has one mahavat. Do you understand? You will confuse him. I don't want to find you out here again.'

'I'm not trying to take your tusker away. It's just I feel safe here.'

'You can sleep with me and Ravi. No one will touch you there.' He leads him back through the mud to their tent. A torch is burning inside and Gajendra sees him in the light and laughs.

'What is it?'

'Look at you. Has Colossus been dribbling over you all night? You are the most disgusting thing I've ever seen.'

He doesn't see Mara's face and it is a good thing. He is still laughing when he curls up in the straw.

CHAPTER 33

There is a river running through the tent and the straw has floated away on it. In the middle of the night they find a dryer spot under one of the carts, but they are barely settled when they are kicked awake again by one of Alexander's sergeants. He wears a savage expression as if he has come to make an arrest.

'What is this about?' Gajendra grumbles, trying to keep the fear out of his voice.

'Alexander wants you – now.'

These Macks; it is clear he would rather slap him with his sword than be his escort.

'Where's the other one? The pretty boy?'

'He's over there.'

'Bring him too.'

'What's happening?' Mara mumbles.

'We're going to see Alexander.'

'We?'

'Hurry up, he doesn't like to be kept waiting.'

The rain has eased off a little. 'Make yourself useful,' Gajendra says. 'Carry the torch.'

They splash through the mud. Gajendra wonders what this is about. He hopes it's not Xatharo and the four soldiers he cut up. Or has Niarchos been killed on his foray against the raiders? His heart lurches between dread and hope.

When they get to Alexander's pavilion, they find him in his cups. He cannot sleep and is prowling the carpets, agitated and nasty. 'Who is this?' are his first words, pointing to Mara.

'He's the slave who saved the captain of the elephants,' the sergeant says. 'You asked to see him.'

Alexander brightens in a moment, remembering his whim. 'Ah. You're the fine fellow who saved my Indian?'

He stands close. He holds out his hand and a slave brings him another cup of wine. His lips are wet. His concentration is intense, as if he is trying to see through billowing smoke.

'You're not long off your mother's teat, I should venture. One of his water boys, are you? A fetcher and carrier? Or a dung pusher. In more ways than one by the look of you.' He takes Mara by the shoulders and pushes him to his knees. 'Kiss the royal foot.'

To Gajendra's surprise, Mara does it.

'What's a dung lark doing killing cavalry?' He turns to Gajendra. 'Where did you get him from, elephant boy?'

'Carthage, my lord.'

'Saved him from being filleted, did you?' He hauls Mara back to his feet. 'I heard you showed great valour. I am curious, why did you do it? What did it matter to you whether my elephant boy lives or dies?'

'I was trying to protect the elephant.'

Alexander murmurs, something between surprise and admiration. Mara has his complete attention now; this is an alternative he has not considered.

'The elephant?'

'I have grown fond of him.'

Alexander drinks and the wine runs down his chin. He snaps his fingers and the royal cupbearer dashes from the shadows with a cloth to dab at his mouth. 'Extraordinary. How do you grow fond of such an ugly creature?'

'They are much like horses. They have valour and loyalty.'

He looks at Gajendra. 'Is he mocking me?'

'It is true.'

He grunts and sways. Gajendra wonders at his little dung lark, and why he still stands so close to Alexander like this. Surely he doesn't intend to kiss him. He wouldn't put it past either of them to fall into carnal embrace right there in front of him.

They hold the moment for long enough that Gajendra feels a pang. He does not wish to share his slave with anyone, even his commander, and this jealousy takes him quite by surprise.

Then his general smiles, smacks his lips to taste the residue of the wine and turns away.

'And you, elephant boy.' He turns his back on Mara so that he is now facing his captain of the elephants. 'I've been watching you. You fancy yourself in a fight, don't you?'

'I am at heart a warrior.'

'Are you, indeed? How did you feel after Carthage when Niarchos got all the credit for your efforts?'

'Did he get all the credit? I didn't know.'

'Of course, you knew. I saw your face. You were steaming about it.' Another gulp of wine. 'You did well today. As I hear it, you organized the defence of the elephants on your own and you had them beaten by the time Niarchos came down the line. I think it's why he chased after the Numidians; he was late for the glory and was rushing to catch up with it. But he's a popular fellow, you know. Among the troops.'

'He seems brave enough.'

'Too slippery for my liking.'

Over Alexander's shoulder, Gajendra can see Mara step closer. He wonders why and is alarmed.

'You still want his wife, don't you?'

'Not just his wife. I want his horse and his commission too.'

Alexander laughs, delighted. 'You're too arrogant by half. You remind me of myself at your age. Except I have royal blood and you have... well, you're just an Indian, aren't you?'

'Yes, my lord.'

'But you did well. I could have lost a lot more of my tuskers if you had not reacted so quickly.'

Gajendra tries to make out the look on Mara's face. If Alexander were to step back right now he would step on his dung lark's toes.

'I have underestimated you.'

'I don't mind. It's happened before.'

Alexander's breath is on his face, sour with wine. 'You are hoping Niarchos does not come back, aren't you?'

It shocks him that Alexander can so plainly divine his thoughts.

'What happened to you, boy?'

'Happened to me?'

'Something impels you. What is it?'

'Ambition. Like every man.'

'No, it's more than that. If you lie, I'll know.'

Gajendra feels cornered. He doesn't know what to say to wriggle out of this.

'Where are your family?'

'They died.'

'Of what?'

'It was a fever. Half my village died from it.'

'And where were you?'

'I was lucky.'

'No, you're lying. There's something else.' Gajendra drops his eyes and Alexander grabs him by the chin and forces him to look up. 'Isn't there?'

Finally, his general turns away. Mara steps back. For Alexander this is enough now. He has grown bored with them both. He needs someone else to entertain him.

His cupbearer splashes more wine in the silver goblet. He gulps. It spills down his white tunic like blood. 'In two days, we will stand before Syracuse. Do well and I will give you the world. Everything you ever dreamed of. It's all up to you now, elephant boy.'

The next morning Mara finds Xatharo in a tent with the rest of the wounded from the previous day's skirmish. He is sitting up, even trying to stand. A bloodied bandage is wrapped around his leg from his knee to his groin, and he is shooing the flies off it.

He sees her and looks irritated. 'May I have my knife back?'

She reaches under the tunic where she has hidden it and slides it back to him.

'How did you know it was me?'

'I may not have had my own private tutor, as some, but I am not stupid. If you ever have to take to the streets, princess, you will make a fine pocket thief. When did you do it?'

'When you were lying on the battlefield.'

'Where's the elephant boy?' His eyes watch for a reaction. He cares less about how she answers than if she can hold his gaze.

'He has taken the elephants to the river with the others.'

'Why aren't you with them?'

'I slipped away to see how you were.'

'I'm touched.' He taps the place where his knife is now hidden. 'Have you slaughtered Zeus's favourite son yet?'

'A jest, Xatharo. I didn't know that you knew of these things.'

'Not a joke. I hear you went to his tent.' He sees her squirm and smiles. 'You couldn't do it, could you?'

'I couldn't get close enough.'

He laughs at this. 'You were in his pavilion. How close do you need to be? Do you want to share his bath before you murder him?'

'I can do it. You forget, I killed a man yesterday.'

'Yes, and I invaded Italy.'

'He had Gajendra on his knees. Did you not see me?'

'All I saw was you running towards the elephant. I ran to save you.'

She cannot believe he had not seen it. 'Ask anyone.'

'You don't have the balls to kill a man, princess. Least of all a man like Alexander.'

'Keep your voice down!' She looks over her shoulder. These men look like they are unconscious, but it doesn't mean they cannot hear.

'You know, I've been thinking what you said. You're right. Someone must stop him, and he should pay for what he has done to our city and to your father. But it's not a job for a woman, especially a pale little wonder like you.'

'You can't even walk. How can you do such a thing?'

'I can walk. This is just a muscle wound. It's a bit stiff but the bone's not broken. You think I haven't had worse? I'll be up and about soon enough.'

'You know what they'll do to you if you succeed?'

'It was your idea.' He makes a stabbing motion, underhand, twists the knife, then holds it to his own throat and draws it across the veins. 'There, that's how it's done. One stroke for him, one stroke for me, and we both go to Hades together, and we'll carry on with it there if he wants. But first I get you out of here, so there's no music for you to face. If you think you can kill a man, then you have it in you to walk to Panormus.'

'We should do it together.'

'It's my way or not at all. I have been knocked out cold and run through twice so far on your account, but this I do for him.' He is sweating with pain. 'You were his whole heart; do you know that?'

'I do now.'

'Your father knew the trouble he would put me through when he gave me this commission. A bloody end was inevitable from the first.'

'I am sorry, Xatharo. I wish I could repay you.'

'You can, by honouring your father in your prayers. He was a better man than you gave him credit for.' He lies back down, grunting at the pain. 'I was always jealous of you.'

She stares at him, shocked. 'What do you mean?'

'Hanno is your father. You didn't have to do anything for it. You didn't have to earn it. You took it for granted. I would have given anything to be his son, his real son.'

The physician comes in, pushes Xatharo back onto his blanket and tells him to keep still, does he not know he has a fever and not enough blood left in him to fill a night jar?

Mara slips away. The sun should be climbing the sky by now but there are still thunderclouds around the mountains and more rain sweeping down the valleys. There is a rumour about the camp that this is Zeus come to help them. She imagines it was Alexander who started this gossip. It would be like him.

The Macks look dark. Fighting Celts and Africans is one thing; soon they must make war on their own.

CHAPTER 34

The forward scouts have found Antipater's army.

He has moved out of Syracuse to meet them, and his army is bolstered by more mercenaries from inside the city. They are outnumbered by three men to every one of theirs. But they are only Greeks, the veterans say. Anyway, whatever battle we fight, we are always outnumbered.

Everyone is on edge. There are extra drills, a double line of sentries posted around the camp. There are grumblings around the campfires; there could be fellow Macedonians in Antipater's army. What then?

Niarchos is safely returned. Gajendra was right; the ambush was not laid by Antipater but by raiding parties sent out by Carthaginian colonies to the north. They have sent another army through the mountains, so Alexander must engage Antipater quickly if he is to avoid being caught in the pincers of two enemies.

Niarchos summons Gajendra to his pavilion.

Gajendra looks around. Niarchos's living arrangements in the field are sparse: there is a bench with a water bowl and a narrow camp bed. He has a boy to look after his horse and a sergeant to run messages. That's all. You don't feel like you've walked into a high-class brothel, as you do when you are ushered into Alexander's pavilion. If Niarchos was back in his crease, he would be ready to drink and wrestle greased pigs with the rest of the boys.

'How are our tuskers?' he asks Gajendra. It is 'our tuskers' now. A week ago, he wanted to leave them in Africanus.

'We lost two. Three others took wounds, including Colossus, but nothing serious. They are still ready to fight. We've taken them down to the river to let them forage for a bit.'

'There's food down there?'

'Elephants will eat anything as long as there's enough of it.'

When Gajendra looks at Niarchos, his thoughts turn immediately to Zahara. He can't help himself. He imagines the two of them together on the camp bed, Niarchos all thumbs. It hurts to think about it.

There is a little wooden figure that Ravi keeps with him, an elephant carved from teak. It has a hundred points marked on its body, and each point means something; you touch here to make your tusker walk, here to make him angry, here to kill him, here to make him walk back…

It seems to him that they could make a similar likeness for a man, and he is sure he knows the pressure point for jealous rage. It is in the pit of the stomach. He feels it pulsing now, cold and sharp, like he has been hollowed out.

Niarchos splashes water on his face and gets his own cloth to dry himself. How he must hate Alexander's affectations.

'Are they ready to fight? Your fate is tied to theirs. I won't be humiliated in the field by a dumb animal.'

'They just need more training. With all this marching we've been doing, loading them onto ships and off again, there hasn't been enough time.'

'Can't you at least get these stupid beasts to stay in formation?'

'Elephants aren't stupid. They're smarter than most people.'

'Including me?' Niarchos says with a leery grin.

'I don't know. I've never tried to train a Macedonian.' It was out of his mouth before he could stop himself. He wonders what Niarchos will do. He is still for a moment and then chooses to laugh and clap him on the shoulder. 'I can see why he likes you.'

'Who?'

'Alexander. Don't tell me you didn't know?'

Gajendra shakes his head and frowns to keep himself from smiling with satisfaction.

'He's grooming you for my position. You wouldn't mind that a bit, would you? I wager you wish that I hadn't come back this morning. You would have hardly mourned my passing, am I right?'

'I'm just an Indian. How can I rise higher than what I am?'

Niarchos steps closer. The smile is gone and so is the good-natured banter. 'I don't know whether he wants you for his bum boy or his general. He likes you people, you know. He doesn't trust his own kind anymore.'

'He's my king as well. I only do as he commands.'

'Be careful of him. He'll take your soul, elephant boy.'

Their eyes lock. Gajendra knows it is insolent, but the challenge is there now, and something in him will not look away. There is a sour smell to the other man's breath. Niarchos has drunk wine with his lunch. It makes him careless with his words.

Niarchos leans in and whispers, 'He loves you now. But he tires quickly of new things. When you are most enamoured of him, he will toss you aside.'

'He pays me for my skill with the tuskers. I just do what I'm told.'

'I don't believe that for a moment.' He turns away, waves a hand in dismissal. Gajendra leaves, seething. He talks to me like I am nothing, he thinks. If the elephants win the day, it is his genius; if they lose formation, he blames me.

Does Alexander truly love me? Then let him love me more. He has promised me the world and that's the very least that I want now.

They are with the elephants down at the river; last night's storms are just a memory. It is a hot afternoon. The scorching wind the locals call the *siroko* has been blowing from the south all day. Mara stands in the shallows, under the trees that bow over the river, watching as Gajendra and the other boys strip off their clothes and plunge in with the tuskers.

Mara starts scrubbing Colossus down with the pumice.

Gajendra wades over. 'I've never seen you with your shirt off.'

'I get burned by the sun very easily.'

He shrugs; all the other boys had stripped naked, brown and gleaming. A thought occurs. He tries to brush it aside; it makes him uncomfortable.

But he can't.

Dusk is approaching as they walk the elephants back to the camp. The sun hovers above the horizon; the air is still, breathless.

He grabs Mara and pulls him aside. 'What did you think of our king?'

'He's shorter than I thought he would be.'

'You were honoured.'

'Was I?'

'To be allowed into the royal tent is no small things.' He gets dressed, feels Mara staring. 'He seemed very taken with you,'

Gajendra says. 'He likes boys, you know. You should have flirted more. Better a slave to a king than a slave to an elephant.'

He slaps at a mosquito.

Mara doesn't answer.

'You're a strange one, aren't you?'

Mara puts on his sandals, one hand against Gajendra's chest to do it. Like he's a tree. Or a lover. He could knock his hand away, but he doesn't.

Gajendra is both alarmed and intrigued. There is a sudden light in those green eyes.

Mara leans forward and kisses Gajendra on the mouth.

Gajendra pushes him away. 'So that's what it is. You have a crush on me. Well, forget it.'

Something shifts in Mara's eyes.

Gajendra sighs, shakes his head. 'How old are you?'

'I have fifteen summers.'

'The truth.'

A long breath. 'Twenty.'

Gajendra runs a hand down his cheek. It is so smooth, too smooth for twenty summers. Without warning he puts his hand between Mara's legs.

Mara gasps and tries to twist away but he stops her.

'Who are you?' Gajendra says.

She doesn't answer.

'Why are you dressed like a boy? And who or what is Xatharo? Let me have the truth if you want me to help you.'

She takes a deep breath. 'Xatharo is my manservant. He was charged with looking after me when you took our city. I suspect he must rue the day he ever set eyes on me. Dressing me like this was his idea.'

'Manservant?'

She bites her lip.

'You have noble blood?'

She nods. 'What will you do if I tell you?'

'I owe you my life. I will repay you by saving yours. But you'll have to trust me.'

'My father's name is Hanno.'

Gajendra lets her arm drop. 'The general who stood against us at Carthage?'

She searches his face. 'Please do not betray us.'

He stares at her in shock.

'Xatharo warned me not to say anything.'

'Well he was wrong. I promised I would repay you and I will.'

Gajendra walks down to the river and stares at the sunset dappled in the water. He needs time to think. Then he walks back.

'Why were you not with your father under his protection?'

'I had renounced my former life to become a priestess at the temple of Tanith. When your armies came I refused to leave. My father sent Xatharo to protect me as best he could when the city fell. There, you have it. What will you do with me now?'

He does not answer her straight away. He slaps at another mosquito. 'I promised I would help you and I will.'

'How?'

'I don't know, I will have to think about this.' He turns away. 'For now, I'm going back to camp. I'm not staying down here to get eaten by the mosquitoes. But no wonder you were useless at shovelling shit.'

When Mara returns to the camp, Xatharo is back on his feet again. He has a stick to lean on for walking. 'Where have you been?' he asks her.

'I was by the river talking to the young captain.'

'What about?'

'I told him I need a new bodyguard, the one I have is an old woman who takes to his bed for the slightest scratch.'

'If he touched you, I'll fillet him from groin to chin.'

'By the time you're ready to fillet anyone again I shall be beyond child-bearing years. How is your leg?'

'What do you care?'

She puts a hand on his arm. It startles him. 'I am sorry.'

It is too dark to see his astonishment, but she hears it in his voice. 'For what?'

'For all the trouble you have been through in my name. If I am ever restored to my place in life, I shall ensure that you are given a vineyard and a pension where you can live out your days in peace.'

'Who said I want peace? Why would you torture me with a vineyard? This is the life I like.' He frowns, thinking about what she has just said. 'Anyway, I thought you did not want to be restored to your former nobilities. You had dedicated yourself to Tanith.'

'Not for ever.'

'What has changed your mind?'

'Time, and an elephant.'

He shakes his head. This makes no sense to him at all, but he is not one for debating such things.

'Shall I get you your dinner?' Mara says.

'You are going to fetch me my supper?'

'I have been ungrateful to you in the past. I want to make up for it.'

His eyes glitter. He still has a fever from his wound. He thinks he is hallucinating. 'All right. See if you can get me an extra ration of bread. I haven't eaten for days.'

She kisses him on the forehead. He pushes her away, thoroughly alarmed. 'I know what you've been doing,' he growls. 'When I'm fit again, I'm going to kill him.'

That night she dreams of her father. He is frowning at her in the way that he did when she was a child. He had never needed to reproach her, he only had to look a certain way when he walked into the room to send her scurrying. It is as if he wants to say something to her, but in the way of all dreams, she cannot hear him.

CHAPTER 35

As Gajendra lies in the straw, he thinks about Mara and Xatharo and what to do about them. He knows he won't betray their secret; it is not in his nature to do that. It is not in his best interests to stay silent either. So what other choices does he have?

He thinks about Mara kissing him. He wishes now that he had kissed her back, to see what it was like.

This moves his thoughts inevitably to that hot morning in the temple of Astarte. In his mind he sees Zahara about to settle her divine flesh onto the pillows her girls had set out for her on the temple stones. He thinks about the look of casual indifference on her face after she went with him into the orange grove, how she settled back against the tree and waited for him to take his pleasure.

What might it have been like if he had taken what the goddess and his coins had promised?

He realises that what he had really wanted was for Zahara to take his face in her hands and kiss him the way Mara had done. Perhaps Mara was right. He didn't want Zahara. He wanted all those things a poor Indian boy was never supposed to have.

His thoughts are in chaos. He sits up. Sleep is going to be impossible tonight. Ravi asks him what is wrong. The way he is groaning and tossing, he thinks he has been bitten by a snake.

Gajendra tells him to go back to sleep.

'I am going to check on the guards,' he says.

Ravi grunts and turns over. Soon he is snoring away like the other mahavats around them.

Gajendra prowls the camp like a ghost. He feels like the world's biggest fool. There are two roads stretching ahead of him, but he doesn't know which way will lead him home. If he helps Alexander defeat Antipater, he can name his price. But if his general discovers he is sheltering his enemy's daughter and has not told him, he could suffer the same excruciating fate as Oxathres.

What should he do?

CHAPTER 36

In the days that follow, Alexander is uncharacteristically cautious. He halts the army ten leagues west of Syracuse and waits. He sends Niarchos to Antipater as his envoy. Gajendra and Ravi watch them ride out.

'What is happening?'

'How should I know?'

'I thought you were part of Alexander's inner circle these days.'

Ravi is mocking him, but the joke is on him. He's right, Gajendra does know what this is about.

'He has a letter for Sostratus from Alexander. Our general is offering terms.'

Ravi looks shocked, not just by the news, but the fact that Gajendra knows about it.

'He will ask for Antipater's head in a basket in return for not destroying the city. He must open the gates of Syracuse to him. And pay annual tribute.'

'That is not terms. That is grovelling.'

'Grovelling is what Alexander calls an accord.'

'What do you think Sostratus will say?'

'I think he will send Niarchos' head back in the basket. That's what I think.'

'Or what you hope?'

'I should never wish another man ill.'

Gajendra wishes this were true. But Ravi is right; should Niarchos not return, he fancies himself the next Elephantarch. Someone must lead the elephants into the next battle, and he is the logical choice. He is a heartbeat away from every dream he ever had, but for the good of his soul he will try not to pray for a deadly outcome to Niarchos' mission.

The pavilion has been fly-rigged open on all sides, despite the baking wind, so the men can see their generals at work.

Soldiers cluster around outside, leaning on their spears, a few murmuring among themselves, but mostly silent, intent. They are close enough that Gajendra can smell their sweat. The Macks hate their general until it is time for the battle. Then they remember they will be lost without him.

There is no sign of Niarchos. Scouts ride in, bringing prisoners they have captured from one of Antipater's outposts, bound and blindfolded. They all sing the same song; according to them Antipater's army is many times the size of theirs. They say the harbour at Syracuse is a forest of masts, and that it took them three days just to land their horses.

It seems that Alexander has finally overreached himself. Or did these men deliberately allow themselves to be captured, in order to sow doubt and fear?

If it is all true, then Alexander looks relaxed about it. He wanders the tent, sipping wine and laughing, as if planning a wedding feast for his latest wife.

He tells his generals what his forward scouts have told him this morning; the truth is only a little less alarming than the rumours. Antipater has with him fifty thousand infantry and ten thousand horses. He has left Macedon unprotected, relying on his allies in the east to do his fighting for him. If he can defeat Alexander the crown is his, whatever happens elsewhere.

And he wants revenge for his sons.

Alexander becomes expansive. 'They outnumber us four to one, gentlemen. They are rested and they are well supplied. They even have a phalanx of Macedonians who are willing to betray their crease. So, shall we give up and go home? Ah, but I forget. Thanks to Antipater, we don't have a home to go to anymore.'

The generals laugh. It is good to see Alexander on top form again.

'We have surprised them with the speed of our arrival. He thought we should still be in Carthage, taking the sea air. If the attack on our tuskers had succeeded, we might be at a disadvantage. Thanks to this brave young fellow here, they did not succeed.'

He claps Gajendra on the shoulder and puts his arm around him, as if they had together held a pass against a thousand men. Gajendra knows it is theatre but feels flattered anyway.

With a flourish Alexander points out the rectangles and arrows he has made on his charts. 'The other news I have is this: Carthage has raised another army from their city colonies in the north and they are three day's march from here.'

There is a murmur of surprise and consternation from the generals gathered about him.

'Antipater hoped to catch us between the horns of two armies, but the speed of our advance means we have deprived him of that pleasure. He will have to face us on his own.

'In our favour, he has no experience of fighting elephants. All he knows is what he has heard from the soldiers who fought with us in India. He will think we will do as we did at Carthage and set them against the infantry.

'But we will not oblige him that way. Instead, we will target his cavalry. You all saw what happened when the Guggas attacked us on the road here. Their horses broke and bolted, would not get close. In a battle they will turn and run again.'

The seasoned veterans stand with their arms folded, looking weary with it all. Gajendra can see them thinking; win this battle, perhaps we can all go home.

They hear shouting outside. A sentry rushes in.

'Niarchos has returned, my lord.'

He has indeed returned; at least, what is left of him. They have tied his hands to the saddle to keep him upright, but in truth it is pride alone that keeps him on his horse. His mount knows its way back to the camp, and that is fortunate, because he is in no condition to ride it.

Several of the guards rush out to grab its reins while others pull him out of the saddle.

Gajendra looks once then turns away. Dying in battle is one thing, this is something he does not even want to think about.

As they help him down, he thinks Alexander might bend to comfort his former favourite, but he just sighs and turns away. 'There is our answer to our offer of treaty, gentlemen,' he says, and saunters back into his pavilion.

'You know what they are saying,' Ravi says. 'That he sent him out knowing what they would do to him; he was getting too popular with the men, so he decided to get rid of him.'

'He could not have foreseen that kind of barbarity.'

'What was in the letter he gave him? No one knows, do they? Only Alexander.'

Gajendra doesn't want to believe it. 'It is what he always does. He attempts a treaty first.'

'Well, it's good news for you. Everyone says it now. His own people are tired of fighting, and he wants someone young with energy and ambition to lead his elephants into the fray. Now Niarchos is out of the way it has to be you. If we are victorious against Antipater…'

'Of course we will be.'

'… then you will be his new favourite. At least, until he tires of you.'

'That's what Niarchos said.'

'He'll use you, turn you, goad you, reward you, and when he has everything he needs out of you, the moment he thinks you are more popular with the soldiers than he is, he'll do to you what he did to Niarchos.'

'He didn't do it, Sostratus did.'

'You know what I fear more? That it won't happen. That you'll become more and more like him until in the end I'll be sorry I ever found that little orphan boy wandering around the Rajah's camp and gave him the chance to make something of himself.'

Gajendra pushes Ravi in the chest. It is not intended as a blow, but Ravi trips and goes down. For a moment they are both too surprised to say anything.

Ravi shakes his head. 'You see,' he says. 'It has already started.'

CHAPTER 37

He should be accustomed to it by now; kicked awake in the middle of the night by one of Alexander's guards, led stumbling half asleep through the camp to his pavilion. What is it this time? The camp is quiet, but Alexander's household is in riot. Alexander himself sits on a stool, surrounded by his toadies and his officers, being comforted by a wife.

The oil lamps hanging from the crossed metal spears in the entrance throw long shadows. Smoke from the pine knots burning in the brazier stings Gajendra's eyes.

He barely recognizes his general. He sits there half naked with a hunted, haunted look in his eyes. He no longer appears indestructible. He scratches at the purple scar on his leg where an arrowhead smashed the bone at Marakanda. They say splinters of bone still work their way out of it from time to time. And in the lamplight, Gajendra can see the hollow where he was hit in the face by a stone hurled from the ramparts of some fort or other. He was blind for a while and could not talk.

Alexander turns his head towards him. 'Boy, I dreamed about your elephants.'

Is this why he has him out of bed at this hour, another dream?

'What did you see in the dream, my lord?'

'Your elephant, the big one…'

'Colossus.'

'He spoke to me.'

Gajendra keeps his face immobile. 'My elephant spoke to you?'

'He said that I had overreached myself.'

'How is this possible?' one of his Persians says. 'A god cannot overreach.'

They look to Gajendra to agree. But he is not of a mind to do so. He did not leave a good sleep to come over here and kiss Alexander's ass.

'Did Colossus say anything else?' he says.

'That I should fall at the feet of Hercules.'

'But you are Hercules,' says one of his toadies from the shadows. Alexander does not look as if this comforts him overmuch.

He gets to his feet, pushes the wife away. He is tired of having his neck rubbed and does not want to have a conversation with her breasts in his face. It is clearly bothering him, like flies hanging around.

Ptolemy gives Gajendra a look. Tomorrow they must engage with their enemy. It will not do to have Alexander agitated and deprived of sleep. Do something, the look says.

Gajendra finds inspiration. 'This is not a bad dream to have,' he says.

'How can it not be a bad dream?'

'In India, the elephant is a lucky sign. When we dream of elephants it means good fortune.'

'Do your good luck elephants also tell you that you have gone too far?'

'It may simply be a warning not to stretch your lines of supply. It means that we should not rush into the battle but take our time to confront the enemy.'

'But what about Hercules?'

Gajendra takes a step closer, his heart in his mouth. He fears he is also about to overreach himself. 'You are not a god.'

Alexander's glance is not hostile, more curious. 'It would not do for others to think that.'

'The gods wish a sacrifice from you. That's all. To show that you are not a threat to them.'

His eyes are shining. Not a god, Gajendra thinks, though quite possibly mad. But what he has said is enough. Alexander shrugs off his mood like a wet cloak. He smiles. 'You think that is all it is?'

'The elephant is a sign that you will win. Sacrifice to the gods and all will be well.'

'Yes, you're right. You're right!' Alexander claps his hands together and calls for wine. He stretches, his face radiant, then puts an arm around Gajendra's shoulder and leads him out of earshot. An idea has dawned. He kisses the tips of his fingers and touches them to Gajendra's cheek. 'I need a new Elephantarch, someone to lead my tuskers tomorrow. Do you think you can do it?'

'From a horse?'

'What do you know of horses? No, from Colossus.'

Alexander's fingers toy with Gajendra's tunic, like a lover. He can feel the drum of his own pulse. All things are becoming possible.

'Help me be victorious tomorrow,' Alexander murmurs, 'and I will give you anything you want.'

He holds out a hand for someone to place a wine cup in it, takes a long draught and grins, his teeth red.

'I will not let you down,' Gajendra says.

'Of course not.' He turns his back as suddenly as he had embraced him and waves an airy hand in dismissal.

'Everything is clear to me now. Go.'

Gajendra is ushered out again by the guards and stumbles back to the straw. In the morning he will wonder if he has dreamed it all.

But the next day he hears that Alexander has gone up the mountain just before dawn and made sacrifices by torchlight to the local gods, to prove to them that he is no threat.

Not that Alexander believes that, but never let the gods know what you're thinking.

Ravi looks panicked. When Gajendra sees the look on his face, he knows what has happened. Ravi pulls him to his feet and leads him out of earshot of the other mahavats. 'This boy, Mara. I found him in the bushes, squatting. To piss.'

'Did she see you?'

Ravi's jaw drops. 'You knew about this?'

'Yes, I knew.'

'Are you mad? I can't believe you kept this to yourself.'

'The less anyone knows, the better.'

'You should have at least told me. Who is she?'

'She's the daughter of the general who stood against us outside Carthage.'

Ravi shakes his head. 'Alexander will have you crucified if he finds out you have deceived him about this.'

'Will he?'

The question takes Ravi's breath away. 'So now you think you're above everyone else?'

'Let me calculate the risk.'

'Let me calculate it for you. We're both dead men if we don't go to Alexander now, tonight.'

'I can't do that.'

'What if someone else finds out? It's only a matter of time.'

'I'll say I didn't know anything about it. No one else has worked it out.'

'And how long will you keep up this charade?'

'When that ugly brute who trails her around can walk again, I'll help them get away. Not a word, all right?'

'Are you fucking her?'

'Of course not.'

He can see by his face that Ravi doesn't believe him.

'She'll be gone soon and there'll be nothing to worry about.' They hear the reveille. The camp is waking. 'Get the water boys up and about. We have work to do.'

Gajendra tries a fresh approach. As the new Elephantarch, he will lead from the front. Instead of archers, Colossus will have a signal boy with flags in the *howdah* on his back so he can direct the others. Gajendra also has large kettle drums mounted on the sides of the *howdah*, so he can send his orders even if there is thick dust and the other mahavat*s* cannot see the flags.

All morning they drill the elephants. The younger elephants are still not up to it. Time and again when the cavalry charges, the young bulls back up or turn out of formation, panicked, disrupting the others.

By early afternoon Gajendra's nerves are ragged, and his mahavats are cursing their elephants and one another. Ptolemy, in charge of the cavalry, is apoplectic. He rides off to tell Alexander that he must change his battle plans.

Gajendra calls the elephants back into line. They try again.

Late that afternoon, Mara finds him in an olive grove, on his knees, praying in front of a small stone god. He looks up. 'What are you doing here?'

'I came looking for you. I have to know what you plan to do.'

'I haven't made up my mind.'

Mara sees the malachite figurine. 'What's that?' she asks him.

He has surrounded the statuette with flowers and olives he has plucked from the tree. The god is like no god she has ever seen; it has many arms, and a head like an elephant.

'It is Ganesha,' he says.

'You pray to an elephant?'

He picks up his god and hides him away in a pouch in his belt. 'He is the Placer and Remover of Obstacles.'

'He does both?'

'He will clear the way to your desire if you ask him. He will put obstacles there, too, if he thinks you need to be thwarted for your own good.'

Gajendra stands up. He looks so sure of himself, she thinks. My husband looked like that the day he got on the ship that carried him to his death. 'And what are your desires, Gaji?'

It is the first time she has called him that. He doesn't rebuke her. 'I want the colour of my skin to be no impediment to becoming one of Alexander's generals. I want to be the one who helps him defeat Antipater's army.'

'And when you are a general, you will be content?'

'Yes, because I will have everything there is to have. I will be rich and feared and I will have the girl of my dreams.'

'The girl of your dreams. You have told her how you feel about her?'

He nods.

'And what did she say?'

'She didn't say anything. She wanted to give me my money back.'

Mara puts her hand over her mouth to try to stop herself, but it's no good. She laughs aloud, and his face flushes a deep bronze.

'You are in love with a dancing girl? The last time we spoke about this, the object of your affections was a princess. You continually seek outside your realm if I may say so.'

'If you tell anyone about this, I will go straight to Alexander and tell him who you are.'

'I won't tell anyone. Who would believe such a story anyway?'

'Laugh at me all you want. Already I am captain of the elephants. My tuskers will win Alexander even more victories and I will be his most important general. Then I may name whatever token I wish from him.'

'Or tomorrow you could die in a battle or one of your tuskers might step on you.'

'I will take my chances.'

'This Ganesha, I am curious about him. I understand how he can remove obstacles, any god worth their salt can do that. But what obstacles do you think he will put in your way, for your own good?'

She can see by his face that he has not thought of this. 'I don't know what you mean.'

'You have fixed your heart on a mirage. When you discover she sweats and has a temper, you are going to be very disappointed at spending your credit with Alexander on a fantasy. Perhaps your little elephant god already knows this.'

Gajendra looks sulky. We all want our dreams. We don't want to hear that there are good reasons why we shouldn't have them.

'There's something you should know,' Gajendra says to her. 'Ravi saw you. He knows you are a girl.'

This news deflates her. She is suddenly not so sure of herself. 'I suppose it was only a matter of time. At least it was Ravi who saw me, not one of the others.'

'He spied you in the bushes. You will have to be more careful.'

She hears Ravi calling for her, down at the river. The water boys have taken the elephants for their bath. She turns to go.

'Wait. Tell me something. Why does a general's daughter become a priestess?'

'I suppose I had given up on life.'

'Given up? All you had to do was lie in a bath all day and listen to your slaves tell you how beautiful you are.'

'You're right. When I was a young girl, I was very spoiled.'

'And then?'

'My father arranged a good marriage for me. My husband was wealthy, but he was also kind and he loved me. I was so happy. I had everything I ever wanted.'

'But then?'

'He had estates in Carthage and also in Sicily. Once a year, he went there to check on his overseer, make sure he wasn't cheating him. The first time he went, he took me with him. The second year, I stayed behind. I was carrying our first child and I was sick all the time.'

'What happened?'

'His ship foundered in a storm, and he was lost along with the captain and crew.'

'I'm so sorry,' Gajendra murmured.

'The spoiled little girl grew up very fast.'

'What happened to your baby?'

'She was born too soon and without life in her. My father blamed it on grief.'

Carthage and the temple already seem so long ago to her now. She remembers how she had returned once to the Tophet, the place where she had given her child back to Tanith. She had stood on the edge, listening to the wind moan through the well. She even thought of throwing herself in.

She had been a priestess then for three months, but seclusion and devotion had not healed even the smallest part of her grief. There had been a constant pain that sat below her breastbone, as if she had eaten something foul. It ached in her all day, and she could not rid herself of it. She was tired of the constant pain.

She suddenly realises, with dull surprise, that the ache is gone. When did that happen? All she can think of these days how much she hates Alexander and the debt she owes to Xatharo for keeping her alive.

Twice Gajendra starts to say something. But he cannot, for there are no words. So he puts his arms around her to comfort her. Her fingers stroke the smooth skin of his shoulder. Their eyes meet. It is a moment of frank appraisal.

He eases his fingers under her tunic seeking her bare flesh. But she gently pushes him away. 'I can't,' she murmurs.

He was smiling, her husband, that last day on the dock. He blew her kisses. She had one hand on her belly and their growing child, blew a kiss back with her other hand. It was a bright day with a cool zephyr of wind. There was no warning of the storm, no premonition in her heart.

There is a part of her that refuses to betray him, as if he is still out there somewhere at sea, trying to get home.

Gajendra pulls back, confused.

'In my heart, I still have a husband,' she says. 'And you still hope for the woman of your dreams. That woman is not me.'

Colossus trumpets somewhere down by the river. Ravi calls for her again. She forces a smile. 'The general's daughter must go and scrub the elephants,' she says.

CHAPTER 38

When she gets back to the camp, Xatharo is waiting for her. He is limping badly, but he refuses to use the crutch they gave him. Perhaps it hurts his pride. He looks at her accusingly, as her father used to. She cannot meet his eyes. It's as if he already knows what she has done.

He has spilled so much blood for her of late. She wants to tell him to lie down, to rest.

As if he would listen to her.

Why is he so loyal? It is unfathomable. They are not even kin. Her father told her Xatharo is from a Balearic island, though others say he popped out of the earth from Hades. None of it accounts for this steadfastness to her father.

'You look pale,' he says. 'What has happened to you?'

She shakes her head and shrugs.

'From now on you will not leave my sight. You are still under my protection.'

'How many more wounds will you take for me?'

'As many as it takes to keep you safe.'

She takes a deep breath. She has to tell him. 'Gajendra knows.'

'You told him?'

She dissembles. 'No, Ravi caught me, in the bushes.'

His hands close into fists. 'I warned you to be careful!'

'They won't say anything.'

'Why not?' His face screws up into a snarl. 'What have you been doing to curry favour?'

'I've done nothing. Gaji is simply kind.'

'*Gaji?* When did you become so familiar?'

'He will not betray us.'

'Of course he will! He's just waiting for the right moment. We have to get out of here.'

Shields, spears and javelins have been stacked outside the tents. Soldiers kneel in the dirt playing dice by the flicker of oil lamps. The flap to Alexander's tent has been left open; there's a guard but even he is lounging.

There's a Persian carpet, a wooden chest with silver handles. His armour has been hung on a centre pole. It gleams dully in the glow of a lamp that swings from a ridgepole.

Alexander is sitting at a camp table writing orders using a stylus on a wax tablet. It is so hot the wax is stripping off the board with every stroke and the words are difficult to read. As Gajendra enters, he does not look up. He raises a finger to indicate he is to wait.

Look at how he lives, Gajendra thinks. Now that he must face Macedonian troops, he has decided to become a Macedonian again. He wears just a tooled leather breastplate over his tunic. There is a royal blue blanket laid on the ground for his bed. He is the complete military man once more, a single guard on the door and a rolled blanket for a pillow.

Finally, he turns to Gajendra.

'You wished to see me, my lord?' Gajendra says.

Alexander stands up, stretches his back so that Gajendra might admire his squat, blond physique. 'Do you know they say we're lovers?'

This is unexpected. 'Who says it?'

'Gossip. It is brought to me occasionally. Apparently because we spend so much time together. But I have more important things to do than fuck. Don't people know this?'

The frightened little boy of last night is gone. He looks cocky, a god once more. It is only the night that erodes his confidence; by day he is king of everything.

'Are the elephants ready?'

'We're ready.'

'I promise you, when the battle commences, you will be in the thick of things. That's what you want, isn't it? To be in the flaming heart of the battle. Test yourself.'

'Yes.'

'We must have our victory. I have learned from my spies that the Gugga general, Hanno, has fled to Panormus, to the north of here. I suspected as much. We did not find his corpse in the ruins when we took Carthage. A tough old boy. He had no side but his own in the end. Do you know the city's Council tried to treat with me before the walls fell? He was to be part of their bargain. Now they are in exile they have rehired him and paid him to lead another army. This is who is coming down to meet us. We will have to account for Antipater quickly before he gets here.'

'Surely Antipater will stall the battle until they are close.'

'You may understand battle, elephant boy, but you don't know the first thing about politics. Antipater will want to win this without the Guggas. This is about the crown of Macedon and who is fit to wear it.'

He stands in front of Gajendra, straightens him up, adjusts his tunic, as if he is sending him off to make a good impression in the provinces. 'They tell me Carthage was your first battle.'

'I was at Jhellum. But I was only a water boy then. I was behind the lines with the baggage train.'

'And killing? Close up, as you and I are now? Your first was when Hanno's raiders attacked your elephants, am I right?'

Gajendra nods.

'Do you dream about him? The man you killed?'

'Sometimes.'

'It is unnatural at first. But this lust is in every man. Any man will become a killer if you put a sword in his hand. You just have to show him how, give him a little skill and confidence. And the more we do it, the more battles we survive, the more we kill, the easier it becomes and the better soldiers we are.' He pats his arm. 'Such a need in you, isn't there? Such a desperate longing. Where does it come from, I wonder? How does it begin? Is a man born with ambition or does something happen to move him? What do you think?'

'I think it's in our nature.'

'No, you don't. You don't think that at all.'

He is so close. His breath is foul. Gajendra winces but tries not to look away.

'I am thinking of replacing you.'

'Replacing me?'

'With someone more able. Ptolemy tells me we cannot rely on your elephants in the thick of battle, that it will be as it was at Carthage, but this time we shall not be as fortunate. Your big tusker, Colossus, he can't do everything on his own. Ptolemy thinks you should be replaced with someone who wants it more than you.'

Gajendra feels the panic rising. '*No one* wants this more than I do. I have trained for this. No one can lead those elephants like I can.'

Alexander shakes his head. 'You are incidental to me. When I need a thing done, I want it done.'

'What do you want from me?'

'I want to know who you are, elephant boy. How you came to be here. I need to know all my generals, from their souls out. Do you understand?'

Gajendra knows what he's asking. He hesitates, but he knows he cannot afford to think about this too long. Alexander is not renowned for his patience. 'I don't remember much of it.'

'I am thinking that perhaps Ravi will be my new Elephantarch.'

'I'll tell you everything.'

'You see? That's better. Now you have clarity. I'm your only friend, elephant boy. We should have no secrets from each other, you and me. Now tell me, what is this old mahavat Ravi to you?'

'He was kind to me.'

'Why?'

'I don't know. He found me, half-starved, wandering around the Rajah's camp and decided to save me. I think it was because he never had a son of his own.'

'How did you come to be half-dead?'

A fine, hot morning when they came. He was inside, listening to his mother and sisters pound the rice. What was he doing inside? Why wasn't he in the field with his brothers? He remembers now. He was sick.

He heard the dacoits shouting, felt the drumming of their horses' hooves through the ground.

'Ah, now we're getting somewhere. So, bandits attacked your village. What happened to your family? Don't tell me the bandits killed them all? Look at me, elephant boy, not the floor. If you are going to tell me, you might as well tell me to my face.'

Their faces were fading now; sometimes he would lie in bed in the morning, in that soft place between dreams and waking, and try to picture his mother and sisters. But it was like trying to catch smoke. His father was almost gone also. All he remembers now are betel-stained teeth and large bony hands.

'You're remembering now, aren't you?'

'My mother was threshing rice.'

'You were there? You saw everything?'

Gajendra winces. He can hear screams. He glances around, thinking they are real.

'What did you do?'

'I ran.'

'You ran away?'

'I ran to my mother.'

'How old were you?'

'I was eight years old.'

His two older brothers ran in from the fields, waving their arms, trying to warn everyone. But there was no time to get away. By the time they realized what was happening, it was too late.

'What did they do?'

'I couldn't stop them.'

'Of course not. You were a little boy.'

One of the dacoits rode into the field and cut his brothers down, like he was harvesting rice. Two, three sweeps of his scimitar and they were gone. They must have screamed. Did they? He does not remember. His mother did, though.

'You can still hear them dying, can't you? You're hearing them now. Do you hear them at night, too?'

'Sometimes.'

'What are they doing? The bandits.'

'They have my mother and my sisters. They're holding them down. They're laughing.'

'And what is my little elephant boy doing?'

'I'm hitting them.'

'Hitting them? That was very brave.'

It is a lie; the little boy just watches. One of the men is laughing when he grabs him by the hair and pushes him to his knees. He tells him that he will give him the chance to save his mother and sisters.

'Did you try to save them?'

'They made me beg.'

'How did they do that?'

'Their leader said he wouldn't kill them if I would do something for them.'

'What did he make you do?'

He crawls, he cries, he begs, hands outstretched. When they laugh, he thinks they are warming to him, so he does it more. For the first time in his life he has an audience and while the bandits laugh, his mother and his sisters are still alive. Then they form a circle and piss on him, still laughing.

Gajendra is trembling.

'What did they make you do?'

'My mother was screaming.'

'You could see her face?'

'I could see her face.'

'And the men, they had you on the ground?'

'They pissed on me.'

'While they were raping your mother and your sister?'

'After.'

They have all taken a turn. Other dacoits are rounding up the cows, stealing everything they can find. The leader takes his turn to piss on him, too, and then he barks an order and they slit his sisters' throats first, then his mother's. They are going to kill him last. Then their chief says: 'Leave him.'

'Why didn't they kill you, elephant boy?'

'I don't know.'

Alexander strokes Gajendra's cheek. Tenderly, he says, 'That torments you every night, doesn't it? Why didn't they kill you? Because you were a coward or because you were brave? You wanted to die with the rest of them, didn't you?'

He nods.

'You dread it, don't you, elephant boy? You dread being weak again. You dread being helpless. That's why you want this so badly. Then your mother and your sister will stop screaming inside your head, is that what you think?' Alexander sighs, and smiles. He kisses him gently on the lips. 'You are going to be a fine general. For now, you are my new Elephantarch. Win for me, Gajendra. Tomorrow you must make me victorious.'

Gajendra finds Xatharo hunkered down in the straw chewing on a stale crust of bread and staring at the mountains.

He looks up, wary, when he sees Gajendra.

'You are going to get Mara away from here,' Gajendra says.

Xatharo thinks it's a trick. He chews and swallows. 'What?'

'You can do that, can't you? It's your job to protect her?'

He doesn't say anything, stares back at him with malevolent eyes.

'You are going to take her back to her father.'

'Her father's dead.'

'No, he's not. He is just over those mountains bringing another army.' Gajendra recounts what he has learned from Alexander.

'Why are you telling me this?'

'Because I do not want her to come to harm. Perdiccas wants you both out of here anyway, after the trouble with the soldiers.'

'Panormus is a long way to walk.'

'I'll get you horses. A few coins thrown the way of one of the sergeants in the baggage train for old nags they don't need any more.'

'Why would you do this?'

'You ask too many questions. Just thank your good fortune and do as I say.' Gajendra walks away, feeling better about himself. At least, a little better than he felt when he left Alexander's tent.

CHAPTER 39

'Your father is alive,' Xatharo says without preamble.

Mara murmurs something between astonishment and disbelief and sits down hard.

'The Hundred wanted to use him as barter, they say. He escaped to Panormus, and those conniving bastards had the gall to ask him for his help. If it was me, I would have cut out their livers. The short of it, he's three days west of here with another army.'

'How can you know this?'

'From our boss. *Gaji*. He says he got all this from Alexander himself. He's kept it from the army. He doesn't want the men to know they may have to fight two battles in two days.'

She draws her knees up to her chest. One back from the dead, then. She had abandoned all hope of seeing her father again and it had grieved her that so many things had been left unsaid between them.

This news changes everything. Now she has a second chance.

'He has arranged for us to get away. Despite what you say, I have to think you have paid him in some way. It can't be in coin because you don't have any.'

'He will help us escape?'

'He says he can get us horses, a couple of nags from the baggage train. But he thinks they'll get us where we need to go.'

She imagines a reunion with her father. She had resigned herself to never seeing him again. Now she gives herself leave to imagine making amends. If I ever get away from here, she tells herself, I will try to forget all I have lost, and instead take better care of all I still have.

A messenger comes from Niarchos. He wishes to speak to his captain of the elephants. Gajendra shudders. He had hoped to avoid this.

Niarchos's tent is dark. It is toward evening, but there is not a candle burning. Gajendra wrinkles his nose at the smell of old blood. Zahara is there, but as he enters she moves away from the bed, the gauze of her gown brushing his skin as she passes. Her scent is the only pleasant thing on the air. A rustle of skirts and she is gone.

Niarchos lies on a bed behind a curtain. His face is in shadow. A slave stands over him with a fan to keep off the flies. All that is visible is his arm, which beckons.

'Come and sit here,' he says.

Gajendra sits on a stool beside the bed. He watches the laboured rise and fall of Niarchos' chest. He can barely stand to look at him.

A hand snakes out and grips his arm. 'So, Alexander's new beloved. You must be satisfied with the way things have turned out.'

'I never wished this suffering on you.'

'Still, it has worked in your favour. But remember what I said, elephant boy. Be careful.'

'Careful of what?'

'Of your general and benefactor.' Blood bubbles through the bandage when he breathes. They have bound up his head with linen so already he looks like the dead.

'Have they given you laudanum?'

'I can bear the pain. I still need my wits about me, and laudanum will take them away. You like Zahara, don't you?'

'It is not for me to think one way or another about her. She's your wife.'

Niarchos laughs at this. 'Why does a man think he can slaver over another man's property and not be noticed? Cheer up, son, when I'm dead Alexander may give her to you.'

There is so much copal burning in the censer next to the bed it makes his head spin. 'You are not going to die.'

'That's the hell of it, isn't it? Death would have been kinder. I am sure Zahara thinks so. Hold my hand, elephant boy.'

There is nothing for it but to do as he says.

'That's it. I can feel the strength in you. I shall need a little of that tomorrow.'

He pulls him closer. Gajendra tries to resist but his grip is too strong.

'It is cold in the shadows when the sun decides to take its warmth elsewhere.'

'I did not ask for this to happen to you.'

'Yet you are responsible. Has he got you in his bed yet? He will.'

'I am more than a pretty boy, as you will all see soon enough.'

'Shall I blame Sostratus for my wounds, or Alexander? I never learned what was in the letter until after it was delivered.'

'You cannot blame Alexander for another man's perfidy.'

'But Alexander can write a letter in such a way that a man's perfidy will work in his favour.'

'Why would he do this?'

'You'll soon work it out. He has been looking for someone to love again since Hephaestion died. I always thought it would be another Greek. He has gone native in more ways than one. Once it was just foreign soldiers, now he is recruiting the natives for home service as well.'

'It's not true.'

'Not yet. But it will be. You are to be groomed.'

He lets his arm fall.

'I thought you loved him,' Gajendra says.

'I thought he loved me. But Alexander's trouble is that he has everything, and the problem with having everything is, it's never enough. It has made him mad. He has a lion by its tail and as soon as he lets go, it will eat him. It will eat you, too.'

'I don't have to listen to this.' He gets up to leave.

'Do you know what happened when we were in Egypt? I was with him the day he went to consult the oracle of Zeus at the Siwa oasis. Three hundred miles across the desert we rode. We were lost once, and the horses nearly died of thirst.' He pauses, has to get his breath. 'And when we finally found the old woman, do you know what he asked her? He wanted to know if his father's murderers had been punished to the satisfaction of the gods. Can you guess why her answer was so important to him?'

Gajendra can guess, but he doesn't want to say it.

'He is terrified of dying, that man. He has good cause. What do they do in Hades to a god who has murdered his own father?'

Once outside, Gajendra takes a deep breath. The smell of dung and campfires and thirty thousand men seems almost fragrant now.

CHAPTER 40

It is dark under the trees along Elephant Row. Colossus moves his trunk along the ground as he catches Gajendra's scent. Gajendra rubs the top of his trunk, feeds him apples. The other elephants are restless tonight. They have set up an incessant rumbling. It's as if they know.

'Tomorrow is our day,' he whispers to Colossus. 'You have to be brave and strong. If we win tomorrow, Alexander will make us the very core of his army. His Elephantarch will be even more important to him than the captains of his cavalry. He will build his strategies around us.' He feels the rough skin quiver under his touch.

A sound behind him. He spins around, a knife in his hand. Mara lets out a gasp as the needle point draws blood from the soft white flesh of her neck. 'It's me,' she says.

He sheaths the knife and leads her away from the elephants. 'What are you doing here?'

'I wanted to thank you. Xatharo told me what you have done for us. You're a good man, Gaji.' She slides her hand down his arm.

'If you get away from here, keep going. Even Panormus is not far enough. Alexander will not stop at Syracuse. We are going to rule over the whole world one day.'

'We?'

'Everything I want…' He reaches out a hand, closes it slowly into a fist. 'It is close enough that I can feel it.'

Mara looks sad. 'I saw her today. The most beautiful girl in the world. She was coming out of Niarchos's tent. That is the one, isn't it?'

'Her name's Zahara.'

'Oh, Gaji,' she whispers. 'You poor boy.' The leaves rustle in the wind and the moon trails a filigree of black clouds.

'You don't have to feel sorry for me. I'm going to be a lord. Ganesha will help me.'

'I'm sure he will.' She kisses him on the cheek and goes to fetch water for the elephants.

When Mara returns, Xatharo is sharpening his knife on a rock. He is stealthy about it; it will not do to have anyone see him armed.

'What are you doing?' she says.

'Alexander is coming to inspect the elephants tomorrow.'

His face is a study in concentration. He wants the blade to be nice and sharp when he slides it between the ribs of a living god.

'But we're leaving tonight.'

'You are,' Xatharo says. 'I'm staying here. Once you're gone, I'll be free to ply my trade in peace.'

'He will be surrounded by his bodyguards.'

'That didn't save his father and it won't save him. I know what I'm about. It's not the first time I've done this, you know.'

'It's suicide.'

'That's what I said to you when you first suggested it, but somehow you made it sound reasonable. Now I am persuaded.'

'They'll crucify you for this, Xatharo.'

'I'll do it and fall on the knife afterwards.'

'What if you don't have time?'

'My life doesn't count compared to what's at stake here. Get some rest. You have a long ride ahead of you.'

She lies on the straw and watches the stars wheel above her. She listens to Xatharo sharpening his knife. She does not want him to do this anymore. She has grown fond of him and wants him to come back with her to Panormus. This is not right.

'I should have done it that night,' she says. 'Instead I have left the burden with you.'

'It's what I was born for.' He puts the knife away, concealing it under his tunic.

'Don't do it, Xatharo. Keep your pledge to my father and ride out of here with me tonight as you promised. Let someone else rid the world of that monster.'

'No one else is capable,' he says. 'Go to sleep, princess.'

CHAPTER 41

Mara and Xatharo creep away from the camp to find the horses. Mara hears the tuskers on Elephant Row. She has never heard the rumbling so loud.

They are grouped together, vast grey shadows in the dark, and as her eyes grow accustomed to the gloom, she sees they have put their trunks in each other's mouths. Colossus trumpets several times, a chilling sound.

They know the battle is coming, somehow, and like soldiers everywhere they are thinking about pain and death.

From somewhere very close she hears another sound, something or someone, howling like a wolf. It sends a shiver through her. 'What was that?'

'It's Kassander,' Xatharo growls.

The horses are where Gajendra has said they will be. Even in the dark she can tell they are miserable specimens. Still, they have four legs, and it will be better than walking.

'Follow the north star by night and Aetna by day,' Xatharo says. 'When you are near the volcano, you ride inland. Swap the horses every few hours to keep them fresh. Your father's scouts will find you before you find them.'

'Come with me.'

He helps her up onto the horse. 'I have served your father faithfully all my life and never questioned any order he has given me. But someone must stop this devil and it will not be done on the battlefield. Even if I came with you and got you safe there, how long would your freedom last, or your father's? This is the only way.'

There is no goodbye, not with Xatharo. He slaps the horse's rump to set her moving and then disappears into the dark.

Alexander is wearing his antique armour, a metal breastplate laced to a leather back plate. There are polished guards for his wrists and shins. He carries a helmet with stiff red boar's hair under his arm. He stalks across the swept ground, like Zeus himself coming down from the heavens.

The water boys are busy with their pots of red and yellow paint, drawing circles around the elephants' eyes and patterns on their trunks and sides. Other boys are sitting astride their backs, rubbing in coconut oil to strengthen the beasts' nerves.

Alexander wanders down the line,. He examines each beast in turn, fingering the sharpened point on the iron protector they wear on their tusks, the tough leather they wear to protect their flanks and the new segmented armour on their legs. It will take the better part of the day to get them ready. They have them in the shade to keep them cool while the mahavats and water boys do their work. His guards lag: by the time he reaches the end of Elephant Row they are struggling to keep up with him.

Xatharo feels for the edge of the blade inside his tunic. It is so sharp it slices open the pad on his thumb. He sucks the blood.

Gajendra accompanies Alexander along the line; this is an unparalleled honour. Alexander is reminiscing about Gaugamela, the first time he encountered elephants. He is in high spirits. He claps Gajendra on the shoulder and tells him, for the sake of his retinue, that no army on the earth can stand against them.

The more timid beasts are being given rice wine. It will get their blood up. There is none for Colossus; give him rice wine right now and he will tear down the camp before he even gets to the battle line.

The mahavat*s* are laughing. It is amusing to see elephants drunk, staggering and spouting wine over each other, playful - for now at least. But that will change once they are on the battlefield, and they have the drums and the flutes around them, the noise making them mad.

'What is happening?' Alexander asks him.

'We are getting the timid ones ready to go to war.'

'By getting them drunk?'

'They are like men. Get enough wine into a book-keeper or a pastry chef and he thinks he is Hercules.'

One of the elephants roars, enraged, and charges at one of its fellows. The mahavats yell and tug on the ropes, using the bull hooks and canes to bring him back into the line. It has started already. The beasts will soon be uncontrollable.

Gajendra tells them to get the tuskers away from the wine, take them to their battle lines, have the archers mounted.

Alexander stops in front of Colossus. 'Why is this one not having any wine? The poor creature looks thirsty!'

Gajendra sees Xatharo and for a moment he is surprised. Last night he had given him horses and a means of escape. Why is he still here? Then he sees the glint of the knife and he knows what he is planning.

He puts himself between Xatharo and his general.

'Don't just stand there,' he says to him. 'Get the water boys to fetch wine for Colossus.'

He sees Xatharo calculate; now he will have to kill Gajendra to get to Alexander. Even if he is quick about it, the guards will have ample time to step in and dispatch him before he reaches the general.

Still, credit to him, he hesitates, thinking it through.

'Quickly, you and you, go with Xatharo and get the wine.'

'You told us this one did not need wine,' Xatharo says, standing his ground.

'I don't have to explain anything to you,' Gajendra says and slaps him hard across the face. Xatharo reaches inside his tunic and for a moment Gajendra thinks he will actually try it.

But at the last he withdraws and, with one rueful look at Alexander, he goes with the others.

Alexander is feeding Colossus oranges. It amuses him. He holds out a hand for more. The water boys laugh dutifully as he tosses them into Colossus's mouth, making a game of it. The King of the World's luck has held again; he should be lying slaughtered right now.

Alexander soon tires of the game. 'We should not keep Antipater waiting too long,' he says and turns on his heel.

After he has gone, Xatharo and the other water boys return with the buckets of rice wine. They are about to pour it into the tub in front of Colossus, but Gajendra stops them. 'What are you doing? You want him to wreck the whole camp?'

'You said to fetch him wine,' Xatharo says.

'I know what I said, give the wine to one of the others. Siru, perhaps. He needs the courage. No, let the other boys do it. Xatharo, come with me. We're taking Colossus to the river.'

'But he has his armour on.'

'Don't argue with me, do as I say.'

They walk Colossus down to the river in his battle armour, lead him under the shade of a fig tree, and Gajendra lets him drink but keeps him hobbled with the chains. When Xatharo turns his back, he slips his hand inside his tunic. Nothing.

'What are you doing?' Xatharo shouts and jumps back.

Gajendra feels like a fool. He is sure he had seen the glint of a knife. The strain of the coming battle must be telling on him.

'Where's Mara?'

'She's gone.'

'You let her leave alone?'

Xatharo shrugs.

'Why are you still here?'

'I like the food.'

'You planned to kill him just now.'

'I don't know what you're talking about.'

Gajendra doesn't believe him. He could easily have thrown the knife in the bushes when he went to fetch the rice wine. The trumpets are calling them to form up the lines; he hasn't time for this now. He shouts a command and Colossus lumbers out of the shallows, dressed for battle, iron clanking, leather gleaming with water.

'This isn't finished,' Gajendra says.

CHAPTER 42

Gajendra leads his elephants through the lines. The infantry is formed up in their phalanx, the brigade sergeants shouting, 'Plugs off, skin 'em back!' The corpsmen strip off the oiled fleece covers from their *sarissas*, each spear the height of three men. It's a dangerous business forming up for battle, the whetted edges lethal in close formation.

Trumpets are blaring, grooms boost riders into saddles. They use their body weight to keep the beasts from bolting; they are high and need a firm hand. The forest of pikes springs into the air as the infantry rise from their knees. There is the smell of sweat, oil and iron.

Nervous horses piss steaming yellow streams on the ground.

Gajendra looks left and right, sees the phalanx wheel in column and line without a word, in perfect unison. The gleaming spear line swings right then left. Suddenly the men beat their spears on their shields and shout their war cry:

'Alalalalai...'

The sound of it shatters the silence. It is terrifying even though they are on his side. He would hate to have to face them on the battlefield.

He looks across the plain at their enemy's massed ranks. Antipater has decided to stand his ground. His heavy infantry is in the centre, his cavalry on the wings. There is no innovation here. He has a massive army three times the size of Alexander's and he clearly thinks he doesn't need strategy.

'Reveal and conceal,' is Alexander's mantra. He has shown Antipater a weakened right flank oblique to the centre, where

Ptolemy has taken up position with his cavalry, inviting Antipater to attack.

Alexander rides along the line, the shoulder wings of his corselet unbattened; he won't dog them down until he's ready for the charge. He's telling his men: look at me, I am utterly relaxed about this morning's little skirmish. Being outnumbered three to one is nothing to a god.

He wears an extraordinary helmet, with two golden wings. He has his usual crowd of pages and staff officers clustered around him. This display is not just his monstrous vanity, though that is part of it. He wants Antipater to see him, to put his best cavalry regiments against him. This way he controls his enemy's moves as if he is issuing their orders himself.

He calls out to his sergeants by name as he rides the line, settles the more restless of his men with a gesture of his hand. His massive stallion is high, his tail up. Froth sprays from his muzzle and along his flanks. His hooves are the size of skillets, his chest armoured, seventeen hands high.

Alexander reins in, addresses them all, his voice carrying even to the furthest ranks. He tells them they are on the road to destiny. Win this and they will become the first army of men in history to conquer the entire world.

'What do I care for Macedon?' he shouts at them. 'You do not fight for land, for a crown. You fight for the gods. You fight for Zeus. You fight for me!'

He says it all in Greek which means that none of the foreigners in his army can understand him. It doesn't matter to them. They cheer as loudly as the rest for the fine spectacle he makes.

Ptolemy had already begun to advance but has now halted, the better for Antipater to see the apparent weakness on their right flank. Antipater will be suspicious of Alexander's tactics. But the trap is set. How long will Antipater be able to resist the lure?

Couriers dash along the lines; the sergeants stand out before their squares shouting instructions, keeping the infantry to order.

Niarchos suddenly appears, seemingly from nowhere, galloping through the line into the killing ground between the two armies. His disfigured face is concealed by his regimental scarf. He tears this garment free as he gallops. Gajendra knows what is now revealed; the nose and ears have gone, leaving a crust of dried blood and torn flesh.

Niarchos raises his right arm; the hand has been severed at the wrist. He then elevates the battle standard in his left. He intends to ride without reins. Impressive.

He wears no helmet and no armour, though his horse's headstall and frontlet are in place. He has only a light combat saddle.

'What is he doing?' Ravi says.

Gajendra thinks for a moment that he has come to steal his glory. Does he still think to command the elephants? But Alexander has made his wishes plain. He is the Elephantarch now, not Niarchos.

He rides back towards their line and raises the standard again in salute. Now Gajendra knows what is on his mind.

The two armies fall silent. Niarchos turns and rides straight at the enemy line. Antipater's archers and *hoplites* wait behind their palisade and let him come. Finally, an arrow arcs from the line, then a volley of them. He does not fall.

There are shouts from their own infantry who believe he might get through. Another volley of arrows and this time he goes down, his horse as well. But there is yet movement as the dust settles. His horse rises slowly and starts to trot back towards their line.

Then, unbelieving, they watch Niarchos rise too. He staggers towards the enemy palisade. Are they mocking him or honouring him by letting him come so close? A last volley of arrows, and he falls and lies still.

The riderless horse gallops back through the lines.

The sweat dries on Gajendra's back. He takes up his position on Colossus, the signal boy in the howdah behind him. He is desperate with thirst; nerves and dust have turned his throat to chalkstone. Colossus flares out his ears, impatient to charge.

There are eight squadrons of Companion Cavalry under Ptolemy halted on the plain on their right flank; he has just two thousand light infantry with him. These men have no armour, just leather shields and a twelve-foot lance. They make a tempting target.

What Antipater doesn't know is that the infantrymen are specially trained to fight cavalry and are on double pay for doing it. Those that survive will have women and wine for a year.

Finally, Antipater cannot resist. The Greeks charge Ptolemy's tiny force. They will overrun them, it is only a matter of time, but they are in for a much tougher fight than they think. It will buy time, and this is what Alexander wants.

Alexander stands in the saddle and raises his sword. Gajendra sees him and turns and waves to the signal boy in the *howdah* behind him. The boy raises his flags.

Alexander and his heavy cavalry transit to the front, a 'misdirection' as he called it when they were gathered around his battle charts. Gajendra follows with his elephants, revealing the mass of the infantry behind. Then he peels off to the right, towards the cavalry ranged on their enemy's left flank. What will Antipater make of this? Now it is his nerves that will jangle.

Because Antipater does not know much of elephants, he cannot anticipate that they can be as fast as horses over short distances. He will think he has more time to react to Gajendra's charge than he does.

Gajendra looks back over his shoulder. The archers in the *howdahs* are barely clinging on. But he is pleased to see that his elephants are keeping their shape. They follow Colossus in perfect order.

Now Antipater is in a fix. If he moves to cover Gajendra's tuskers, he will lose the opportunity to drive home the attack on Ptolemy. If he doesn't, he leaves himself exposed.

Meanwhile, Alexander's cavalry is charging his centre. He has but a few heartbeats to divine Alexander's plan and form a counter strategy.

Gajendra can imagine nerves at breaking point around the old general. His staff will be shouting at each other up there on the hill; if Antipater moves more infantry across to cover Gajendra's charge, Alexander may break through the centre; if he doesn't, can his cavalry alone withstand the elephants.

Antipater will be doubting himself at every turn. He will overthink it, knowing Alexander's reputation for battlefield surprises. Alexander could win this just with the legend of his own invincibility.

From up here the battle sounds like an earthquake. Mara can see nothing. The armies are too close to each other to make out what is happening. Gajendra told her it was the same for any warrior, even a general. Battles only made sense when you drew them out afterwards in the sand – if you survived – after talking to your fellows and to prisoners. You were always too close or too far away, too scared or too confused to know what was going on.

'You came back,' Xatharo says when he sees her.

'Are you surprised.'

'I should be more so. But it is like you. I wish you had heeded me. You should be almost to Panormus by now.'

'I couldn't abandon you.'

'Now I have failed your father on two counts. Until now, I had never let him down in anything he asked of me.'

'Yet I am relieved. I thought I should find Alexander on a funeral pyre and you on a cross.'

'Your friend Gajendra found me out. He saw the knife I hid in my tunic. He could have had me thrown in front of Alexander in chains, but he chose not to do it. I have not worked him out at all.'

'Neither have I.'

'Is that why you came back, because of the Indian?'

She doesn't answer.

He folds his arms. 'Well, perhaps Alexander will lose, and your elephant boy will go down with him. Then all our problems will be solved.'

The ranks of their heavy cavalry shimmer in the heat haze. All they have, to go against these tens of thousands, is forty elephants. For once Alexander has not yet teased a break in the line. But they cannot go back now. Colossus keep lumbering forward. At least one of us is not afraid, Gajendra thinks.

At the last moment he sees Alexander break off his own charge and wheel his Companion Cavalry to the right, traversing the line towards them. Yet another feint, one he has not even told his own generals about. Or perhaps this is Alexander making do in the heat of things.

He sees cavalry pennants whipping in the wind in front of them. The serried ranks of the *hoplites* are ranged between the horses, in pot and plate, forming up into lines of bristling steel. Their archers are taking aim.

Gajendra prays for movement and sees it.

A horse shies, then another. It is like a ripple spreading through the water. It starts from around the centre and moves outwards along the entire line. He has seen this in drills and in casual encounters, a horse's utter panic at the sight or smell of an elephant. The officers try to hold their mounts and cannot. The line breaks, slowly at first, but then it crumbles away as more horses bolt, terrifying their fellows.

The first volley of arrows arcs down. But the archers have miscalculated the speed of the tuskers. There are three ranks of bowmen in front of the cavalry; the front row gets off two volleys, the second one, but by then the third rank is already running.

The horses are shoving and kicking their way back through their own ranks and, when they find their way blocked, they gallop over the top of the soldiers positioned between them. An infantry phalanx relies on order and discipline for its effect; once it is fractured the individual soldiers are powerless. The panicked horses create corridors through their ranks and Gajendra turns and points to his signalman, who is holding grimly to the sides of the *howdah*.

They must all follow me!

And they do. Instead of attacking the entire flank along its length he leads Colossus through the widest gap, trampling anything in his way. There is scarce any resistance at this point in the line. The enemy's own horses have created chaos in their retreat and Gajendra's squadron punches a hole through Antipater's left flank.

His elephants charge through the line. Gajendra turns and sees Alexander's famous golden helmet as he follows them through with two thousand heavy cavalry coming in behind. In a moment, he flashes past them and ploughs into the rout.

There is a danger that in the rush of victory they may push too far through the lines. If he were Alexander, he supposes he wouldn't care. Alexander is immortal. But Gajendra knows he must hold back, wait for the infantry following behind or there will be no one to protect the elephants. He turns and gives the order to pull back to his signalman in the *howdah*. It is too late.

Ravi is in trouble.

Antipater has some rebel Macks among his infantry who deserted from Kraterus. They are veterans of the Jhellum River and know how to fight an elephant. They target Ran Bagha. They know to attack the mahavat first, one of their scouts whirls a sling above his head and brings Ravi down with a stone. Archers take out the men in the *howdah*.

After that, it would have been better for Ran Bagha to retreat and leave Ravi behind. Instead he stands his ground, one massive foot either side of his mahavat. He flares his ears, trumpeting his defiance.

Two of the soldiers run in and one is sliced clean through by his iron tusk. The other he catches with his trunk and slams him onto the ground. But an isolated elephant cannot last long against a determined attack from brave men. The Macks have surrounded him now.

Gajendra sends Colossus thundering over. Alexander's light infantry, his stingers, are not far behind but they will not be able to get to Ran Bagha in time. Hard men like these Macks fight to the death. They are well drilled and know their business.

Ran Bagha fells two more of his attackers with his iron-tipped tusks, but a third slips in behind with a battle axe and chops at his hamstring. The elephant bellows and turns to face his tormentor, all the while keeping himself above Ravi's stricken body.

The man raises his axe again and Ran Bagha swings with his armoured trunk and knocks him aside, like kicking a stone off the path. The man does not rise.

There is another behind him, his battle axe hacking again at Ran Bagha's unprotected lower legs. A soldier is underneath him, thrusting up with his spear. He roars and his back legs give way, crushing the soldier while impaling himself further on the spear. But still he holds himself up with his forelegs. If he goes all the way down Ravi will be crushed.

He swings again with his trunk and another soldier cartwheels across the ground.

They are attacking his eyes now and looking for the gaps in the lamellar. But he won't go down. There must be at least a dozen Macks, dead or wounded, around him.

The soldiers see Colossus coming and wheel around to face him. He barrels into them, and they go down under his feet, screaming. He is in a rage and Gajendra does not have to tell him what to do. He uses his tusks and his trunk and his feet. Gajendra wonders at the courage of these Macks, for they try to stand up to him. Brutes, the lot of them, but they don't know the meaning of defeat.

As Colossus wheels around Gajendra uses his heels to give the order: *Let me down*. Colossus hesitates a moment but is too well trained to disobey. Gajendra leaps off and rushes over to Ravi, grabs him by the shoulders and pulls him clear just as Ran Bagha collapses. The ground shakes when an elephant goes down; you can feel it through the soles of your feet.

Colossus continues the slaughter unaided. He is a warrior for all his gentle ways with Mara. Now here come Alexander's stingers, rushing in and taking out the last of the Macks.

Gajendra sinks to his knees beside Ravi. Colossus has finished with the war also and stands over Ran Bagha, searching for life with his trunk. Finally, he raises his head and bellows.

Ravi's eyes blink open. He does not know where he is or what has happened. There is a dent in his helmet the size of a fist. Gajendra takes it off. He has a bloody split in his scalp, but his brains are still there. His head has been given a good rattling is all. He would have been dead if not for his elephant.

The battle rushes over them like a wave and the slaughter continues somewhere else. His signal boy is shouting at him from the *howdah*. He must lead the line again or the attack may yet falter. He runs back and tells him to raise the flags.

They sweep into the remains of Antipater's phalanx a second time. He glimpses Alexander far ahead in the thick of things, surrounded on every side, tireless in the way he swings his sword, laughing. It is the only time he ever sees him truly happy, when he is about death's work. Spray him with another man's blood and, in his mind, you pelt him with flowers.

The Gauls that Antipater has brought with him have dropped their weapons and run. The Macks and Greeks stand their ground, but their lines are broken, and it is simply a matter of doing the slaughter.

After a time, killing is just heavy labour. The soldiers will be exhausted tonight. Antipater's men die in their thousands. Some fought side by side with Alexander in India. It must be done. These men have turned once, and they cannot be trusted to be loyal again.

Impeded by their own baggage train, decimated by their own cavalry turning back on them, Antipater's thousands count for nothing. Once a soldier starts to run, he can save himself or he can die, but he cannot hurt you anymore. Many fall prey to Alexander's cavalry and the light infantry that follow in behind.

Behind the army, Antipater's baggage train is in ruins; tents are mere rags, carts no more than firewood. Whores stagger about stealing money from dead soldiers and offering their services to their new masters even before they have finished swinging their swords.

The day wears on and the battle degenerates into bargaining; soldiers buy women with rings torn from dying men; prisoners are dragged behind horses for sport; captains and corporals stagger about draping themselves in plundered gowns and women's jewels.

It was supposed to be the great battle that would decide the future of the world. In the end it was no more than a skilled fighter grabbing a bully by the hair and pitching him out of the window.

CHAPTER 43

It is demanding work taking the armour off wounded elephants.

They are distressed and it is a dangerous task. The leather armour on Colossus's flanks bristles with arrows. One has somehow found its way through and blood streams from his neck. The physician is the same one who tends Alexander. Alexander himself has ordered him to look after the tuskers.

There is an air of celebration; men never drink so much or laugh so loud as when they have cheated death. Exploits are recounted in the extravagant boasts of men who cannot believe they have survived such a slaughter.

The elephants are rewarded with food, mountains of it brought in carts and stacked in front of them to distract them while the physicians do their work. Later they are taken down to the river where the grime and blood can be washed off.

Most days they trumpet and spray water everywhere. But today the elephants are impatient with their handlers, and several are hurt by their surly charges.

Gajendra urges his boys to caution. The tuskers have lost comrades. They are wild animals, but sometimes they can act like men. They are angry. It is grief, pure and simple.

Mara slips away to the battlefield. Kites circle screaming over the corpses. Some soldiers are still looking for a favourite spear they've left in someone's guts or drinking all the wine from enemy canteens.

She walks among the dead and dying, tries not to look too closely at what she sees. Twice she slips in blood pools. She keeps her hands over her ears, so she does not have to listen to the things she hears. Why doesn't someone put these men out of their misery?

Ran Bagha is not hard to find, a massive grey mountain of flesh on the plain. Pennants flutter around him, placed there by other mahavats. Ravi sits alone and cross-legged. He does not look up at her approach.

She sits down beside him. They mourn together.

Alexander's sword is stuck to his hand with blood. A physician is stitching a gash in his shoulder with thread. Alexander drinks another cup of wine and appears oblivious. His body is a patchwork of old wounds and cicatrices. He has scars on his scars.

His face is flushed with the glory of it. His armour lies on the floor, slimed with gore. Both shoulder pieces of his corselet have been sheared away, and the facing of his breastplate is so battered he cannot identify the Gorgons that were so painstakingly worked into the gold.

His tunic is discarded also, a rag of blood and sweat. His physician now attempts to seal a gash on his head with copper dog-bites and stitches.

Gajendra is cheered as he walks in. Hands clap him on the shoulder. He is not an elephant boy anymore; he is the hero of Syracuse.

Alexander finally manages to detach himself from his sword and he stands and embraces him. There is a general euphoria. The dead are forgotten. How could they be so remiss as to expire in such a complete victory? It is plainly their fault that they are missing this celebration.

They have had word from their spies in Syracuse that Antipater has proved himself inconvenient to his hosts and has been murdered. Sostratus is suing for peace, and with Alexander's navy now blockading his port, it will come at a heavy price. The rebellion has been crushed. Kraterus will retake Macedon; Italy is next for Alexander, and then the world is his.

Even the grumblers are silent now.

'Your elephants won the day,' Alexander says to Gajendra, and gives him wine and a seat beside him. Blood still streams from his shoulder and mixes with sweat and grime. He is in his element. He takes a long breath, savouring the moment.

Gajendra has found his heaven also. No one is going to piss on him, not ever again. An elephant boy has become a general.

So why is it that all he can think of is Ravi and his beloved Ran Bagha? He imagines the flies will be at work already. Soon it will be the turn of the maggots and the worms. It was just a wild beast, not even one of the best warriors. They can buy and train another. A thousand men dead out there, what does one tusker matter?

'What shall be your reward?' Alexander asks him. 'Name it.'

'Zahara,' he hears himself say.

The smile falls away. Those standing close turn to listen. Even Alexander is perturbed. 'You will not give her time to weep?'

'She will not weep for Niarchos. She was a trophy to him like any other.'

'Yet it would be best to wait.'

'You asked me what I wished for as a reward. I have told you.'

A chill silence settles on the room. Niarchos has earned a hero's death today and this smacks of disrespect.

'This is not right,' he hears someone mutter. 'Should a wife not be a widow for longer than a day?'

Gajendra is shocked by his own audacity. But he wants his due, what he has risked and worked for, and he wants it now.

Alexander smiles. 'So, you can be ruthless after all. The elephant boy is a general.'

'It seems so.'

'They will not like it,' he says, looking at the other captains, those who cheered him hoarse a few moments before.

'I do not care what they think of me.'

Alexander is bleeding more heavily now. The doctor again attempts to finish stitching his head. He pushes him away and claps Gajendra on the shoulder. 'What are you all staring at? Is he not the hero of Syracuse? We shall give him his due!'

They are used to being bullied by Alexander, but they don't have to like it. All he gets is sullen looks.

Alexander laughs and calls for more wine.

CHAPTER 44

Alexander has blessed the wedding and it is he who will sponsor it.

His pavilion is decked out with flowers and garlands. There are censers burning to disguise the smell of the corpse fires further down the valley. Some guests are still bleeding.

After the ritual sacrifices, they retire to the pavilion for the feast. There is an air of forced gaiety. Alexander has commanded his musicians to play for them. He has ordered general happiness and watches for glumness like his guards watch for assassins.

The men and women sit at different tables. Alexander sprawls at the heart of this grim celebration eating little and drinking much. His lips are wet, his eyes wild with dissatisfaction.

He stews. Something nameless gnaws at him.

Gajendra remembers what Niarchos told him. He thought then it was just env, but now he wonders how much truth there was in it.

One of his lads tries to tempt Alexander with a tray of sesame seeds mixed with honey, but he pushes the salver away. He grabs Zahara's wrist and drags her across the room to Gajendra.

'She has no father here, so I shall be the father.'

Gajendra stumbles to his feet, unprepared.

Alexander draws back her veil and thrusts her arm at him. 'I give you this woman, that she may bring children into the world within the bond of wedlock.'

'I accept her.'

'I agree to provide a dowry of three talents with her.'

'I accept that too – with pleasure.'

'There,' Alexander says. 'It is done.'

His boys form up the procession and lead the way, holding torches. Others whirl ahead, dancing to the flutes and drums. There are even elephants. Colossus is notable by his absence.

There is much shouting and laughter, though none from the generals. The din of music is so deafening it almost drowns out the screaming from the hospital tent. He lifts Zahara onto the ritual cart. The mules break into a trot.

Alexander leads the cheering. The Macedonians grudgingly join in. What choice is there?

Alexander has granted Gajendra his own pavilion, as befitting his new station as Elephantarch. It belonged formerly to Niarchos, as did the slaves. There will be no more sleeping in the straw or with the tuskers, no more washing in the river.

Gajendra lifts his bride from the ritual chariot and waits as carpenters rip off the axle. It is chopped and a pyre built with kindling and saltpetre. Zahara is handed a brand to light it. It is tradition; it signifies that she has taken a new home and will not now be returning to the old one. The Macedonians smirk behind their hands. Isn't this the tent she just came from?

Alexander posts guards at the door of the pavilion. Her women remain outside with drums to scare away the underworld spirits.

Gajendra's every desire has been fulfilled. This is the greatest day of his young life. He would like Ravi to see this; Ravi who said such things could not happen to an elephant boy. But Ravi is still out on the battlefield sitting with his dead tusker and will come back to the camp for no man.

CHAPTER 45

She takes off her clothes and lies under the sheet. There is a glimpse of honey flesh, the heady scent of Arabian perfume. He draws back the sheet to gaze at her. Her beauty is breath-taking. This moment is perfect.

He lies down beside her; she is silky, compliant. She allows him to kiss her. He explores what he has so long desired, every soft place, every curve, every delightful rounding of the flesh. He waits for her to respond.

But he cannot wait long. He must possess what he has ached for. He puts his arms around her and pulls her towards him. He mounts her, disappointed and enraged.

It is over quickly.

Is that all there is to dreams?

Afterwards, he rolls away from her and lies still as the sweat cools on his body and his breathing slows to its normal rhythm.

'Do you remember me?' he says to her.

'Remember you?'

'We met at the temple. You came to make sacrifice to Astarte.'

'That was you?'

'Do you remember what I said to you?'

'I was too shocked by what you did. What did you say?'

He is about to tell her but realises there is no point. 'It does not matter now.' He sits up, angry with himself, with her, with the world.

'Who is Mara?'

'What do you mean?'

'As you were loving me. You spoke the name twice.'

'Did I? I don't remember.'

'Where are you going?'

'Outside.'

'But we are married now. Should we not share the same bed tonight?'

She means it, he thinks. She is present and decorous. It is what is expected. How can she understand that she has not fulfilled her part of the bargain? It was my dream, not hers.

'Did you have any feelings for Niarchos?'

'Why should I have had feelings for him? I hardly knew him.'

'Of course. Forgive me.'

He goes outside, looks up at the moon, just a sliver of it in a dark sky. He stares at the stars. He has everything he wanted and once thought impossible to obtain. He is awash in glory. How can triumph taste so bitter?

CHAPTER 46

Gajendra cannot sleep. He goes to Elephant Row but cannot find Colossus. Several of the elephants are missing, and the water boys mumble incoherent replies when he demands to know where they are. At first, he panics. If Alexander finds out about this, he will lose his position as Elephantarch as quickly as he has gained it.

But then he realizes – he senses – what has happened. He has seen it before in India. A young female elephant had died after being mauled by a tiger and for days the other elephants stayed by her side and would not leave her. And every year after that they came back to the same place, looking for the bones. It was as if they were grieving.

Ravi had showed him this curious ritual. They had hidden in the jungle, out of sight of the herd, to watch. By then most of the bones had bleached or disappeared.

'It is like they understand what death is,' Ravi had whispered. 'Tell me one other animal that knows what a grave is!'

Gajendra trudges across the battlefield. Most of the bodies have been stripped and dragged away, but debris still litters the grass. He trips on the shoulder piece of a corselet in the dark. There are discarded scraps of uniform everywhere.

He hears his tuskers before he sees them. They are not trumpeting or shrieking; it is the rumble from their stomachs that alerts him that they are close by. They are all gathered around Ran Bagha.

Ravi sits cross-legged at his head. There are two other silhouettes. As the moon skims from behind high clouds, he recognizes Mara and Xatharo.

He sits down and watches. He makes no move to join them and supposes they have not seen him. He is downwind, so the elephants do not catch his scent. He would like to join them but feels he has no place there.

He listens to the elephants and the wind rustling in the grass.

Mara and Xatharo sit side by side, staring at the vast grey mountain that once was Ran Bagha. The corpses have long ago been hauled away by the carters, but the elephant is a different proposition. They will have to burn the carcass soon. As he lies out here in the hot sun, the gases are building up inside his giant body and there is a danger he will explode.

Ravi will not leave him. He has sat here all day, without shelter. If the water boys had not taken it in turns to bring him water from the river he would have died from thirst. He has not eaten. He has hardly moved.

Mara will not leave Ravi, and Xatharo will not leave her. So they stay. No one has come to order them back to camp. Gajendra is too busy with his new wife to chasten his slaves, Mara supposes. Besides, he wants us to escape. He is giving us another chance.

Flies cluster around the dried blood on Ravi's scalp. He will not go to the physicians to have the wound tended. He just sits there, rocking back and forward.

Just after dawn, Mara sees a knot of riders approach from the camp. The early morning sun reflects on their armour and hurts the eyes. She knows they are officers by the way they ride. As they get closer, she recognizes Alexander in the lead.

He jumps down from the saddle. 'Well, this is a fine pass. What do we have here?' He walks around the beast and then looks down at Ravi. 'He's starting to smell. Time you moved on.'

'He gave his life for me.'

'Well, then we shall remember him fondly. In the meantime, I wish you to remove back to the camp. We need good Indians to replace the mahavats I lost in the fight.'

'What will you do with him?'

'What would you have me do? Build a mausoleum?' He sees Mara and Xatharo. 'What are they doing?'

He does not seem perturbed that they do not answer.

Instead he turns to Perdiccas, watching from his horse. 'I want the foot,' he says.

'The foot?'

'I shall need a footstool. I heard the King of Taxila has one. If it's good enough for an Indian, it's good enough for me.'

'You will cut off his foot?' Ravi says, in a daze.

'Not just his foot, we will have his ivory, too. By the black breath of hell, he stinks!' He turns and is about to remount his horse. Suddenly Mara comes out of her daze, grabs the knife that Xatharo has concealed in his tunic and rushes him. Alexander hears her coming, turns unhurriedly to face her. He registers no alarm, even when he sees the knife flash in the sun. A man who has spent his whole life in battle is accustomed to having drawn blades thrust at him.

As she brings the knife down, he casually steps aside and knocks her down with a fist. At the same moment he wrenches the knife out of her hand, waving aside his guards with a flicker of annoyance. I do not need wet nursing, the look says.

My father would be ashamed, she thinks, as she lies there, stunned. I had two chances to rid the world of this beast and both times I failed.

Xatharo is a different proposition. Alexander is not expecting this. The little fellow hits him on the run and takes him out at the knees. He goes down, winded, and drops the knife. Xatharo snatches it up and is about to slash Alexander's throat in the same movement when one of the bodyguards reacts and takes him down with his spear. Xatharo screams and grabs the shaft, which has smashed his thigh, the same one he wounded days ago. This time it smashes the bone. A man, even one as brave as Xatharo, cannot stand on a broken leg. He falls to the ground.

Alexander is on his feet in an instant, takes out his sword and plunges it through Xatharo's chest. Mara sobs as she sees the light go out of his eyes.

Alexander turns to her. She tries to get up. He forces her down with his foot and puts his sword at her throat. 'Don't hurt her! She's a girl!' Ravi shouts before he can administer the killing stroke.

Alexander stands back, frowning. He strides over to Ravi and squats down on his haunches. 'What did you say?'

'She's just a girl.'

'A girl?'

Ravi nods.

'Does your Elephantarch know about this?'

Ravi shakes his head, no, but he is a very bad liar.

Alexander gives a nod of the head, a signal to his bodyguards to take the prisoner away. He looks down at Xatharo's lifeless body in disgust. Mara knows what he is thinking: how did a fellow like this become so useful with a sword? If it weren't for his bodyguards, he would be bleeding into the dirt right now.

This will bear looking into.

CHAPTER 47

When Gajendra walks into Alexander's pavilion, Mara is lying on the ground at his feet. She has been beaten, but not badly, not yet.

Alexander looks up at him and says, 'You heard what your elephant boy did to me? Only he's not a boy, is he? Did you know?'

He thinks about lying, but there is no longer any point.

He nods.

Alexander strikes him once, with his fist. It is like getting kicked by a horse. He goes down.

'Why did you keep this a secret? What was it, did you feel sorry for her?'

Gajendra gets up slowly. 'I imagine that I did.'

'I gave you a woman. Was that not enough for you? A princess! What is this scrawny wretch here? What could possibly be the attraction? You haven't fucked her, have you?'

He does not answer.

'What shall we do with her? She came at me with a knife. I think we should crucify her, don't you? It would not do for others to think that they can test me with a blade and not suffer the consequence.'

'Please,' Gajendra says.

'What did you say?'

'Let her live.'

'Why should you care if she suffers and dies?'

'I have grown fond of her.'

'Fond of her?' Alexander decides to laugh. This is a wonderful joke. 'How fond?'

'She only did this because of the elephant.'

'The elephant?'

He sees her look up at him, through her bruises. She is astonished that he is arguing for her.

'She loved the dead elephant as you love your horse.'

'A horse is different.'

'Not to her. She was enraged, I am sure of it. She did not plan to do you harm. It was a moment's madness.'

'But if she had been quicker, I should have a knife in my back whether she planned it or not. How badly do you wish my leniency, elephant boy?'

'I'll do anything.'

'Will you? Get down on your belly, then.'

He knows what Alexander is about to do. He drops to his knees and lies flat, his forehead touching the carpets.

From here, he sees that Alexander's sandals have blood on them. He wonders whether it belongs to Mara or to Xatharo.

'Beg me.'

'Please.'

'Say it louder. Say it like you mean it.'

'Please, don't hurt her.'

'Again.'

'Please let her go. I beg you, my lord. Have mercy on her.'

Alexander draws up his robe and Gajendra feels his warm stream on his head and shoulders. He can hear his mother and sisters wailing again.

'I didn't hear you. Say it again.'

'Please let her go...'

Alexander finishes and adjusts his robe. 'I am disappointed in you, elephant boy. I thought I saw something in you.' He bends over and whispers, 'You stink of piss, and they have all seen you grovel now. You'll never walk among generals again. You'll always be just a piss-ant.'

'Let her go.'

Alexander sighs. 'All right. If that's what you want. Now get out.'

But even as he scrambles to his feet, he knows the promise is a lie. Grovel all you want, elephant boy, he's going to kill her anyway.

CHAPTER 48

The news spreads through the camp: the hero of Syracuse is disgraced.

Ravi finds him sitting alone by the river. There is mist on the water but with the heat of the new day it burns off and he can see Syracuse in the distance, Aetna rising beyond.

A heron fishes in the shallows. It flies off as Ravi approaches. He squats down next to Gajendra, puts his arm around his shoulders. After a while, he leads him down to the river and scrubs Alexander off him.

'He is going to execute her,' Gajendra says.

'He'll do it slow, so that you have to watch.'

'You think so?'

'You know him better than I do. What do you think?'

Gajendra's limbs are shaking. It is as if they belong to someone else. He tries to tense his muscles to still them. He does not want anyone to see him like this, even Ravi.

'I'm going to get her away from here.'

'How? Overpower Alexander's entire army?'

'I don't have to overpower an army. I just have to distract a few guards. Will you help me?'

'What choice do I have?'

'All you have to do is get me two good horses.'

'Steal horses and help a prisoner escape? Oh, well, that's all right then. As long as it's not something that would get me tortured and killed.'

'I know someone. Find him and pay him, he'll know what to do. He's done it before.'

'No wonder you're in trouble, Gaji.'

'Packhorses will do. As long as they have four legs. You'll do it for me?'

'I'll do it. I was growing fond of her too. What is the plan?'

'I'm going to set fire to Alexander's camp.'

There is just one guard outside the tent where Mara is being held. She's only a woman after all, and who is going to take her? The man has drawn the guard duty as punishment from his squad sergeant for sleeping at his watch and now he sits slumped on the ground, resenting it.

He stands up, though, when he smells the smoke. He can hear the elephants trumpeting on the other side of the camp and there is a commotion with the horses. When he sees the orange glow spreading up the sky he starts to panic. What is he supposed to do now?

Then he sees Gajendra. The captain of the elephants is in disgrace. What is he doing here? He has heard how Alexander made him grovel and then pissed on his head. But he is still the Elephantarch. Should he salute him or jeer at him?

He has no chance to do either.

'There's a fire, the elephants have got out!' Gajendra shouts at him.

The guard hears screams coming from Elephant Row, he imagines those dangerous brutes running amok through the camp. They will trample the army and be halfway back to Carthage by the time they have the fire out.

In the fire glow, the soldier's face is a study in confusion. 'Someone has unshackled them,' he says.

'Yes, it was me.'

The elephant hook hits the lad on the back of the head, under the helmet. He falls face down into the dirt.

Gajendra takes a smoking torch and goes inside the tent. Mara is curled up on the ground, tied hand and foot. One eye is swollen shut where they have beaten her.

She sits up, startled, and backs into the corner, expecting more maltreatment.

'It's me,' he tells her. He does not waste time explaining to her what is happening. He scoops her up in his arms. She is as light as a bird. He carries her out and runs off into the darkness.

Ravi is waiting with the horses.

'Did you have any trouble?' Gajendra asks him.

'That sergeant tried to raise the price on me at the last moment,' Ravi says. 'I had to put a knife to his throat to get him to keep to our arrangement.'

'You have a knife? Here, let me have it.' Gajendra takes it and slashes through the ropes at Mara's wrists and ankles. They had bound her tight, and the bonds come away bloody.

'Help her on her horse,' he tells Ravi.

'Where are you going?'

'I'll be right back.' He runs off into the dark. It isn't hard to find what he is looking for; he lets his nose lead him.

It is a dangerous notion because the cage he is looking for has been left close to Alexander's pavilion. But it is unguarded, as he thought it would be. Everyone has gone to the fire.

Kassander yips and snarls behind the bars of his prison. Gajendra comes closer. It may be no mercy setting him free; he is covered in sores and all manner of filth; his beard is down to his belly and his eyes are like a madman's. He cannot imagine what will become of him.

But he slips the latch on the cage and throws it open. At first, Kassander does not move. He cowers in the corner, thinking it is a trick. It is only when Gajendra steps back that the cunning returns to his eyes. When he finally makes the decision to escape he is a quicksilver shadow, one moment there, the next vanished into the dark.

Gajendra silently wishes him better fortune, a quick death at least.

He heads back to the camp. Men are running everywhere, pointlessly, not really knowing what to do. No one pays him mind. When a man is caught between a mad elephant and a good roasting, he could be carrying away Alexander's pickled head in a jar and no one would stop to look, let alone draw their sword.

The smell of smoke is overpowering. He cannot hear his tuskers trumpeting anymore, though. They must have escaped. It will be days before they round them all up again.

Mara sags in the saddle of her horse. Gajendra wonders if she will be strong enough for this. He mounts his own nag. He is no horseman, but he has ridden enough times to know how it is done. It is strange to have a saddle and no ears to hang onto.

Mara's horse staggers and she sways and nearly falls off its back. Even with her sparrow's weight, the beast looks as if he has been asked to carry a siege engine. Pack animals both of them. If the sergeant hadn't sold them, they would have been in the soup by the end of the week.

'Go well, my friend,' Ravi says.

'Until we meet again.'

Ravi grips his hand.

They trot away, through the drifting smoke. He sees a few brave souls rushing the other way to help fight the fire. Not many.

Mara, weak from the beatings, can barely keep herself upright. Gajendra holds the reins, leading her horse behind his. Well, I let you piss on my head, Alexander. You thought you had me beaten. But that was misdirection, as you call it. A feint.

You were a good tutor. I learned well.

He stops on the ridge to look back. The fire has grown bigger than he intended. It has lit up the plain and the orange glow of it is reflected on Mara's face. She has recovered a little, has taken back the reins, at least.

She puts her hand on his arm. He thinks she is about to thank him. Instead she says, 'We have to go back.'

He stares at her. 'Go back?'

'I cannot leave Xatharo to rot in the sun.'

'Xatharo's dead.'

'More reason to save his honour.'

'Save his honour? I am trying to save your life!'

'I will not leave him. Go without me if you must. But my father did not raise a wretch who will leave her champion to be eaten by carrion crows.'

He admires her, even though he would like to slap her off her horse. Perhaps she will do the same for him one day. He would like someone to save him from the birds if he were lying out there.

There is nothing for it but to go back.

CHAPTER 49

In the dark it would have been impossible to find him, but with the glow of the fire spreading across the sky, the battlefield is lit like early morning. He sees a huge silhouette near the brow of a low rise; what is left of Ran Bagha after the crows have been at their work. Xatharo will be very close by.

But getting the body is not going to be so easy.

Alexander has posted two men to protect the elephant's ivory tusks, which have yet to be removed. They will have to be dealt with.

He'll crucify me if I get caught, Gajendra thinks. It would be three days dying because of this madwoman.

The air is ripe with dead elephant and the guards have been forced to stand a little way off with scarves over their faces. They have been dozing, but the fire has woken them. They are too scared to leave their post, so they stand there, gawping, pointing to where the flames have taken hold.

There are two of them: are they veterans or green recruits, Macks or Persians? It will make a difference to the outcome.

Gajendra and Mara leave the horses in the shadows, tied to a solitary olive tree. They creep closer. 'So,' she whispers, 'do we say, good morning men, we just want this body, sorry to trouble you and now we'll be off? Is that your plan?'

'You will have to distract them,' he says.

'How?'

He shrugs.

'You want me to play the tart when, for all these months, I have convinced everyone that I am a boy?'

'They won't mind what you are, as long as you show willing.'

If it were daylight, she would not look the seductress, not with this swollen face and bleeding wrists. But every woman is beautiful in the dark, or that is what they say, and besides, there is no choice. This was her idea, so she will have to do her part.

He waits in the shadows. She stands up, takes a deep breath and starts to walk towards them. She affects a provocative sway of the hips, a parody of a Babylon streetwalker, which makes him almost laugh out loud.

These men are little use as guards; they are both so entranced by the progress of the fire in the camp that she is on them before they realize she is there. They shout in alarm when they finally see her approach, and they run for their weapons.

He could not truthfully say that Mara has any talent for harlotry; the sum of her abilities is to hitch up her tunic, show the boys what is on offer and ask for a gold coin donation. It astonishes him that they do not consider the situation more carefully, yet it has been his experience that when a man receives such an invitation, his prick always works faster than his brain.

They must assume she is a camp follower, so short on business that she has needed to leave the comfort of her own tent to find work. And in the middle of a conflagration, too.

In their defence, they are young, and they are bored from a long night sitting too close to a decomposing elephant. But he'll give them this: they are quick about it. One is already on top of her and the other yelling encouragement by the time Gajendra can even get into position. They have handily left their weapons, together with their helmets and clothes, to one side. The one looking out for his friend does not even turn around. The first he knows of Gajendra's presence is when the shaft of his own spear strikes him on the back of his head and down he goes, blacked out before he even hits the ground.

The second is immediately of a mind to rise and scramble for his sword, but Mara wraps her arms and legs around him, impeding him. Gajendra swings again but because the boy wriggles and throws up an arm it takes three clouts and a knee in the vitals before he is subdued.

When it is done, Gajendra looks around for her. He thinks to find her weeping on the ground, but she is already on her feet, brushing dirt off her tunic.

'What took you so long?' she says to him. 'He had almost violated me.'

'You make a poor harlot.'

'And you are a useless bodyguard.'

CHAPTER 50

The fire stripes the bodies of the two soldiers with ochre. Gajendra does not think he has killed them. He hopes not; they were only doing their job. It is the first time he has fought without weapons, and without an elephant to compensate for what he lacks in size.

Xatharo lies in the shadow of Ran Bagha's corpse. The smell is unbearable, and he does not linger over an examination of the body. He puts one of the soldier's blankets over him and picks him up. He is surprised at the weight of him for such a short fellow.

He throws him across the saddle of his horse. Mara has already mounted her nag and is ready to leave. Her tunic is torn, and she has had to tie a knot in the shoulder to hold it together. There are fresh scratches on her arm and her throat.

They only stop when they reach what Gajendra judges to be a safe distance. The moon appears between high scudding clouds, and he can hear the sea breaking on the shore. A pink glow is spreading up the sky to the south. The army still haven't put his fire out.

Alexander won't be pleased.

He helps Mara from the saddle and down onto the sand. The moon is bright enough to distinguish shapes from shadows.

'We are safe here,' he says. 'We can find somewhere to bury him in the soft sand.'

'We are not burying him here. We are taking him back with us to Panormus. My father will want to see the body and give him a proper burial.'

He sighs. He thought that was what she would say.

'You don't have to do this,' she says. 'You can leave me now. I'll manage.'

'Well, that's as foolish a declaration as I ever heard.'

'Is it? Only I do not wish to burden you further. I have ruined everything for you, it seems. You had everything you wanted until you walked into Alexander's tent and pleaded for my life.'

'Did you really try to kill him because of an elephant?'

'He wanted Ran Bagha's leg for a footstool.'

Gajendra sits down on a rock. His earlier elation has evaporated. A small victory such as this is not salvation. 'You're right, I'm nothing again.'

'Can you not go back?'

'It's too late for that, even I wanted to. And I don't want to.'

'My father will be grateful.'

'Your father is not Alexander.'

Mara goes to her horse and pulls back the blanket they have wrapped around Xatharo's body. 'He doesn't even look like himself anymore.'

'Would you really have killed Alexander?' he says to her.

'I keep asking myself why I didn't. But that night I went with you to his tent he seemed so charming, nothing like the man I imagined. And perhaps it's not in me to kill like that, in cold blood. But then this morning, when he saw he wanted them to saw off Ran Bagha's leg and tusks, something snapped. I have never hated anyone so much. I couldn't see for spite. If he had not turned at the last moment, I would have stuck that knife in him as far as I could make it go.'

Gajendra looks at the sky. 'We had best keep riding.'

'Thank you,' she murmurs, 'for saving me. You have given up everything for me.'

'There is nothing back there I will miss,' he says. 'Except my elephant.'

They ride through the night, as far away from Alexander's camp as they can, and stop just before dawn to rest the horses. The sun throws a lemon stain above the hills. It is cold and Gajendra's muscles are stiff and sore.

He sits with his back against a tree, closes his eyes for a moment. Exhaustion overtakes him. After a while, he feels the drumming of horses' hooves through the earth. He thinks it might be that dream again, and that he is back at Taxila, asleep on the floor of the hut. But then he comes fully awake and realizes that the hoof beats are real.

He jumps to his feet and searches the horizon in the early morning gloom.

'Get up,' he says to Mara. He pulls her, protesting, to her feet. He can see the riders now, silhouetted against the rising sun. They were headed south, but they have seen them and have changed direction.

'We might be able to outrun them,' he tells her. Were they Alexander's men, or deserters, bandits? With any luck they would never have to find out.

'What are you doing?' he says to her. She is trying to haul Xatharo's body towards the horses. 'We don't have time!' He tries to pull her away.

She shrugs him off. 'I won't leave him!'

There is nothing for it but to drag Xatharo over to the horses and across the poll of his own horse. He covers him quickly with the blanket.

And all the time the riders are getting closer.

Mara is a poor rider, even less expert than him. She pulls too tight on the reins and is unsure of herself in the saddle. The nags they are riding are no match for the good horses of their pursuers, especially when one of them is weighed down with a corpse. Gajendra looks over his shoulder and sees them gaining ground, fast. This is hopeless.

There are four of them, Bactrians by the look of them, and they know their business. As they get closer they spread out, ready to encircle them.

They reach a creek and that slows them further. Gajendra realizes they will not make it. Mara's horse baulks in the riverbed. It doesn't matter, because two of the Bactrians have already leaped the banks and are trotting towards them through the shallows, grinning.

CHAPTER 51

Once they have them surrounded, the Bactrians relax. There is no longer any reason to be desperate about it.

Their leader is a big man with a nose that makes his horse look handsome. He has a face like an old leather bag, ill-repaired, and not a tooth in his head that did not appear at least part rotten.

'I wish you good morning,' Gajendra says and walks his horse up to him. No one yet has produced a weapon. But in such a situation, he supposes, there is no need.

Gajendra studies the ragtag of men with him. He knows the type; they will run face first into walls to make themselves look more fearsome. If they were just bandits he would be more hopeful, but these men look like mercenaries, professionals. Violation and murder are set into such men's souls like iron rusted into a wall.

They are no doubt deserters from someone's army. He doubts it is Alexander's, for the general takes care to keep his men well-paid and well-fed. They speak rudimentary Greek with bad accents; he supposes men like this don't even speak their own language very well.

'Where are you headed?' the ugly one asks him.

'Panormus,' Gajendra says and then he adds, 'This is General Hanno's daughter. There is a massive reward offered for her safe return.' He looks from one to the other. 'We can all share it if you like.'

There is stunned silence and then the horsemen all pound their saddles with their fists and guffaw. The ugly one gives a nod and one of the riders grabs Mara and pulls her off her horse. 'Looks like a boy to me,' he says, 'but we'll soon find out.'

'Leave her!' Gajendra tries to put his nag between her and them, but he is no horseman and only succeeds in losing control of the beast. After they have finished laughing at him one of the men draws his sword and hammers the hilt into his face, knocking him to the ground.

He lies there, stunned. He cannot breathe. His mouth and nose are clotted with blood, and he has to roll onto his belly to spit it out.

The men find this amusing. 'Come on, boy, get up,' their leader jeers at him. 'Let's see you make a fight of it.'

The brute gets off his horse and aims a leisurely kick at his ribs.

He hears Mara screaming, curses mainly, but they haven't really tried to hurt her yet.

The man stands, legs apart, right in front of him. Gajendra crawls forward, hand over hand. Never mind that he laughs and dares you to fight like a man, he thinks. Just keep your head down.

Poor Mara. For a general's daughter she has borne a lot of rough handling this last year; now here are four men intent on violating her, either as a girl or as a boy, depending on their fancy. He shuts out her screams. It is distracting him.

He reckons he has broken some ribs when he came off the horse.

'Please don't hurt us,' he says. 'Take our horses, take whatever you want, but please don't hurt us.'

The ugly one likes that. 'You hear that? First he offers us a general's daughter, now he's offering us the horses.' Another kick. 'If we wanted them we would take them, but I wouldn't even carve these nags up for the pot. Are you sure that one is a girl?'

There is consternation among them, however, when they find Xatharo's body across his saddle. This is unexpected and alarms them. It is a perfect distraction.

When your opponent thinks he has won it is your time to strike, Gajendra hears Alexander say. He concentrates all his will on bringing his knee up so that he is ready to spring and then reverses his grip on the knife in his tunic.

As soon as the ugly one looks away for a moment, Gajendra is on his feet. His head smashes the other man's nose, while his knife plunges in to the hilt. Xatharo could not have done better.

Even before he has finished his dying, Gajendra has the man's sword in his hand and has lopped off the arm of one of the other bandits. He does not linger over him. In his experience, a man who has lost a limb in such dramatic fashion quickly loses his appetite for the fight.

He concentrates instead on the two men bending over Mara. They are covered in scratches; she has made a good fight of it. She holds onto the soldier who is on top of her and keeps him from rising. Twice in one day. It is almost becoming routine.

While the other one fumbles for his weapon, Gajendra swings down with all his strength. The edge of the sword cleaves the man's face from scalp to chin.

The one on top of Mara screams in horror and punches her twice in the face to get away. But she has delayed him enough. Gajendra dares not swing the sword a second time in case he strikes her instead, so he lunges with the point.

He is inexpert but he is in luck. It takes the man through the centre of his chest. He puts a foot on his breastbone to extract the sword and then walks over to the man whose arm he took off. He is still rolling around bleeding everywhere and howling for his mother. He dispatches him quickly.

Gajendra has never known such cold rage. He would chew their bones with his teeth and spit their gristle in the mud if he could. He is of a mind to mutilate them even though they are dead, but that would serve no purpose. They are not the bandits who raped his mother and sisters.

But they might as well be.

Mara is on her knees, spitting blood. He goes to comfort her, but she waves him away. She does not wish to be touched, even by her rescuer.

He hesitates, then reaches for her a second time. This time she relents, hides her face in his shoulder and clings to him. Her face is a pulpy mess of bruises.

He pulls the stopper from a waterskin and washes the blood off her face as best he can. If they reach Panormus, her father will think he did this. If he recognizes her at all.

'It will be all right,' he whispers. He looks down at himself. He is covered in gore. Some of it is his. Just like Alexander, then. The elephant boy has learned his lessons well.

CHAPTER 52

Hanno strides out of his tent. His scouts have brought in two prisoners and at first he assumes they are deserters from Antipater's army. The news has already reached him of Alexander's victory at Syracuse.

He watches the slow approach of the horses. A captain leads the escort up the slope. The two captives do not wear armour. One is a young man, an Oriental, in a rough and blood-crusted leather tunic; the other is a young boy, in rags, slumped over the saddle, with rope burns at his wrists and ankles. He has been badly used by the looks of it.

His men pull him from the saddle. He cannot stand unaided, and they let him slump to the grass. The other prisoner goes to help him, cradles his head and appeals for water.

'Who are you?' Hanno says.

The Oriental looks up and addresses him informally. 'Are you Hanno?'

He thinks to strike him for his impertinence but something about this scene disturbs him. His worst fears are confirmed when his soldiers haul a corpse from one of the horses and uncover it. 'Xatharo,' he murmurs.

But this isn't right. He looks back at the Oriental, who nods.

'Mara,' Hanno says when he realizes the bleeding wretch at his feet is his daughter. His little girl! One eye is swollen shut. Her lip is ripped and swollen, her hair is butchered and there is a pulpy bruise over her cheek the size of an orange.

It will not do for his men to see him weep. His hand moves to his sword. Who is there he might kill and vent this rage on?

'Alexander,' he says.

He bends to pick her up, bawling for his physician, and carries her into his tent. Gajendra is allowed to follow. Someone hands him a waterskin. He gulps at it gratefully, then slumps onto his knees, exhausted.

CHAPTER 53

Hanno has Gajendra brought to his tent.

He has just come from burying Xatharo. They lit a pyre for him, gave him all honours. Now the general stands, legs akimbo, in the middle of his pavilion, feeling uncommonly grateful to this Oriental who has saved Mara from God knows what.

Seeing Xatharo's body has shaken him almost as much as the unexpected reunion with his daughter. He takes a moment to compose himself. 'She says I have you to thank for her safe arrival here,' he says.

'Yes. That's about right.'

'No false modesty from you then.'

'I killed four men for her.'

'Four?'

'They misjudged me.'

'I promise not to do the same.'

'Your man Xatharo was the bravest fellow I have ever seen. I hope you're going to build him a statue somewhere. He died trying to slay Alexander for you.'

'Would that he had succeeded.'

'He did his best. I have seen thirty-year veterans with fewer scars on him than your man.'

Hanno goes to the stand and splashes water on his face.

'What were you to Alexander?'

'I was his Elephantarch.'

'And what is that?'

'I was chief of the elephants.'

'An officer?'

'You are surprised because I am Indian?'

'I am surprised because you are so young.'

'Alexander was younger than me when he won his first victory. In comparison, I feel I have been slow in my development.'

'You compare yourself to him?'

'He's just a man, general.'

'Really?' Hanno steps close. 'And can you tell me how to defeat this... man?'

'Yes.'

Hanno frowns. He has not expected so blunt an answer. Not even a moment's hesitation. But there must be something to this fellow. He has saved his daughter and survived when Xatharo could not. That alone makes him remarkable.

'Why would you wish to help us?'

'If I do not show you how to do it, my life is forfeit. Alexander never forgets a slight; cheating him of his prisoner he will regard as a deadly insult. That, and I set fire to his camp.'

'That was you?' For the first time since the interview began, he is amused.

'It was not done in malice. I needed to create a distraction.'

'Gajendra. Is that your name?'

A nod.

'How do I know I can trust you, Gajendra?'

'Ask your daughter.'

It is a brave thing to say. Hanno grunts, wondering whether this boy has been more to his daughter than simply protector. 'Your arrival here has caused much discussion.'

'I can imagine.'

Hanno scratches his beard. 'Some call you a spy, others think you could change our fortunes.'

'They are right to have their suspicions. Once, all I wanted was to serve Alexander, lead his army, become his favourite general. Now I want to destroy him more than anything in the world.' He looks out onto the plain where Hanno's army is camped. 'Is this all the men you have?'

'Carthage is not a race of warriors. Most of that rabble are mercenaries, and mercenaries by their nature cost money. There's not much of that left, Alexander took it all. Carthage now is just a few forts and colonies on the north of this island. Even to raise an army this size will bankrupt us for generations. If there are any future generations.'

'Well, numbers do not matter overmuch if you employ the right tactics.'

'When they heard of Alexander's latest victory over Antipater, my officers favoured retreat back into the mountains, to the safety of our forts there.'

'If I were one of your generals and recognized my deficiencies, so would I.'

Hanno is amused. 'Really? Are you a general now?'

'I am ready for that responsibility,' Gajendra says with such sincerity that Hanno looks twice at him, thinking it is a joke. But it's not. 'Now you have me here,' Gajendra says, 'you could win the campaign, if not the battle.'

'Where did you learn such conceit?'

'From the most conceited man in the world. If he were not so sure of himself, he would not have come this far. And if I were not so sure of my own abilities I should not be standing here right now, telling you how to defeat him.' He leans on the table, his knuckles on the wood. 'I know his mind. There is no one outside of his close circle who knows it better. I can make all the difference.'

'Antipater knew his mind.'

'Antipater let his thirst for revenge get the better of him. You have to fight a battle in cold blood.'

'Even if you do know the way to do it, look around you. I had a much larger army at Carthage, and he decimated it.'

'I know, I was there. You played right into his hands.'

Hanno reigns in his temper. 'Well, I have no intention of doing that again.'

'Then what is your plan?

'We are here at Antipater's urging. He wished to catch Alexander in a trap. But he moved before we were ready. He wanted all the glory for himself.'

'Alexander forced his hand. If he had not come out to meet him, he would have penned him inside Syracuse while he dealt with you. It was much discussed among his generals. Anyway, what is done is done. It is time now to deceive the great deceiver.'

'Should we succeed, and that is far from certain, what is it you want?'

'I could say that I want your daughter in marriage, that I want elevation to the nobility, a villa, an estate, a vineyard. Are you able to give me any of those things?'

Hanno does not hear this list of demands; all his inner functioning seems to skew at 'daughter in marriage.'

'My daughter?'

'And the villa with the estate and the vineyard.'

'You impertinent pup. I should gut you like a hog and hang you on a pole outside my tent.'

Gajendra meets his stare. He is unperturbed by this turn of menace. 'Your daughter would not take kindly to that. I have seen her plunge a dagger into a man's back to save my life, so you would do well not to make an enemy of her.' He smiles. 'Filial devotion only goes so far.'

'She is fond of you?'

'I don't know why but yes, that is how it seems.'

Hanno wonders what has happened to his daughter since he left her behind that day. Right now, it is too much to take in. For now, he has to see if the lad, this little demon, is all boast, or whether he truly has found a loose thread in Alexander's cloak of invincibility.

In this moment, in this year of exile, of despair, he sees an ember of hope. He sees, too, a place in history if he is the one finally to defeat the undefeated.

'Tell me how this can be done,' he says.

Mara wakes to the murmur of insects, hears her father talking in whispers outside. She is lying on a camp bed. There are linen bandages around her wrists and ankles, and her head drums with pain. She touches her face, but it doesn't feel like her own. Her lip is swollen to twice its normal size and one eye is closed.

Women come in, fuss over her. She sends them away. She can hear her father outside interrogating the physician.

He hasn't mellowed then, she thinks.

The tent flap bursts open, and he stands silhouetted against the volcano. 'I thought I should never see you again.' He has lost weight. Once he was a big man; now he just looks very tall. 'Who did this to you?'

'Everyone. First, Alexander's men. Then the bandits we met on the road.'

'The Asiatic?'

'He was the worst of all of them. You should have him executed. Look.' She holds out her hands to show him the yellow filth under her fingernails. 'I have blisters. Dirty nails. And calluses. It's all his fault.'

He doesn't understand she is making a joke. He looks bewildered.

For the first time he looks old to her. She notices the grey in his beard, the lines around his eyes. 'Tell me truthfully, what should I make of him?'

'Alexander was about to execute me. He saved my life.'

'What is he to you?'

'We have become close friends.'

'How close?' He presses his lips together until they are white. She can imagine what he is thinking. Bad enough a foreigner has violated his daughter, now he has to thank him for it.

'Close enough that he risked his life for me. Not so close that you need to be concerned for my virtue.'

'The boy claims to be Alexander's Elephantarch. A grand word. He says it like he's King of Persia. What is such a thing? I have never heard of it.'

'He is not a boy. At least you did not think so when his elephants walked over your phalanx outside Carthage. He was surely not a boy when he killed four men to bring me safe here.'

'He said there were four, also. He did not exaggerate then?'

'He may look young but so does Alexander. Gajendra is a warrior, father, like you.'

He strides around the tent, agitated. Then he falls on his knees, takes her hand and presses it to his heart. There are tears on his face. She is too astonished to speak. It is like seeing one of the marble gods in the temple step down from its plinth and start weeping.

Finally, he stands up and turns away from her, embarrassed at this unseemly display of emotion. 'We have given Xatharo to the flames with all honour.'

'It was the least that he deserved.'

'It was also brave and honourable of you to bring him back.' He wipes a hand across his face, in control again. 'He had surely suffered enough, judging by the scars on him. There were fresh wounds on his thighs and his chest. He was a patchwork.'

'They were all earned in my name and in your service.'

'How did he die?'

'Trying to defend me. Alexander dispatched him with his sword.'

He closes his eyes, trying not to imagine it too vividly.

'Why was he so loyal to you?' she asks him.

'It is not easy to explain. I am not sure you would understand.'

'Try.'

He sighs. 'You know, of course, that your mother was not the only woman in my life.'

'I had assumed.' There is a long silence. 'He was my half-brother?'

'Did he look like your half-brother?'

'I never had another brother to compare him with.'

'Well, he wasn't yours. His mother was one of my mistresses. She died many years ago. Xatharo was her boy, she already had him when I knew her. He was by another man who left her when he saw the misshapen son she had given him. She always worried what would happen to Xatharo if she died, and I swore I would always look after him. I kept my promise.'

'How old was he when you took him in?'

'Just a lad.'

'Yet I never saw him.'

'I raised him elsewhere.'

'You trained him, too?'

'I had him trained. He welcomed it. He had a warrior's instincts. He was the perfect conduit for those requirements of office that had to be performed without official sanction. Who would suspect that such a little fellow like that was so lethal? He was loyal to me because I kept my word to his mother. I believe he looked upon me as his father, or the closest anyone had ever come to it.'

'In the end, he repaid you in full.'

'Yes. He kept you safe, and now I will do the same. I am sending you back to Panormus.'

'I appreciate your concern for me, papa, but I will not go.'

'I have ordered it. That's the end of the matter.'

'No, Father. If you die here, what is there for me in Panormus? From now on, I want to stay close to the two men who are important to me.'

'The two men? So you do have feelings for this Gajendra?' He sits down on the bed, puts his arms around her and holds her, gently. He kisses the top of her head. 'Very well. If that is your wish.'

'There is nowhere left to run,' Mara says. 'No matter what happens, we live or die together now.'

The generals are gathered around the chart they have thrown across a bench. They stare at Gajendra as he walks in. He would imagine friendlier looks at his own execution. He can read it in their faces; he is too young, too unschooled, too *foreign* to be of any use to them.

'Who's this?' one of them says.

Hanno leans on the table. 'He's my counsellor.'

Gajendra regards his former enemies; they regard him. Neither is much impressed. It is like a gathering of crows, he thinks, waiting for their quarry to stop shuffling about so they can pick out the juicy bits for dinner.

Alexander would not have done this, was never one to stand back and let other men insult his charges. He would have his arm round me now, push me forward right in their faces, dare them to be uncivil.

But Hanno's authority is not as certain.

Gajendra studies the chart, the planned dispositions. The generals watch him, arms folded. They are waiting for a brilliant plan, he supposes, as if that alone would defeat Alexander. But he knows whatever they do, Alexander will adapt.

Gajendra has some stones in his fist, and he drops them on the map, places them at strategic points. 'Here is Alexander, here his cavalry, there his heavy infantry and elephants. This is how he will line up against us. But expect this to change almost immediately battle commences.'

He has exhausted almost all his pile of stones before he sets out their own positions. It requires not nearly as many pebbles.

'He has that many soldiers?' Hanno asks.

'Those mercenaries who survived the rout at Syracuse have gone over to him.'

'Then we're fucked,' someone says.

Gajendra nods. 'In a conventional battle you might as well fall on your swords and save the Macks the trouble.'

A grim silence.

'The first thing you must do is show him how you intend to win. Because he will be wondering and waiting.'

Several of them turn to Hanno, and one asks, 'You are not contemplating going against him without Antipater?'

'I have sent couriers to Antipater and Sostratus, asking them to return to the field and attack him in a concerted pincer movement, allied with us.'

'But Antipater is dead! They had him executed so they could make terms with Alexander.'

'He is not aware we know this,' Hanno replies. 'Alexander will capture our couriers on the road, read our letters then send back another letter, under Antipater's seal, agreeing to participate in a joint attack. Alexander will think we have been duped and led into his trap.'

He smiles at them, thin-lipped.

'What difference will it make?' one of the generals growls. 'We are hopelessly outnumbered. What advantage does this give us? And they have *elephants!*'

'There are several other things we must do,' Gajendra says, and all heads swivel back to him. They are frowning now, fearing themselves being drawn into something they wish no part of – a fair fight.

'We shall need someone to take Hanno's place on the battlefield. A decoy.'

'Take my place?' Hanno says. This has not been mentioned before.

'This man must wear your armour, general, and ride under your standard, take up your position behind the line, as you would.'

'Why?' someone asks.

'It is a baited hook, to lure Alexander into a trap. One final thing: we shall need pigs.'

They stare at him in utter disbelief. 'Pigs?'

'As many as you can find.'

There is stunned silence. The wind whips at the pavilion.

And then they are all shouting at once. Even the Macks never had this much enmity for a common Indian, Gajendra thinks. They give Hanno their opinion of him and his plans at the top of their voices. How can we trust this boy? He has spent the last two years taking it up the arse from the King of Macedon and that's the closest he ever got to his inner sanctum.

And no one can go against elephants! Even Alexander almost lost a battle in India when the Maharajah brought his tuskers into the fight. They ran through our infantry at Carthage and just a week ago chased off Antipater's cavalry.

And they had superior numbers! But this water boy thinks we can beat them with a few pigs? You can't trust Asiatics. They'd sell their own mothers if there was a profit in it.

The generals crowd around and compete to shout each other down. Gajendra is astonished. If this is the calibre of men Hanno surrounds himself with, no wonder Alexander won so easily at Carthage.

Hanno makes Alexander look like an hysteric; he keeps his arms crossed and his face still through their tirade. He does not give away what he is thinking. His gaze flicks around the room. He reminds Gajendra of a hawk, with those deep black eyes.

At last, they are done. He nods at Gajendra, gives him leave to speak again.

'If you all run back to Panormus,' Gajendra tells them, 'you know what will happen. He'll cross the island at his leisure, tear down the walls of your forts and towns and crucify any that survive. Then he will take your women and children as slaves.'

'Why didn't Antipater wait for us?' one of them grumbles.

'What Antipater did or did not do is no longer our concern. All we have is our present circumstance. And if you run away from that, you delay the inevitable. Here you have one advantage. You can yet choose the terms of the battle.'

'No one can beat Alexander,' another braveheart says from the back of this inglorious huddle.

'I can,' Gajendra says. He turns to Hanno. 'The first thing we must do is defeat his elephants; your men will not be able to stand against them. They do not have the training or the discipline, and when your horses smell them on the air, they will turn and bolt.

'Alexander will engage our army and direct his elephant squadron at what he perceives is our weakest spot. As soon as they make their move, we drive the pigs among them to scatter them.'

'Scatter them?'

'It will be like releasing a pack of snarling dogs among a herd of sheep. Once the elephants turn, it will create panic among the Macedonian ranks. It will appear to Alexander that this is our chief strategy, but before he can resolve the problem, we will present him immediately with a solution.'

There is silence. They are all staring at him.

'As soon as the elephants are in retreat, we will send our foot soldiers after them.'

'And slaughter them.'

Gajendra looks at the man as if he is mad. 'With this puny army? Perhaps Antipater might have done that. We shall have to be a little more realistic about our abilities.'

'Then after the elephants have retreated, what is your plan?'

'Our infantry's advance will create a break in our line. Alexander will be looking for that. Our men will be halted by Alexander's phalanx, meanwhile he will take the opportunity to attack with his heavy cavalry. We let him. We lure him in.'

'So, letting him win? That's your plan?'

'No, this is the plan: we can't kill their entire army. And we don't have to. We just have to kill Alexander. Wait for him to come so deep in our lines that we can cut him off from his own men. And we kill him. Then we retreat.'

'They'll come after us.'

'Those Macks will be too busy fighting among themselves for the next hundred years to bother anyone.'

There is silence in the tent. One by one they realise that what the Indian boy has suggested might really work.

'How do we know he will take the bait?'

'Alexander always leads the charge from the front. He lives for it. Besides, he always said that a general could not commend his men to valour if he himself sat behind the lines on a fine horse with a servant holding a shade umbrella.'

He looks around. That is precisely what these fine men will be doing.

'This, good men of Carthage, becomes our best chance to rid the world of Alexander.'

'What if the elephants don't run?'

'They will run.'

'How can you be so sure?'

'Because I was Alexander's general of the elephants. I know the tuskers. I know Alexander. If you want to get off this island with your lives, I am your one hope.'

And that finally shuts them up.

CHAPTER 54

The next day, he finds her in the temple.

She looks so different now. She wears a diaphanous gown and has her ladies attending her, while her guards keep at a respectful distance. There are bangles on her wrists and at her throat. She has a wig, with blonde ringlets. She is still skinny, but now smells of patchouli instead of elephants.

The bruises on her face are healing, though it will be a while before she looks as pretty as she did when she was a dung lark. But the transformation is nevertheless astonishing.

'There you are!' She dismisses her entourage, who wait for her at the temple gate. She takes his hand with the familiarity of a wife and leads him out of earshot. 'My father this morning could not break bread without one officer or another bursting in and decrying you for a charlatan. I could hear them all shouting though my tent is a hundred paces away from his. What have you been doing now?'

'I have been advising them on tactics. His men of war have been telling him to run away and hide. They don't like it that I have told them how they might actually win a battle. Their knowledge of warfare goes no further than tactical withdrawal.'

'Well, when Alexander is the opposing general, all men take pause.'

The temple is deserted. Leaves rustle across the marble and weeds grow through the cracks.

'Look at you!' he says. He pretends to examine her fingernails for elephant dung. 'This is more like it. No more breast binding, I see. And what is this gown, are you trying to seduce me?'

She snatches her hand away and feigns outrage. 'I could have you as my slave. One word in my father's ear, to confirm his officers' worst suspicions of you, is all it would take. Perhaps I'll do it anyway. I need a boy to fetch water for my bath.'

'This one would get in it with you.'

Her fingers stroke his cheek. Their eyes meet. 'Can the elephant boy really defeat the god of war?'

They are interrupted by another summer storm. The shadows of clouds race up the hill towards them, as fast as mounted raiders. The rain explodes with unexpected force on the marble flagstones like a barrage of stones.

They run across the forecourt to the tabernacle to take shelter, but they are not quick enough. In moments she is soaked through and the filmy gown clings to her body.

Gajendra looks beyond the gates where her ladies and soldiers have taken shelter under the trees. He pulls her out of sight. Almighty Zeus is unimpressed with his clumsy efforts at seduction; he lies on the floor of his tabernacle, fractured, one arm outstretched. He seems to be saying, not again elephant boy, haven't you learned your lesson yet?

She pushes him away. She is a general's daughter again, not to be fondled without consequence.

'Gaji, I asked you a question. Can you beat him?'

'He's just a man.'

'Yet for a long time, it seemed to me that you revered him as a god.'

'It was hard not to think that. They all said he should have died countless times in battle. He does seem immortal sometimes. He believes he was fathered by Zeus.'

'Do you still believe it?'

Gajendra does not answer.

There are rats running behind the altars and the courtyard is littered with debris. Mara steps over the threshold and looks around. 'What happened to this place?'

'Struck by lightning, or so they say. People here took it as a sign and cleared out. It's Zeus's symbol, you know, lightning.'

On cue, lightning flashes over the mountains and for a moment the tabernacle is backlit. The light is greenish and strange. He wonders if it is an omen.

She stands on tiptoe and whispers, 'When did you first know that I was not a boy?'

'I'm not sure. I may need further proof.'

He tries to kiss her, but she pulls away, laughing. 'After all this is done, you will come back to me, won't you, elephant boy?'

He tries to slide a hand into her gown. She pushes it away.

'If you conceive here, you could say the father was Zeus.'

'Give him the blame while you have the pleasure. Is that your game?'

The breasts she had tried once to keep hidden are now pushed forwards, inviting caress. He can see over her shoulder into the forecourt. Her people are still huddled under trees outside. While it rains like this, they are still private.

'It is a game we might both enjoy.'

'You'd best be quick, elephant boy,' she whispers. 'This downpour can't last forever.'

Her skin glows in the storm light. Her shoulder is bare, and he kisses it. The rain stops as quickly as it came. Her ladies come out from under the trees looking for her.

'Enough of that. No tenderness from you until you have defeated Alexander. Promise me you will win.'

'Ganesha will have to play his part.'

'Are you frightened?'

'Of course.'

'You do not appear to be frightened. You look very calm.'

'I am scared only of not appearing brave in front of other men.'

She strokes his hair. 'I don't care if you are not brave. Just come back. I have grown a little fond of you.'

'I will do my best,' he says.

But the gods are fickle, especially Ganesha. He wonders what other obstacles he will put in his way or if his elephant god thinks he has learned his lessons well enough.

Pray all you like, elephant boy. In the end, the gods do whatever they choose.

CHAPTER 55

Hanno rides up to him. He has his helmet under his arm. He wears plain armour, looks like any other cavalry officer. It is Gajendra who wears Hanno's plumed helmet, his red general's cloak, and rides his high-stepping Arab with silver trappings.

Another dream he has fulfilled, though not as he had once imagined it.

The battlefield is in motion. The atmosphere is charged. If fear could condense on the air, a man might not be able to breathe. An infantryman drops his weapon and a horse rears on its hind legs in panic. A man pisses where he stands, his water running down his leg. He doesn't even notice.

The infantrymen plunge the butt of their spikes into the earth and drop down to one knee, their bronze and oak shields slung across their chests. Boys run in and out of the lines with waterskins of wine. Beside the *hoplites* are the Iberians with their bossed wooden shields and javelins. They have little in the way of armour, just buskin boots and a woollen cloak. That is not going to help them much if they come up against the Macedonians' *sarissas*.

'This is madness,' one of Hanno's generals says. They will not let this go, these liverless bastards. Too late now for anyone to change their minds, but still they grumble about it.

'Get to your positions,' Hanno tells them, brooking no further discussion. He steps his horse up beside Gajendra. 'You really think this will work?'

'It will work,' Gajendra says, though privately he believes the odds are against them. 'Remember, we do not have to defeat their army, we only have to kill one man.'

Hanno nods.

Another storm is moving in off the sea. Gajendra feels the ground quake under the next roll of thunder.

Hundreds of Hanno's men have deserted during the night, though not as many as he had feared. Mercenaries are sometimes more loyal than conscripts.

Gajendra stares straight ahead. Alexander has formed up his army on the plain below. He can see their spear points glitter as the sun appears through a rare break in the clouds. The grass has been soaked by the rain and glows emerald green. It looks pretty, for now.

'I want to thank you,' Hanno says.

'For what?'

'For bringing my daughter safely back. She has told me what you did to protect her. I shall be forever in your debt.'

Gajendra smiles. 'You may regret saying that if I ever call in my marker.'

'It is my creditors who should be more worried today than my debtors. Goodbye, Gajendra.'

'Aren't you supposed to say – I will see you after the battle?'

'It's more likely one or both of us will be dead.' Hanno puts a hand on his arm. 'Take care, my boy. My daughter seems to think something of you.'

The standard bearers and signal corps cluster around. Hanno puts on his helmet, a plain thing, bronze, with face pieces something like a beard. He looks like all the rest now. As he rides away Gajendra is surrounded and cramped on every side by bodyguards and couriers.

Yet he has never felt so alone.

CHAPTER 56

Alexander has presented as Gajendra thought he would. The elephants – his elephants – are at the centre, the stingers in between, the phalanx at the rear. The cavalry is at the flanks, at the oblique, of course, but not static. Alexander will never present to the enemy a static line; already he is on the move, his light cavalry crossing to the right, further weakening his other flank and inviting attack.

There he is, a flash of gold, Alexander in his gorgeous armour, moving down the line. His flag bearers and officers ride behind him as he inspects the lines, cajoling, encouraging. This is his idea of heaven. Gajendra has never seen him bad-tempered before a battle. Without war, Alexander could not exist.

Alexander's only fear, Niarchos once told him, was that he would reach the end of the world, only to find everyone had surrendered.

'Always attack,' Gajendra remembers him saying, many times. 'Attack makes men bold; defence makes them timorous. Always attack, even when you are outnumbered. Always.'

Does he know I am here? Gajendra wonders. He must surely suspect. But he will have dismissed my importance as Hanno's ally. He still thinks me just an elephant boy and he will underestimate me.

He thinks we are holding the valley waiting for Antipater, the general who will not come, thinks we are unsuspecting of his private arrangements with Sostratus. That is one advantage we have already.

He assumes we are relying on the caltrops we have spread in front of our infantry to blunt his attack. He will be unconcerned; believes he can trample us into the mud with the elephants along our flanks.

Cloud shadows race across the grass. Another hour and the storm will be on them. They will be fighting this battle in the mud; Colossus will like that.

They are a fearsome sight, these Macedonians. They have been drilled to the point that they could fight this battle in their sleep.

Gajendra can pick out Colossus at the head of the battle line. He holds his head high as his massive forelegs come down to shake the earth. He appears to double in size with each advancing stride.

Gajendra has promised himself he will carry this off today without hurting the elephants. He will not see his boys come to harm, not a single one of them.

They come at them like a wave, not the phalanx of Silver Shields, not the cavalry, not the elephants. The swarm is composed entirely of the camp followers, pouring across the plain in their thousands. A gasp runs through the serried ranks of the *hoplites* behind the palisades.

No one thinks to ask Gajendra what is happening, not even Hanno; if he had, he would have told him. He may be the only one on this side of the line who is expecting this. He expects it because Alexander has told him this is what he will do if ever this situation arises.

After the battle of Carthage, Gajendra had said to Alexander: 'What if, instead of sharpened wooden spikes, they had seeded their front with caltrops - spiked metal balls - to impede our elephants?'

'I would respond with greed,' he had said.

'Greed?'

'I would send a man to the rear, to the whores, the cooks, the carpenters, and the hangers-on and offer a silver coin for every caltrop brought to my quartermaster by hand.'

'No one will risk his life for a few coins!'

He had laughed at that. 'You are so young. It's almost touching how innocent you are.' His lips had curled into a smile. It was always a surprise, how ugly his smile was, when the rest of him was so very pretty. 'You have no idea what people will do for a little money.'

Hanno is watching proceedings from a hill above the temple of Zeus, far to the rear. A courier is sent all the way back to ask for orders. The response is too slow to be effective. By the time the archers have been told to deal with these irregulars, half the field has been cleared.

What surprises Gajendra is how brave these whores and cooks are. Or how stupid. Even when the first arrows slice in, and their neighbours start to fall, they stay out there trying to gather as many of the spiked metal balls as they can. Only a few of them flee. After the second volley many more retreat, carrying the caltrops in their arms or in sacks over their shoulders. But even then a few persist.

It is only after the fourth volley, when a hundred or so tarts and barbers lie twitching in the grass, that the field is empty again. By then, most of the caltrops are gone. If the elephants advance now, there is nothing between them and the hoplites.

For a while silence prevails.

The thunder growls in the high passes. The wind whips at the clothes of the dead and wounded lying in front of the timbered palisade.

Even from where he is way back in the rear, Gajendra can hear the pigs. So much depends on whether the little herd of porkers can be herded to the right place on the battlefield in time. Come on, Alexander. Make up your mind. Where will you strike first?

He uses the hiatus to admire how fine his elephants look. Colossus is worthy of his name; he is immense. He imagines Ravi on his shoulders and feels a twist in his gut. Stay safe, uncle. Don't die for Alexander, not today. He's not worth it.

Ravi starts to bring them forward; has Alexander made him the new Elephantarch? The whole line is disciplined and moving at the oblique. He sees the stingers jogging between the tuskers, brown-skinned and lithe. He feels a surge of pride; he trained them well.

Now the pigs are downwind, and he can smell them as well as hear them. Out on the flanks the horses catch their scent too and skitter in their places.

He hopes Hanno remembers all he has told him and does not deviate from the plan. He has some gutless timeservers on his staff who will yet try to sway him; when the generals are all picked by a council, you will always be served a dog's breakfast. But if Hanno lets them interfere now, then this will turn into a bloody rout and none of them will get out of this with their lives.

There is movement in the front ranks. Men run through the lines with flaming torches and spears. Alexander will not like this. He seldom has to face the unexpected on the battlefield.

Here are the pigs now. There are hundreds of them brought up on chains, at the trot. They run through the phalanx and are only released when they are out beyond the palisades. Their men prod them in their rumps with their spears and flaming torches to make them run. They set off across the field towards the elephants. A few have been soaked in pitch and set on fire so they will run faster than the rest.

He never ordered that. He did not think it necessary.

For a moment nothing happens. The pigs run, and both armies watch. Some of the porkers run in circles, others turn back in the direction they have come, confused. But that is the reason he has specified there should be so many. He needs just a portion of their number to run straight up the hill towards the elephants for this to be effective.

The trumpeting of the elephants is deafening. They raise their trunks and squeal in terror. They back up, despite the desperate efforts of their mahavats to keep them in line, and then they turn and dash through their own lines, trampling everything in their path. *Howdahs* topple and are crushed under the feet of other tuskers running behind.

The infantry scatters. He can hear men screaming on the wind. He feels sorry for his mahavats. When an elephant loses its mind there is nothing to be done. You would have better luck ordering the tide to turn or making an avalanche stop dead on the side of a mountain. The tuskers leave a trail of bolted horses, crushed infantry and dashed flags in their wake.

Carthage cheers. They sense victory.

What happens next is entirely predictable. Hanno's *hoplites* give their battle cry and rush through the palisades. A lesser general than Alexander would panic, but Gajendra knows that instead, Alexander will be pulling on his helmet and looking to gain advantage from this reverse.

The whole line is in motion now, the infantry running over the open ground to the ragged gap left by the departed elephants. The tuskers' rout has left a gaping hole in the line, piles of bleeding rags that once were men littering the ground behind them. The squares of the phalanx have been scattered.

Other soldiers might have dropped their weapons and fled, and it may have degenerated into a massacre. But these men are Alexander's Silver Shields, scarred veterans of Issus, Gaugamela and the Jhellum River. They rapidly re-form. By the time the *hoplites* arrive, they find them unchastened by this reverse and ready to do murder.

Gajendra's horse twitches underneath him; he feels uneasy. If it were Colossus, he would know how to calm him, but this beast is as foreign to him as riding a camel. It's as if it knows what is coming.

The *hoplites* arrive at Alexander's phalanx and face a serried rank of eighteen-foot-long *sarissas*. They cannot fall back, neither can they break through. The easy victory of a few moments ago now looks like a serious misjudgement by the captains on the line. Instead of leading a rout they are stalled by the points of the Macedonian spears and have themselves left a break in the line behind them.

Alexander has Ptolemy and his heavy cavalry engage Hanno's Numidians on the left, and charges through the gap with his own cavalry. He has seen Hanno's colours now, indeed he has looked for nothing else.

There is just a squadron of bodyguard cavalry and a phalanx of mercenaries between Alexander and Gajendra now. Alexander supposes I am Hanno, Gajendra thinks. This is the moment he has been waiting for.

Although Gajendra has invited Alexander's attack, the speed and ferocity of it startles him. He has seen him do this at Carthage and at Syracuse, but then he was behind him, and could not appreciate how demoralizing it might be to see his heavy cavalry coming straight for you.

Gajendra's bodyguards ride out to meet him, but the force of the charge breaks their ranks almost immediately. He can see Alexander clearly now, his plumed helmet, his beautiful golden armour. They fight like Furies, these Macks. He cannot but admire him, even as he wishes him dead.

Hanno's cavalry tries to hold the line but is soon overwhelmed. The first stragglers arrive, galloping hard. It does not take much to win a battle. Once an army turns, it is like a crack appearing in a fortress wall. Everything is then concentrated on that one weakened point, and after months of siege it is all over in hours.

Alexander thinks he has found the crack in the wall.

Gajendra is still. He does not want to snatch away the lure too soon, but suddenly realizes that the lure is in danger of being swallowed whole, along with the line and the fisher. He turns in the saddle and orders retreat. His standard bearers and his bodyguards follow. The rest are swallowed up in the mêlée.

He takes one backward glance at the battlefield. It is chastening to see how quickly heavy cavalry can decimate infantry if they are not properly organized. Hanno's mercenaries, the Greeks, Celts and Gauls, are simply no match. Never mind their fearsome looks, their bearskins, tattoos and beards, they scream and die along with everyone else under the horses' hooves.

Alexander has just one focus. He has seen Hanno's battle standards and he is hacking his way inexorably closer. He will be determined that this time Hanno will not escape.

He is close enough now that Gajendra can see the breastplate on his horse. It has been pierced repeatedly and the animal has a chunk out of its hindquarters that would make a steak big enough for three men. Its chest and forelegs are stiff with matted blood. Yet still it charges on, maddened by pain and rage. Alexander is no less crazed.

Gajendra turns away and leads what is left of his command up the hill. He sees Zeus's temple on the knoll above, the glimmer of the sun flashing for a moment on a soldier's armour.

'Hanno!'

He hears Alexander, his voice roaring over the din. Gajendra turns his horse to face him. The battle now has deteriorated into scores of single combats, but it is this one that will carry the day.

The plan has gone badly awry. The trap has not had time to spring closed. Alexander's charge has been too swift. Gajendra hurls his javelin, and it strikes Alexander's shield and bounces harmlessly away. Alexander responds by throwing his own. It strikes Gajendra's breastplate and snaps off, but the force of it is enough to take his breath away and knock him off his horse. He lands on his back in the grass.

He struggles to his feet, draws his sword and looks for Alexander. Alexander jumps from his horse and charges at him, but he does not use his sword, instead he batters him with his shield until he goes down again.

Gajendra is disappointed he has not put up a better show, but then he supposes there are few bravehearts who can say they have not been bested in combat by this demon.

Alexander does not dispatch him immediately. Instead he leans down and rips off his helmet, for Alexander will show mercy to any man who will ask for it, if he has fought bravely.

He sees it is Gajendra and his face drops. It is the only time he has ever seen Alexander confused.

'Elephant boy?' he says.

CHAPTER 57

Alexander's momentary bewilderment gives Gajendra a moment's respite to roll over and vomit. He is stunned, exhausted. He spits blood. Where is that coming from? Falling from a horse in full armour is a chastening experience.

Ptolemy arrives and leans from his saddle looking similarly bewildered. 'What is he doing here?'

Gajendra tries to crawl away. Alexander puts his foot on his throat to stop him. He thinks he intends to choke him to death. But no, Alexander is just giving himself leave to think, to piece together what has happened.

Gajendra knows he must break his promise to Mara. He is going to die and there is nothing to be done about it.

He looks up at the knoll and wills Hanno to make his entrance now. His advice to him was to wait until Alexander was fully distracted. How much more distracted can Alexander be?

'What have you done, elephant boy?'

'Kill him and let's get out of here,' Ptolemy shouts. 'This is no time to be off your horse berating this lunatic!'

Alexander raises his sword for the killing stroke. 'Well, elephant boy, you want a reckoning with the gods, you shall have one.'

He hears yelling from the ridge and looks up. Hanno and his cavalry are swarming down the slope. It gives Gajendra a moment to scramble out of range. Alexander looks faintly irritated by this turn of events. He points his sword at Gajendra. 'I will settle with you shortly.'

He picks up a javelin from the ground and hurls it at the first of Hanno's cavalry. It takes the rider in the breastplate and bounces off, but just as it did to Gajendra, the force of it knocks the man off his horse and sends him tumbling to the ground.

Gajendra shakes his head in astonishment. The man is not human. He is a god after all. Does he never miss his aim?

Without breaking stride Alexander jumps back onto his horse and he and Ptolemy ride out with the rest of his vanguard to face the cavalry charge. The two ranks of horses collide. Alexander's enthusiasm for the fight is undiminished.

One of Hanno's officers wheels his horse around and comes at him from behind. He swings wildly, and his sabre almost crushes Alexander's helmet. Alexander slumps in the saddle and for a moment Gajendra thinks he will fall, but somehow he recovers.

Now Perdiccas is there, and his spear takes Alexander's attacker out of his saddle.

Alexander shakes his head like a wet dog. His skull must be bone right through. It is true, then. You cannot kill this man.

Gajendra's body is racked with pain, but he concentrates his will on standing up and getting ready to face Alexander a second time.

The rain sweeps in, blinding him. As the lightning arcs across the sky, he sees Hanno's men in full retreat. Alexander is still in the saddle. Gajendra's plan has worked but Alexander, the god, is bigger than one man's plan.

Gajendra sways on his feet. It is hard to breathe, and his vision is blurred. He finds a sword and buckler, though, and drops to one knee to gather himself.

As Alexander approaches, he raises himself to his full height. That he should do so is an irritation to the great man. He jumps from his horse and hammers his sword into Gajendra's buckler, sending him back onto his knees.

'I treated you like my own son. I would have given you the world if you had wanted it. All I asked was your loyalty!'

Gajendra half rises and staggers backward towards the temple.

Alexander removes his helmet and throws it on the ground to register his disgust. 'Why did you do this?' he says.

'Do not think to win the battle... think to win the campaign. Think not to win the campaign, think... to win the war.'

'This was your plan?'

'When you die, you Greeks will go back to fighting among yourselves and leave us alone.'

'You Greeks? Who are you fighting for now?'

The sword hammers on the shield again. He will pound him into the dirt like a nail at this rate. Gajendra reels backwards against the temple gates.

'This cannot be over a woman, can it?'

'You pissed on my head.'

'It *is* over a woman!'

Gajendra retreats as Alexander batters him with his sword. Finally, he summons what strength he has left, hammers his buckler into Alexander's face and thrusts with his *falcata*, tearing through his corselet and finding the flesh between his ribs and the inside of his left arm.

Alexander staggers back, his face registering his outrage that an elephant boy would dare to stab at the royal person.

He puts his hand beneath his armour and when he takes it out it is covered in blood. He stares at it in disbelief.

Gajendra runs across the courtyard, slips on the wet stone and goes down. The fall from the horse has damaged something inside. The pain seems to be everywhere. He rolls onto his side and retches.

Alexander shakes his left arm, as if he can hurl aside the wound in his side like a stray insect. 'What a soldier you make,' he says. 'Not a mark on you, and you are rolling around the floor like you are dying. Come on, elephant boy, get up and let's make a proper fight out of it, then.'

Gajendra cannot feel his arms and he cannot hear Alexander's voice anymore. His sword feels as if it weighs as much as his horse. Alexander is standing over him. His lips are moving so he must be saying something. His teeth are black with blood and dirt.

Alexander stabs down, but it is not a killing stroke. He hasn't finished talking yet. Alexander likes to talk, and he has plenty to say when he feels like it. The battle is over. What is to be established here is the more important question of why he is not properly loved.

Gajendra writhes as the point of Alexander's sword goes in. As his general stands back, he slithers away. Of all the telling moments of his life is this how it will end, down here on the floor again, like a worm?

He rolls his head to the side and sees Zeus there on the temple floor beside him. It can happen to me, Zeus seems to be saying, it can happen to you.

He is lying in a pool of blood, but he is not sure it is his. There have been other combats fought in here today. One of Hanno's officers lies outstretched, his spear at his feet. It is a short, stabbing spear with a four-square iron point.

Gajendra concentrates his will on crawling towards it. Inch by inch, now, never mind about what he is saying about you. When your enemy thinks you are beaten is when you are at your most dangerous. Another of Alexander's lessons.

Alexander is still ranting. He rolls him over with his foot, so that Gajendra can better hear the rest of his speech about loyalty.

Gajendra's fingers close around the broken shaft of the spear.

As Alexander raises his sword to deliver the killing stroke, he steels himself for one final effort. He grasps the spear and thrusts upwards, seeking the vital flesh below the lip of Alexander's breastplate. But he hasn't the strength left to do it and Alexander seizes it with his left hand and forces it out of his grip.

The world turns black.

When he opens his eyes again, there is chaos.

The stone gate crashes in, and he hears an elephant trumpeting. Colossus stands in the courtyard, ears flared.

Somehow, he has lost his mahavat and the archers in the *howdah* are shrieking and clinging on for their lives.

Alexander turns around.

'What have we here?' he says. 'Have you come to rout my enemies or protect your little elephant boy?'

Only Alexander would stand bareheaded before an enraged elephant with nothing but a sword and buckler. His soldiers would come and help him, but they are too far away, and his bodyguard are engaged by Hanno's men, who have regrouped for a second attack.

For the moment, the King of Macedon is on his own.

Colossus raises his trunk and charges.

Alexander reaches for the javelin he has wrested from Gajendra's hand and hefts it in his right hand. He aims for Colossus's eye.

Gajendra rolls onto his side, finds the dagger at his belt and plunges it into Alexander's calf. Alexander screams and the javelin falls easily wide of its mark. He turns and stabs down with his sword a second time. Gajendra cries out in pain.

Colossus picks Alexander up with his trunk and hurls him across the courtyard. He slams against the temple wall. He lies still for long moments, then shakes himself and gets to his feet, dazed. He looks about for his sword.

Colossus charges a second time. He swipes him again, sending him sprawling across the marble. Alexander lands against his fallen idol, Zeus.

No ordinary man could survive such punishment, but Alexander is no ordinary man. He lies on his back, his right hand feeling for his sword. Giving up the search, he rolls onto his side and starts the slow climb to his knees. He leaves a smear of blood on the marble.

Colossus takes him a third time, charging with his tusks, which have been sheathed with iron tips. The force of the charge is enough that the tip of one tusk penetrates Alexander's golden armour and pierces him through, pinning him to the wall of the tabernacle. Colossus shakes his head like a dog with a rat and Alexander lands on the altar, leaving gouts of blood on the stark marble.

Ptolemy is first on the scene and shouts his dismay, 'Alexander is dead!'

Even Hanno's men leave off their fighting to stare. It is a scene so improbable that no one can quite believe it.

Ptolemy rides his horse into the temple to try to retrieve his body. Colossus will have none of it. He charges and Ptolemy retreats. But even that is not enough, for he barges now into the Companion Cavalry and scatters them as well. In moments he has cleared the field. He turns and trudges slowly back to where Gajendra lies stricken.

He nudges him with his trunk, rolling his body, looking for life.

Lightning cracks around the mountain. Hanno climbs down from his horse. They have done what Gajendra has promised, they have killed the man who called himself King of the World.

Their reprieve is temporary. Alexander's cavalry will regroup; Hanno's own army is in rout. Only the thunderstorm and the confusion that will inevitably follow Alexander's death will save them now.

Hanno's men are trying to retrieve Gajendra's body, but the monster elephant will not let them close. They hesitate and look back to him for orders.

Mara appears from nowhere. She is supposed to be at Hanno's camp on the other side of the mountain, with the supply train. It surprises no one that she has defied her father's orders.

She jumps off her horse, pushes his men out of the way and walks straight towards the crazed elephant.

This makes up his mind.

'Kill him! Kill the monster now!' Hanno shouts.

His men reach for their javelins and the two bravest run in with their swords.

CHAPTER 58

Mara slips on the blood pooled underfoot. She gets up and runs at Colossus who flares his ears and roars at her.

'*Ida!*' she shouts at him. '*Ida!* Step aside!'

His trunk snakes out and tests her scent. Then he lowers his ears to let her know it is safe, and steps back.

She kneels at his feet and cradles Gajendra's head in her arms. There is gore everywhere, over her hands, over her dress. Once again, she is standing over the pit. She sees the goddess reach up for Gajendra, all black blood and greed, but she pushes her back.

Gajendra's eyes blink open. 'Mara.'

'Call yourself a warrior. One little scratch and down you go. All you are good for is minding tuskers.'

'Get Colossus away from here.'

'Don't concern yourself, elephant boy, I am taking you both.'

Hanno's men forget about their terror of Colossus. They rush in and carry Gajendra away. They pay no mind to Alexander, leave him where he has fallen. His own men will be coming for him soon, already they can hear the thunder of their horses' hooves.

Let them fight over what is left on the earth, she thinks. She will settle for this one simple victory over Tanith's oblivion. It is not much compared to all that Alexander conquered, but today he is the one lying on the marble, cold and dead, and she is the one riding away, wiping the blood on her dress and smiling.

EPIC ADVENTURE SERIES

Colin Falconer's EPIC ADVENTURE SERIES of stand-alone tales draws inspiration from many periods of history. Visit the fabled city of Xanadu, the Aztec temples of Mexico, or the mountain strongholds of the legendary Cathars. Glimpse Julius Caesar in the sweat and press of the Roman forum, ride a war elephant in the army of Alexander the Great, or follow Suleiman the Magnificent into the forbidden palace of his harem.

2000+ five-star reviews.
Translated into 25 languages.
3000+ pages.

'A fantastic read' - Wilbur Smith

All books are available on Amazon in Kindle eBook or 6x9 inch paperback.

Find them at www.colinfalconer.org.

ABOUT THE AUTHOR

Born in London, Colin Falconer started out in advertising, then became a freelance journalist. He gravitated to radio and television, and started writing novels. He is best known for historical adventure fiction – stories on an epic scale, inspired by his passion for history and travel. His books have been translated into 24 languages.

If you enjoyed this novel, please consider leaving a review online.

If you would like to be kept up to date with new releases from Colin Falconer, please follow him on Facebook or visit his website, www.colinfalconer.org.

Printed in Great Britain
by Amazon

86267585R00185